BLACK RIVER FALLS

Also by Ed Gorman

Hawk Moon
Blood Red Moon
Cold Blue Midnight

BLACK RIVER FALLS

Ed Gorman

HEADLINE
FEATURE

First published in Great Britain in 1996
by HEADLINE BOOK PUBLISHING

A HEADLINE FEATURE hardback

10 9 8 7 6 5 4 3 2 1

British Library Cataloguing in Publication Data

Gorman, Edward
    Black River Falls
    I. Title
    813.54 [F]

ISBN 0-7472-1351-8

Typeset by Keyboard Services, Luton, Beds

Printed and bound in Great Britain by
Mackays of Chatham PLC, Chatham, Kent

HEADLINE BOOK PUBLISHING
A division of Hodder Headline PLC
338 Euston Road
London NW1 3BH

For Bob Tanner – agent, friend, very patient man.

Prologue

4th Precinct
Patrolman William F. Sievers
7 June, 1995

*I was investigating a stolen car complaint when a woman from down
the block asked me if I could stop by her apartment house later.*

*After finishing up with the stolen car. I went down to see the woman.
She lived in one of the old Victorians on the corner of 34th Street and D
Avenue where a lot of university students, a lot of poor blacks, and a lot
of drug dealers live.*

*The woman said the apartment manager wouldn't do anything about
the stench in the apartment next to hers and I would I check it out. I got
the manager to give me the key and that's when I found the girl in the
bedroom.*

8 July, 1995
She came almost every night now, and always did the same thing, just
stood there in front of the shabby Victorian that not even the
moonlight could save, and stared up at the window of the apartment
where she'd lived with the dead girl.

The people in the neighborhood knew who she was, of course; her
name was Alison. She'd lived among them for a good while, an
earnestly pretty girl with big somber eyes and a quick sad smile.

Sometimes it rained but the girl came anyway, not seeming to
notice when she got soaked, not even seeming to notice when one of
the old black women came up to her and said, 'Darlin' why don't you
come inside and let me make you some coffee?' The girl was always
grateful for the kindness but never accepted it.

She just wanted to stand here, watching, remembering.

1

Hot angry summer gave way to chill solemn autumn, and then the girl didn't come quite so often, nor stay quite so long. The old ladies who watched her from their windows had despaired of helping her. All they could do was wonder why she came back here, what she was hoping to learn by standing down there on the sidewalk, frail as a child, staring up at the dark apartment, the place not having been rented since the murder.

What could she possibly want here?

4th Precinct
Patrolman William F. Sievers
7 June, 1995

I guess the thing I noticed right away, even before I took a good long look at her wounds, was her face. She looked a lot like my little sister, Janice. And I got scared. I wanted to get on the phone and call my Mom back on the farm and make sure that Janice was all right. She was sixteen now and driving and going out with boys, and these days girls can get in a lot of trouble.

The young woman was sprawled on her back on the bed. She had blonde hair so you could plainly see where somebody had smashed in the left side of her skull. A fly sat on the wound making angry buzzing noises.

She'd also been cut up pretty bad. Her hands lay open so you could see the defense wounds in the palms, where she'd been trying to keep the knife away. Her breasts were cut up pretty bad, too.

I guess because she resembled my sister so much, I had a hard time looking between her parted legs. Women always look so vulnerable down there. There was heavy red blood on the inside of both her thighs. She'd probably been raped. I wondered if she'd been alive when it had happened.

I wanted to cover her, cover her sex if nothing else, give her a little bit of dignity, but I'd done that on another homicide investigation and the detectives chewed my ass off for altering the crime scene. So all I could do was say a quick little prayer for her.

I went downstairs and called in the precinct and told them what had happened and how we'd need Homicide and an ambulance and the medical examiner.

Then I dug in my wallet and pulled out three ones and laid them next to the phone and said to the lady who'd asked me to investigate, 'I'm leaving the money here for a long-distance call.' She nodded.

Janice wasn't home but Mom was, and when I told her what had happened and how the dead woman looked so much like Janice, Mom said, 'Honey, do you really want to be a policeman? Why don't you get out of that city and come back here and work the farm with your Dad?' Then she assured me that Janice was just fine helping Dad work in the north pasture.

I felt a lot better, then, you know, about my sister Janice. I went back upstairs to guard the crime scene, but I stood outside the door. I just didn't want to see the dead woman again. Right now working in the north pasture, with all those beautiful chestnut horses running in the hills, sounded pretty darned good.

15 October, 1995

Sometimes, one of the neighbors would remember the odd white girl who'd stood vigil all summer outside the apartment house where she'd lived before her friend had been murdered.

Wonder whatever happened to her? the neighborhood women would say. I always felt kind of bad for her. Skinny little girl. And those big sad eyes. Wonder whatever happened to her, anyway?

Winter came early that year, and with it another murder on the block, a drunken white husband beating his fourteen-year-old daughter to death for letting one of the neighborhood black kids have sex with her.

A good grim story to be savored and cherished by all the neighborhood people; a story so good, so grim that it made them forget about the summer's murder, and the girl with the big solemn eyes standing vigil even in the rain.

ONE

1

3 June
One year later

Ben knew right away that he would have to kill her.

There was no choice now.

After checking the rest of the cages, he went back outside into the barnyard and the sunny June morning.

Ben Tyler was nineteen years old, a slim blond boy who spent the warm months in a white T-shirt and a pair of jeans and a scuffed pair of white Reeboks. Dressing up for a date with Alison meant wearing a blue button-down shirt from Penney's instead of a T-shirt.

But this morning he wasn't thinking about Alison.

He was thinking about death.

He kept busy the next twenty minutes cleaning out the barn which housed the dairy cows that another farmer milked for them. The farmer got a cut of the profits. This left Ben's mother free to keep up her practice as a veterinarian. She had converted the smaller and older barn into her office and hospital.

In the big dairy barn, Ben swept the floor and scraped and hosed off manure. You had to work vigilantly to keep a dairy barn up to government spec.

When he was finished with that, he went into the vet office and filled up three baby bottles, careful to avoid looking into the room where his mother kept the cages for the dogs and cats.

Then he went back to the big barn.

He spent another twenty minutes this morning bottle-feeding the new calves. He liked the warm and milky smell of the hay in which they lay, and he liked the urgent sounds they made sucking on the rubber nipples. They were sweet, ungainly creatures, and he felt sorry for them and loved them, the way he did most animals. There was so much harm waiting to befall such young creatures.

He tried hard not to think of how he'd been bottle-feeding Elizabeth lately. To no avail.

When he was finished with the bottles, he knew it was time to go back to the office and tell his mother what he'd found out. Like her, he was going to be a vet someday: he drove forty-six miles to the state university every school day. Because of this, his mother had suggested that he handle Elizabeth entirely on his own. He'd said fine, he could do it, but now that the time was here, he wasn't so sure. Of all the animals on the farm, he loved Elizabeth the most.

His mother, a slender woman with a pretty face dominated by outsize brown eyes, looked up when he came into the office. She wore a chambray work shirt and jeans. Her dark hair was pulled back into a loose chignon. Ben's blond hair he got from his father, a man who'd died in a tractor accident when Ben was eight.

She was going over bank statements, a job she hated. She'd just assumed that when she'd bought the computer at Sears, with all the software the salesman had bragged on about so much – she'd just assumed that her bookkeeping chores would be cut in half. Not so. The care and feeding of a computer was just as time-consuming as the care and feeding of a ledger. The only advantage was that you got a print-out.

The office was small, containing a used Steelcase desk and two used Steelcase office chairs. There was a cork bulletin board filled with photos of cats and dogs Lynn had taken care of. The Mr Coffee in the corner birthed at least two full pots a day.

She looked up at him and smiled sadly. 'I checked on Elizabeth.'

'Yeah. So did I.'

'I'm sorry, honey.'

'I know.'

'She's such a little sweetie.'

'She sure is,' he said.

'But it's time, honey.'

'Yeah.'

8

'I'll do it if you want me to.'

'I'll do it.'

'You sure?'

He nodded. He had tears in his eyes. He loved little Elizabeth so much. He'd found her three months ago, a stray down by the rope corral where they worked the occasional horse Lynn Tyler had as a patient. A tiny gray mutt, Elizabeth was, filled with fleas and tics, and at least two pounds underweight. Ben was normally more a dog man than a cat man but he got this mad crush on the tiny kitten right off. And he'd made her his special project. He'd bathed her, put her on a good diet, fixed a nice warm box in his room for her to sleep in, even though most nights she crawled under his covers and slept with him. He could never recall feeling anything as slight and delicate and precious as Elizabeth sleeping next to him, all fragile ribs and small long kitten sighs.

She didn't gain weight. No matter what he fed her, or how often, she didn't gain weight. At first, both Ben and Lynn assumed she just needed to adjust more to her environment. Cats were skittish creatures. Then she started vomiting up everything she ingested, including water. And then, secretly so as not to alarm Ben, Lynn gave Elizabeth a feline leukemia test. The results came back positive.

Ben tried to accept it but he couldn't. Not quite. He kept hoping for some kind of miracle turnaround. If she held down a teaspoon of water for more than a minute, he convinced himself that his miracle had happened. If she looked especially spry for a brief span of time, he ran to tell his mother. Maybe she can beat this thing, he'd said so many times. And Lynn, knowing better but not wanting to hurt him, said, 'Yes, honey, maybe she can.'

Over the past week, she'd lost even more weight. She slept, and did very little else.

The time had come.

Lynn said, 'I'll help you with the needle.'

'I'd appreciate it.'

She shut off the computer and stood up and held out her arms. He came over and let her hug him.

He felt embarrassed by his tears but he couldn't help it. He loved little Elizabeth so much.

'When we get done here,' she said, 'why don't you go into town and see your brother? He's got the afternoon off. Maybe you two could go canoeing.'

Michael was twenty-three, handsome, poised. Even though he'd dropped out of college sophomore year, he'd lucked into a video-store franchise that paid him good money. And he was still a hero. Everybody remembered his basketball years at the Black River Falls high school. He was also Ben's hero and always had been. When he was down, Michael could make him laugh. When he was troubled by something, Michael could help him deal with it. Michael never seemed to mind that his younger brother had bad eyes, hair that never laid down quite right, few social skills, and was considered by most of the townspeople as something of a freak and a burden to both Michael and his mother.

'Well,' Ben said, 'I need a haircut so I guess I could stop in and see him while I'm overtown.'

She looked at him. 'You don't have to do this, you know – with Elizabeth, I mean.'

'I know.'

'You think you're ready?'

'I think so.'

She kissed him on the cheek and then she went in the back where the big rumbling old refrigerator was. She kept all the vaccines and other medicines stored in the thirty-year-old Frigidaire.

That's where she also kept Beuthanasia, the drug she used to put animals to sleep.

'I'm telling you, Michael, I think he suspects.'

'He doesn't suspect anything.'

'He does. I can tell.'

'You can tell. Right.'

In his crisp white shirt, buff blue sport jacket, black gabardine slacks and black suede loafers, Michael Tyler had the air of celebrity about him. He just didn't seem to belong in a Midwestern town of 25,000. The ladies especially liked the dark, curly hair and the gleaming movie-star smile. Nobody quite liked the hard distant intelligence of the brown eyes. There was something troubling about those eyes.

At 8:48 a.m., Michael should have been getting everything ready for the day. The store opened in twelve minutes. A summer day like this, the kids were here soon as the doors opened, videos and interactive games their summer vacation plunder.

Michael liked to dust off the counter, make sure the pop machine was filled up, and the candy stand packed tight with Snickers and Mars and Good 'n Plentys and six or seven other kinds of treats. Candy made Michael good money – sixteen per cent of gross income last year.

But he wasn't getting much done with Denise Fletcher following him around the shop for the last fifteen minutes. She'd been banging frantically on the back door while he'd been letting himself in the front door. Denise was pretty, and had spectacular breasts. Real ones. Not the silicon ones half a dozen local women had bought themselves in the state capitol over the past year. Denise had been a heartbreaker back in their high school days. Her father was a very wealthy banker. That's really why Michael had gone out with her, even more than her breasts. He liked the status she gave him. These days, seeing Denise was even more fun, or had been anyway, till he'd started to tire of her. Her husband of six years was Paul Fletcher, the local Buick dealer and the most arrogant boy in their class. In ninth grade, Paul had read a class paper about the local murder that had involved Michael's grandfather. The class giggled and squirmed and blushed, all eyes fixed on Michael. Paul had done this because Michael had been elected student class president, a job Paul had devoutly sought. Michael had never forgiven him. So balling Paul's wife offered exceptional pleasures. What the dumb bitch didn't seem to understand was that Michael *wanted* Paul to find out. Michael told everybody he knew about the little thing he was having with Denise, knowing that eventually it would get back to Paul, good old Paul.

'So what'm I supposed to do if he asks me for a divorce?'

'Give him one. You'll get a nice settlement.'

'Not if he can prove that I've been sleeping with you.'

He was dusting a display of Clint Eastwood videos, then paused. 'Denise, you could nail him right back.'

'I could? How?'

'You could prove he was unfaithful.'

She looked stunned. 'You think Paul's been unfaithful to me?'

Michael grinned. 'Babe, everybody's unfaithful to everybody. It's the way life is.' He thumped his heart. 'Human nature.'

'I mean, is there something you know that I don't?'

'Huh?'

'You know, about who Paul's been screwing.'

'How would I know?' he said, and went back to his dusting. 'I don't follow him around.'

She was mad at the thought that Paul had been unfaithful to her. All right for her to ball Michael (and before Michael, a few others) but not all right for Paul to sleep with anybody else. 'You think it's Katie Myles?'

'Do I think it's Katie Myles? I don't know what you're talking about.' Dusting a display of Warner Brothers cartoons now. Bugs, Elmer, Tweety-Pie, everybody.

'That he's been screwing. Katie Myles, I mean.'

'Why do you think it's Katie Myles?'

'You remember that party last month at Keith McKenzie's?'

'Uh-huh.'

'She was watching him.'

'Watching Paul?'

'Right. All that weight he's lost at the Diet Center?'

'Huh-uh.'

'He looks kind of studly again.'

'Paul looks studly?'

'Well, for Paul he looks studly. You know what I mean. I mean it's all relative. Compared to you, he doesn't look studly. But compared to Paul thirty pounds ago he looks very studly.'

'I see.' He was putting the candy right now. Dumb little bastards messed up everything.

'I knew she would get to him, the way she was watching him that night out at Keith's. I knew it. Little whore.'

8:56 a.m.

'Babe?'

'I know, I know. You've got to open up the store.'

But before he could protest, or even move away, she slid her arms around him and brought him to her and pressed herself hard against him. Their mouths found each other and he couldn't help himself, he

12

pressed himself right back against her. Maybe he wasn't as tired of her as he'd thought.

'I'm going to give you one tonight you're never going to forget for the rest of your life,' she said when they'd parted.

He laughed. 'Wow. You should get mad at Paul more often.'

'He wants to be unfaithful, I'll show him what unfaithful really means.'

'Same place?'

'Same place. Same time.' She made a face. 'That little whore.'

'You came here all upset that Paul was going to find out about us.'

'If he was here right now, I'd go down on you. Right in front of him. That's how much I care about Paul right now.'

She slipped him her tongue one more time, and rubbed up against him some more, and then she was gone, trailing the scents of perfume and cigarette smoke.

He was properly rattled, overwhelmed by desire (he was a morning man anyway) and still amused at how angry Denise was at the thought of Paul being unfaithful.

People were so crazy sometimes. They wanted it all. They wanted to be unfaithful – but have their mates be virgins.

Crazy.

Lynn held Elizabeth gently but firmly in one hand as she tugged a small plastic bag over the top of the kitten's backside. Sometimes, at just the last moment, animals messed themselves.

Ben was just finishing up with the hypodermic needle. He was sweating and felt as if he were going to vomit. He tried to stop his hands from trembling. He couldn't.

When the needle was ready to go, he turned around and looked down at the gray kitten in his mother's hands.

God, could he actually do it?

'You all right?' Lynn said.

'I guess so.' Then, 'She's so little.'

Lynn stroked the kitten's tangled fur. For the past forty-eight hours Elizabeth had mostly slept, a sweaty and troubled and final sleep. Lynn looked sad now, too.

They were in the back office. There was a new, large white Amana freezer in the corner. This was where the dead animals were kept until they could be driven to the crematorium in town. If the owner wished, he could have the ashes.

Ben touched the kitten and abruptly jerked his hand away, as if he'd been stung.

He'd felt her heartbeat.

She was real.

He was going to kill her.

'Ben,' Lynn said. 'Are you going to be all right?'

'I guess so.'

'It's for her own good, honey.'

'I know. I love her is all.'

'I know you love her. You know I'll do it if you want me to.'

Ben leaned down so he could see her tiny face better. She had such a cute, needy little face. She loved being held. He leaned down and kissed the top of her head. The fur felt damp from sweat. She was very, very sick.

He stood back from her and raised the needle.

With his free hand, he stroked her twice and said, 'I'm sure going to miss you, Elizabeth.'

Lynn watched him. Her brown eyes filled with tears.

Ben put a hand on Elizabeth's back to steady her and then he put the needle in.

'So long, Elizabeth,' he said.

He tried not to think about death. The older he got, the less inclined he was to believe in any kind of afterlife. Not for animals, not for humans.

He felt her small frail body stiffen and then heard her long last breath being expelled.

She was dead.

Lynn went about everything quickly, now. Elizabeth hadn't fouled herself so Lynn put her in the same plastic bag that had been tugged over the kitten's backside. Then into the freezer.

Ben went out on the porch and stared down at the sorrel in the rope corral. The sunlight was just starting to burn the dew off the grass. The shadows from the outbuildings were still moist. Took longer, the sun having to shift, to warm them away.

He thought for a moment about alcohol. Two years ago, when he'd fallen rather foolishly in love with an older high school girl, he'd gone on a three-month drinking jag and learned – to the horror of both himself and his mother – that he had strong alcoholic tendencies. He woke up one morning vomiting blood, and it had really scared him. Ever since then, he'd gone real easy on beer and liquor.

But at the moment, the blessed oblivion that liquor brought ... sounded awful good.

His mother came up and slid her arm around his shoulders and gave him a hug.

'You did the right thing,' she said.

'I know.'

'You're going to make a very good vet.'

He looked at her and smiled sadly. 'Just like you.'

She mussed his hair with her long, quick fingers. 'You go into town and tell that brother of yours to take you out on the river.'

'That sounds good, actually.'

'And take the Bronco.'

'Really?'

The new Bronco was her official office car. He always had to take the old Chevrolet truck.

'Really,' she said, handing him the keys.

He stared some more at the sorrel. It was obvious he wanted to say something else.

'You know how you raised us to be religious and all, Mom?'

She nodded.

'Do you believe that stuff yourself?'

'I'm not sure what "stuff" you're talking about, sweetheart.'

'You know, about there being an afterlife.'

'Oh.'

He studied her face. 'I want you to be honest.'

'Well,' she said, 'then that's what I'll be. Honest.'

She glanced away for a long moment, seeming to track something in the piney hills to the west.

She turned back to him. 'Sometimes I believe in it and sometimes I don't.'

'That's how I am.'

'I guess that's only natural.'

'I mean, sometimes I think we only believe it so we won't have to be scared of dying.'

'That's what I think, too,' Lynn said. 'Sometimes.'

'But if there is an afterlife ... Well, do you think dogs and cats could go there, too?'

She smiled. 'You mean Elizabeth?'

'Yeah. Elizabeth.'

'If there's an afterlife, Elizabeth will be there for sure.'

'Yeah,' he said, 'that's kind of what I was thinking, too.'

He nodded goodbye and then went and got the Bronco.

2

They had a ritual, Ben and Chet the barber. Ben always said, 'Leave it pretty long on the sides, would you, Chet?' and Chet would say, 'Sure thing, youngster,' and then go right ahead and give him the shortest haircut this side of bootcamp.

Chet was one of those mysterious adults who didn't seem exactly young but didn't seem exactly old, either. He always wore a white crew cut and a buff blue polyester barber jacket. On the mirror behind his lone barber's chair was a picture of him and three other soldiers in Viet Nam. None of them looked as old as Ben was now. Ben had been coming to Chet's since he was a boy. In all that time he'd only ever heard Chet refer to Viet Nam once. 'Should've kept the soldiers home and sent the politicians over,' he'd said to a man one day.

Chet kept the place clean. He always swept up the green and white tiles soon as you stepped down, ready for the next customer. The place smelled of sweet red hair tonic and the floury talc Chet used as his finishing touch. Ben's shoulders were always sprinkled white when he left there.

Chet's place was a masculine province that both pleased and frightened Ben. Pleased him because he liked the easy, self-confident way the men talked about things, speaking as if they never for a moment doubted anything they said. Frightened him because he knew he could never be one of them. He couldn't even pretend to be that self-confident.

Al was in there today. Al was old and bald. One of his blue eyes was glass and seemed too large for its socket. He survived on some kind of disability pension from WWII. His life seemed to be measured out in visits to downtown places like the barbershop and then Purvy's News & Cigars and then the Chevrolet dealership, where he always bitched that it was too bad General Motors dealers had to sell foreign cars to survive.

Chet always had the latest *Playboy* on the magazine table, along with *Field and Stream* and *People* and *Soldier of Fortune.*

Al picked up *Playboy* and let the centerfold drop and then grinned at Chet with clacking dentures. He nodded to the naked girl.

Tits like melons and pussy tight as a drum, Ben thought to himself.

Chet said, 'Tits like melons and pussy tight as a drum.'

That's what he always said.

And Al of the clacking dentures always cackled when he said that.

Chet went back to cutting Ben's hair.

'You and that gal Alison are keepin' pretty steady company these days,' he said, and winked at Al.

'Yeah, I guess we kind've are,' Ben said, his face hot, hoping he wasn't blushing. He still didn't know how to respond when people asked him about Alison. He looked at her as a gift that some mysterious force had given him. He was afraid that if he talked about her, his gift would be taken back.

'She's sure a cutey,' Chet said.

'Yeah.'

'You better watch that brother of yours don't cut in,' Al grinned. 'Ass-bandit he is.'

Ben felt his face grow hot again. The truth was, he'd had the same fear himself, afraid that if Alison was around Michael she'd fall in love with him.

Somebody was going to take Alison from him, that much he knew. Nobody as bright and funny and cute as she was, was going to be around somebody like Ben for ever.

That was the weird thing about his feelings for her. He was crazy in love with her but he spent most of the time in utter terror that she was going to dump him.

'You going steady or steadi*ly*?' Chet said.

'I guess I don't know the difference.'

'Well, we used to say, if you were seeing a gal on an exclusive basis, then you were going steady. But if you were seeing a gal and either one of you were free to see other people, then you were going steadi*ly*.'

'Oh. I see. Well, I guess, uh, steady.'

Chet winked at Al again and then went on cutting Ben's hair.

And then Chet cleared his throat and Ben knew just what he was going to say next.

'You know, I was talking to the coach the other day, and he said that the best athlete that ever went through the Black River Falls school system was that brother of yours.'

Too damned bad he had to break his leg, Ben thought.

'Just too damned bad he had to break that leg of his,' Chet said.

And then continued on.

Haircut palaver was in three parts: part one was always about anything going on around town, the more lurid the better, somebody getting arrested or beaten up hopefully: part two was always about Ben's personal life, how things were going with his mother and the animal hospital and things like that: and part three was always about Michael and the glory days of his high school years, and what could've been if only he hadn't broken that damned leg of his.

Michael was the town's only celebrity. He'd not only won two state championships for his team, he'd appeared, along with two other high school boys, on the cover of *Sports Illustrated*, and Dick Schaap on ABC-TV had done a profile on him for the *Evening News*.

Everybody wanted Michael in his club, which explained why he was in Jaycees, Rotary, Lions and a voting member of the Chamber of Commerce board. And he was only twenty-three years old. One other curious fact: the town fathers sort of liked it that he was a hell-raiser. Drank a little too much; drove a little too fast; was a mite heartless about all the ladies, including the married ones, who were always around him. Anybody else, they would have begrudged this kind of behavior. But not Michael. Never Michael.

'That brother of yours gets more pussy than Robert Redford, I'll bet you,' Al said.

'He sure does,' Chet said, and then looked up as the bell tinkled over the door and Alison came in.

Any number of boys from Black River Falls had crushes on Alison. You couldn't help it. Not only was her face sweet and pretty, and her body tempting in a slender quiet way, but there was her merry laugh and curiously solemn gray eyes to contend with. She never seemed aware that she was breaking hearts but she broke hearts regularly.

19

Today she wore a simple white blouse and jeans and a tiny blue barrette in her blonde bobbed hair.

'I was just walking back from lunch,' she said to Ben, 'and I saw you in here. Thought I'd just say hi.' Alison was an assistant at the library. She hadn't finished college and the job was only minimum wage but she lived frugally in a tiny apartment at the back of the print shop down on Main. 'Thought you might walk me back to work.'

Ben hated how he felt, ecstatic over seeing her, yet embarrassed, too. Michael would know just what to say. Do everything nice and easy. Ben was afraid he'd say the wrong thing and look stupid. That's why somebody was going to take her away from him someday. Because she'd be sick of Ben saying stupid stuff.

'I'm just about done with him here, Alison,' Chet said. 'Trim up them sideburns and then you can have him back.'

Ben caught Al looking at Alison's bottom.

Even old guys liked her.

He had no chance of keeping her.

No chance at all.

Steve Conners would never have seen the man breaking into his trailer if he hadn't forgotten his tools that morning.

Steve did carpentry for four different local construction outfits. He always brought his own tools, the way pool hustlers he knew always brought their same cues.

But he'd had a late night with one of the waitresses out to the new line-dancing place between here and the state capitol. He'd been so beer-fuzzy this morning that he'd forgotten to take his tools with him. The morning had gone all right. He'd helped unload trucks was all. But now he needed his tools.

He was roaring down the road, his Firebird lost in the chalky dust of the gravel, when he saw the heavy-set guy park his car on the far side of the oaks that formed a windbreak, and then work his way over to Steve's trailer. Guy was driving a light green Dodge.

Steve pulled over on the shoulder of the road, stopped the car completely, a slender young man of six two with long blond hair so curly it lent his malevolently handsome face an almost feminine aspect. Women loved his face; men wanted to smash it in on sight.

Too much to drink last night, as every night. Dehydrated now, swigging Diet Pepsis, and suffering a bad case of the trots. And now somebody was breaking into his trailer.

But who? And why?

And then he realized that even if he didn't know who, he had a pretty good suspicion of why...

So it had finally happened.

Somebody had finally found him.

He slipped out of the car and started toward the windbreak. While the guy was breaking into Steve's trailer, Steve was going to return the favor by breaking into his car.

From his days on the Chicago police force, Weyrich had learned all about burglary tools. He was especially good with picks. This particular lock, with his pick, took less than three minutes.

The place was an old Airstream that sat alone beneath two willow trees near a slow-moving clay-colored stream. The Airstream was completely isolated, the nearest neighbor a good three-quarter miles away. Perfect place for parties. To the east of it was an elderly Ford up on blocks and sanded down to bleak primer. The windshield was smashed. The day smelled like burned grass.

The name on the front door, just below the bell that probably didn't work, was STEVE CONNERS.

As David Weyrich worked, a fly kept buzzing in his face and aggravating him. A chunky man with a monk's bowl of white fringe hair, he was wearing a winter-heavy camel coat and dark slacks that had some wool in them. Even his necktie had some wool in it. He made himself a promise to get some summer stuff.

Sights as he opened the trailer door: a worn brown fabric-covered couch. On it were an empty Domino's pizza box, several empty Bud cans, a crumpled pack of Winston cigarettes, a threadbare pink summer shirt with some kind of brown stain on the front, and a paperback dangling off the edge. The cover was a photograph of two women. One was doing the other in a prone position. The title was *Lick Me Long!*

Smells as he opened the door: stale beer, cigarette smoke, marijuana smoke, mildewed carpeting, and a kind of generalized filth – dirty dishes, dirty clothes, dirty walls and floors.

He stepped inside and closed the door behind him.

The first thing he had to do was tinkle, tinkle being a word he'd picked up from this lady, this very well-endowed lady he used to bowl with a couple times a month. She always used the word and somehow he'd just picked it up from her.

The bathroom was disgusting, though he figured he probably had it coming. You break into a guy's house and the first thing you do is tinkle in his john. Not a real professional thing to do.

He had to flush the toilet before he used it. Then he had to hold his breath from the stink. The toilet and a shower were packed into the area of a very small closet. The smells were smothering. He was happy to zip up and leave.

He set to work methodically, reasoning that the two places most likely to yield useful stuff were the battered desk on top of which were piled cases of empty beer bottles, and the bureau in the bedroom.

The trouble was, he was wrong on both counts. Nothing useful in either place, unless you considered a pack of Trojans and a couple pairs of ladies' underwear from Penney's useful.

The phone rang.

It sounded loud and accusatory, as if the caller knew that Weyrich was here.

There was no answering machine. Finally, the ringing stopped and the familiar sounds came back. The trembling refrigerator motor; the bark of neighboring dogs.

All right, Sherlock, Weyrich thought, now what? The Sherlock line he'd picked up on some late-night private eye show. He'd used it ever since when he was being down on himself.

Now he looked in all the places *not* likely to be useful. Under the couch. Under the couch cushions. In the back of the TV set. In the refrigerator. In the closet where Conners kept the cleaning stuff that he obviously never used. In the closet where he kept his clothes. In the cedar chest. Nothing.

The phone rang again and unnerved him.

Why should it bother him so much?

When it quit ringing, he went back to searching. Then he remembered the Ford outside. Car up on blocks that way could make a good hiding place.

He went outside, thankful to be in fresh air again.

The Ford was a 1967 Fairlane. Big ass engine. The interior smelled of heat and urine, courtesy no doubt of a local cat or dog.

He was just checking in the glove compartment when he heard the car approaching. All he had found was a section of newspaper folded over into quarters. He grabbed it, slammed the compartment shut, leapt out and started running.

His only hope was to get back to his car.

Steve Conners was doing 60 mph by the time he reached the road that turned toward his Airstream.

He was taking great pleasure from watching the overweight man try to run. Guy would probably have a heart attack and drop down dead. Serve him right.

Conners hadn't learned much about the guy by searching his car. Name was David Weyrich and he lived in the state capitol, at 4670 Elm Street. No suggestion of what his occupation might be.

Conners pulled up to his trailer and slammed on the brakes. By now, Weyrich had reached his car and was sliding behind the wheel.

Conners still had to smile, thinking about how Weyrich had looked, so scared and all, running across that field of buffalo grass. Fat slob.

But Conners' smile faded as he thought again about why Weyrich had likely broken into his trailer.

Somebody had found him.

Somebody had finally found him.

On the drive back to town, Weyrich, still out of breath and glazed with sweat from running from trailer to car, took the folded newspaper from the pocket of his winter sport coat. It was dated 7 June, 1995 – almost a year ago to the day. He got the paper laid out all flat on the seat next to him, patting it down for good measure with his big competent hand, and then he looked at the news story that had a circle drawn around the headline:

WEALTHY COLLEGE GIRL
FOUND MURDERED

Bingo, Weyrich thought.

Bingo.

This Steve Conners was just the man he was looking for.

The town was two towns, really. One was the downtown area with buildings, mostly red brick, that read 1893 and 1902 and 1911 on their cornerstones. In this part of town there was the city park and bandstand. There were also all the old stores and shops. Five years ago the Chamber had convinced all the merchants to buy matching awnings, so on sunny days the exterior of the stores and shops were the bright colors of candy canes. The Carnegie Library was here, too, the place where Ben had discovered Andre Norton and Ray Bradbury and Theodore Sturgeon, and later Ernest Hemingway and William Faulkner and F. Scott Fitzgerald.

The other part of town sat on the edges, east and west. This was where all the new places were, the Wal-Mart and Pizza Hut and Country Kitchen and Hardee's and McDonald's and Motel 6 and three different supermarkets. This was where town and country met, the housewives from the town guiding their carts up and down the same aisles as the farm wives and farmers and farmhands. You saw trucks and cars and even an occasional tractor in the parking lot.

Ben preferred the old part of town.

For instance, now, this lazy noon-hour time of day, it was pleasant to walk across the concrete bridge with the stone lions on either end, and look downstream to where kids in rowboats stood throwing out their fishing lines. It was also pleasant to stop in front of the bandstand and have a drink of fountain water so cold it hurt your teeth. And pick your girl an illicit flower from the garden.

He picked Alison a daisy.

She took it, smelled it, gave him a kiss on the cheek, and continued walking along with him.

'Tonight's the night I make you dinner, remember?'

'Uh-huh,' he said.

She grinned. 'You're scared, aren't you? Think I'm going to poison you, don't you?'

'A TV dinner would be just fine with me.'

She jabbed him in the ribs with her elbow. 'I'm going to make us a casserole and you're going to eat it.'

'Yes, ma'am.'

'And like it.'

'Yes, ma'am.'

A car honked and some boys Ben knew whistled at Alison. Then the driver laid some rubber and they went wailing down the hot asphalt street.

'God, I hate that,' she said. 'They're such little boys.'

'Not all grown up and sophisticated like me, huh?'

'You're doing it again.'

'Oh. I forgot.'

'I don't know why you have to put yourself down all the time, Ben.'

'I was just joking.'

'No, you weren't.' She paused on the sidewalk and looked up at him. 'You really don't have very much respect for yourself.'

He shrugged. 'I'm sort of a dweeb.'

'Yeah? Who said so?'

'Most of the people in this town.' A lot of people had a smirk for gangly Ben; the weird one, they always said, couldn't be more different from his brother if he tried. The weird one. They whispered and giggled about him a lot and sometimes he overheard them and it hurt him a lot, though he pretended that it didn't. The thing was, Ben knew he was weird. He didn't like sports or drugs or hot cars or fist-fights. He spent more time with animals than he did with people, and the truth was, he preferred it that way.

'Yeah, well they're not half as smart as they think they are,' Alison said. 'You know what I think of the people in this town, anyway.'

He didn't want to get her going on the subject of the townspeople. She could get nasty. Three things had happened in the last year that had really angered her. A white friend of hers had gotten herself pregnant by this black man she'd been seeing. The town wanted nothing to do with her. She lived now in a little shack by a little stream, an outcast. The second incident had involved a high school senior who'd started wearing two earrings and a ring in his nose. A bunch of school bullies had beaten him up pretty badly. They'd long suspected he was gay. And when he fled town to go to hairdressing school in Dubuque, they were sure of it. They still told jokes about him. They all predicted gleefully he'd end up with AIDS. The third incident had to do with Mr J. D. Salinger. A group called Christian Women for Decent Literature went to the school board and demanded that *Catcher in the Rye* be taken out of the high school library. Alison and Ben had gone to the school board meeting and told people how much the book had meant to them. The school board elected to leave the book on the shelf. After a movie two nights later, Alison and Ben came out to find the door of her black Honda Civic spray-painted with two words: *Jew lover*. Alison saw this as proof that most folks in Black River Falls were bigots. But Ben said that there were bigots everywhere. White teenagers had lynched a lone black boy in New York last year. And in Chicago, a Latino family had been burned to death by racist neighbors. And in LA a black kid had murdered four white people just because they were white. That's why Ben preferred animals to people. Few animals were malicious. But Alison was wrong about Black River Falls. It wasn't any worse or any better than any other town or city.

When they turned the corner to the library, Ben saw Michael sitting on the park bench to the side of the library steps. He had a woman with him, of course, he always did. This was one of the downtown married women who always dressed up real nice to go to work. They were always fluttering around Michael, just as they had in his high school days.

Michael watched them approach and smiled and waved. He then said something to the woman and she touched him lightly on the knee and got up and left.

Michael stood up and walked over to them. He had a celebrity's walk, self-conscious, purposeful, with just a hint of swagger.

'Hey, kiddo, how's it going?'

Kiddo. He'd called Ben that most of his life.

'And here's the lovely lady,' Michael said as he reached them.

'Hi, Michael,' Alison said.

Though Alison had never said so outright, Ben got the impression that she didn't exactly care for Michael. And the funny thing was, Michael seemed to feel the same way about Alison. They were always pleasant to each other, yet it was clear there was no warmth there.

'You tell her what we're doing this afternoon?' Michael said, sliding his arm around his brother's shoulder. 'Taking the canoe out by the Falls.'

'I wish Ben didn't do that,' Alison said. 'It scares me.'

When Michael was ten years old, he started taking an aluminum canoe downriver to the very edge of the Black River Falls. Then he jumped out of the canoe at the last moment. If you ever went over the rushing, tumbling Falls, which was a 300-foot drop, you'd die for sure. At least four people had died there over the past twenty years or so.

Ben had gone along with Michael sometimes. Not all the time, because the Falls scared him so much. But every once in a while ... They never told their mother what they did. Far as she knew, they just had a nice ordinary time on the river. She'd be terrified and angry if she'd known what Michael had convinced his little brother to do.

'You be sure to wear a life preserver,' Alison said to Ben.

Michael laughed. 'Hey, he's already got one mother. He doesn't need another one.'

'You hear me?' Alison said, ignoring Michael.

'I'll wear one,' Ben said.

'Promise?'

'Promise.'

She made Ben feel important. Here was this really great-looking girl very worried about his safety. Right in front of Michael.

'I'd better get into work,' Alison said. She looked at Michael and said, 'Nice to see you, Michael.'

'Yeah, it's always a pleasure.'

Icy, insincere words on both their parts.

She squeezed Ben's hand and then reached in her pocket and dug out a key. 'I'll probably be late getting home. You can let yourself in.' She smiled. 'You said you'd look at my toilet tank, remember?'

'Oh, that's right.'

'There're three beers in the refrigerator.'

'Thanks.' Talk of beer made him feel more grown up. The truth was, a six-pack lasted Ben and Alison a week or better.

Alison said goodbye again then walked away.

'She doesn't like me, does she?' Michael said.

Ben shrugged. 'You two just seem to rub each other the wrong way, I guess.'

'You could do better, kiddo.'

'Than Alison? Are you crazy?'

'I could introduce you to some girls who would make Alison look pretty plain.'

27

And then the words just came out, and he didn't stammer or blush or anything: 'I love her.'

Michael started to laugh but apparently realized that Ben was serious. Then he looked startled. 'Wow, you're really growing up, kiddo. Loving somebody, I mean.'

'I know. But it's true.'

'You're a little young.'

'Mom and Dad got married when they were twenty-two. I'll be twenty in five months.'

'Wow,' Michael said, shaking his head. 'My little brother really is growing up.' Then he cuffed him on the side of the arm. 'Sorry to hear about Elizabeth. She was a cutey.'

Ben appreciated how Michael never put him down for loving animals so much. He knew that Michael never got attached to them the same way.

'You want to stop off somewhere and get a life preserver?' Michael said.

'I guess not.'

Michael smiled. 'You had me scared there, kiddo. I think it's really nice that you fell in love with her, I really do. But you don't want to go overboard and start getting pushed around by her, now do you?'

'No,' Ben said, wanting to give his brother this one moment, wanting his brother to think that Ben was a regular guy after all. 'I sure wouldn't want to be pushed around.'

But Alison *had* pushed him around to some degree, and the awful truth was, Ben loved it.

A girl wouldn't push you around if she didn't love you.

3

As her sons were heading to the river, Lynn Tyler was in the truck heading east on a gravel road. Her destination was a farm owned by a man named Harvey Quinn. He'd been the foreman of the jury that had found her father guilty of first-degree murder.

There was a lot of talk in the press these days about how the rights of victims didn't seem to be as important as the rights of criminals. Lynn agreed with that. Most people never really recovered from having a spouse or child murdered.

But there was a group of victims most people never gave a thought to: the families of the killers.

Her father, a resolutely handsome and charming man, a doctor of great medical skill and even greater human skill, had been accused of bludgeoning to death the girlfriend neither his wife nor daughter had known anything about.

Lynn had been nine years old at the time. Her world ended. At school, the once-popular girl became a pariah, a figure to be snickered at and whispered about. All she could do was believe devoutly in what her mother told her – that this was somehow all a horrible mistake and that the jury would find her father innocent. And then their lives would go back to normal.

She could still remember holding her mother's hand on the days they visited her father in the county jail, where he was being held during the trial. Everything – walls, tables, chairs – was battered and drab and cold to the touch. The air smelled harshly of disinfectant. Her father never said much, just sat in his chair at the small wobbly table covered with the carved initials of previous inmates. An armed guard stood ten feet away. The conversations never seemed to be very dramatic. Her mother would always ask how he was doing and he would always tell her about life in the county jail, how bad the food was, and how the inmates were always asking him various medical questions, and how he really appreciated the two Baby Ruths she brought him on every visit.

One day her mother went to visit her husband alone and when she came home, she went to the liquor cabinet and got down a bottle of very expensive scotch, and then went up to the den and stayed there most of the night. In the course of this, somehow, she managed to fix Lynn a toasted cheese sandwich and to give her her vitamins, and to tuck her into bed. She weaved and wobbled as she did all this. Then she went back to the den and her drinking. Lynn was worried about her and couldn't sleep. Late into the night, her mother began sobbing, wailing really, and then rushed into the bathroom and threw up. Lynn was terrified, kneeling down next to her mother as she vomited. She did for her mother what her mother always did for her at such a moment, got her to sit on the closed toilet lid and then washed her face up with hot sudsy water on a clean nubby washcloth. Her mother kept right on crying and Lynn didn't know what to do and then her mother said, 'He did it, honey, he killed that girl, he told me so himself.' Lynn half-dragged her mother into bed and then crawled in next to her. Lynn's bed was just a single and so they were very crowded. Lynn held her mother until she finally drifted into a fitful sleep. Lynn wasn't so lucky. For her there was no sleep at all. She just kept thinking about what her mother had said. That her father had admitted killing the girl.

There are always a few people who are kind to outcasts and Lynn met a few of them during the four months of her father's trial. Mostly her new friends were other outcasts, the ones who were marked and maimed in some way, too fat, or lame, or with a speech impediment or who were always getting into trouble. It was then that Lynn also realized how much solace and succor animals were able to give her. There were deep woods behind her house and she spent more and more of the daylight hours there. She befriended a raccoon she named Bess, and a possum she named Seymour, and a hawk who could not quite fly right she named Caesar. She spoke to them in a silent tongue far more beautiful and articulate than human words could ever be, and they understood with a compassion and wisdom no human could ever offer.

Two years later, two weeks before Thanksgiving break, her father was put to death in the electric chair. A lot of the locals were surprised. There'd been bets that because he was a doctor who had powerful friends in the state capitol, he would be spared at the last moment. The governor, a Democrat who wanted to prove that class should hold no sway, had denied her father's final appeal.

By this time, her mother's drinking was out of control. She stayed home and drank. She created little humiliating scenes, as when she drunkenly walked into Bob's Supermarket dressed only in her slip. The police chief forced her to sell her car so she couldn't drive. Lynn was pretty much on her own. In addition to her schoolwork, Lynn did all the housework and took care of her mother. This frequently meant feeding her and bathing her and forcing her to bed so she could get some sleep. The family doctor had warned Lynn about delirium tremens, saying they came on when the alcoholic didn't sleep enough to dream properly. Delirium tremens were nightmares the mind had saved up.

In the autumn of tenth grade, after a brief pass through the woods to check on Seymour and Bess and Caesar, Lynn found her mother asleep in the recliner. On the TV screen played one of her mother's favorite soap operas, 'The Edge of Night.' She twice tried to wake her mother before realizing that her mother would never be awakened again. The family doctor said heart attack and the county coroner agreed.

Lynn spent the last two years of her high school days living with the family doctor. He was a widower and needed a great deal of help around the house. He was also a decent man and a good and patient friend. Lynn suffered from several long spells of clinical depression and he helped her through each one of them. On occasion, and this was worst of all for her, she saw the family of the young woman her father had killed. They were a poor family, and so there was class anger on top of their sorrow and loss. Sometimes, she left flowers on the young woman's grave, never letting people know who left them there. She did not approve of the young woman's affair with her father, but her father had no right to kill her.

The murder had created so many victims, and in both families...

31

She was forever marked by the town, of course. No matter what else she did, or became, she would always be the daughter of that doctor who savagely murdered his young mistress because she'd wanted to break up.

The snickers and smirks might have gone now, all these years later, but there would always be the whispers. Each new generation of Black River Falls learned about Lynn and her father, and each generation looked upon her with a curious mixture of pity and contempt.

Now she was about to visit the foreman of the jury that had sentenced her father to death...

Conners kept looking out at the road and the boss kept yelling at him for doing it.

Conners was trying to see if the fat guy who'd broken into his trailer was lurking out there somewhere, watching.

Conners' hangovers were pretty well known to the local construction trade. If he was stone sober, he was a good carpenter, a *rough* carpenter, one who assembled the framework of the house or building, and then placed the sheathing and siding on the structures. He wasn't worth a damn, drunk or sober, as a *finish* carpenter, however, meaning he never did anything that took great finesse. A finish guy would come in and hang the doors and windows and lay the floors and things like that.

Today Conners wasn't worth a damn at anything at all.

Three houses were going up on the side of a hill overlooking a leg of the Black River. The construction was at least five weeks behind and every few days or so the owners would show up in their fancy-ass cars and gnaw a little bit on the foreman. The owners all had commitments to sell their current houses – and let the buyers move in on a certain date – so they had good reason to be anxious.

And the schedule wasn't being helped along any by a carpenter who kept tripping over the edges of the sub-floor and dropping his saw every few minutes as he worked.

The foreman, a big red-faced sweaty guy named Clete, came over and put his hands on his hips and spat a stream of tobacco that almost hit Conners in the face. The other workers kept on hammering, the sounds creating echoes in the hills. On the edge of the woods, a sweet young doe watched them work as, overhead, a raccoon squatted on a branch, trying to figure out if the construction site had any food it might steal.

'Where'd you have lunch?'

'Wendy's, why?' Conners said, squinting up into the sun. It was a lie – he'd been too upset to eat after seeing the guy breaking into his trailer – but he knew what Clete was after here.

'You stop by a tavern?' Clete said.

'Nope.'

'I don't want any lies.'

'I'm not lying, Clete. Honest. I didn't stop by any tavern.'

'Then what the hell's wrong with you?'

'There's nothin' wrong with me.'

'Then how come you're trippin' over everything, and you keep droppin' your hammer and saw?'

'Catching a cold, I guess.'

Clete wiped his sweaty forehead with a meaty arm. 'You know how far behind we are?'

'I sure do.'

'Then concentrate a little better, you understand me?'

'I sure do, Clete. And I will. Concentrate a little better, I mean.'

Clete let another stream of tobacco go, glowered a moment at Conners, and then walked away.

Conners got back to work.

He also kept a nervous eye on the road.

The fat guy could be anywhere, watching him.

Whoever he was, wherever he was from, the fat guy obviously knew all about Steve Conners and what Steve Conners had done.

Steve should never have come back to Black River Falls. After he'd done those things, he should have just kept going.

He wondered how long before the fat guy got the law down on him.

He wondered how long before he'd be in a prison cell for the rest of his life.

Should have just kept traveling. Yessir.

A whimper caught in his throat, the kind of whimper a little boy makes when he's terribly afraid of something. That was how Conners felt, his shirt off and him baking in the summer sun out here in the boonies, just like a helpless little kid.

33

The roof of a car sparkled in the sunlight. Conners' eye followed it as it climbed up into the piney hills. This didn't look like the car the fat guy had been driving but then maybe he'd switched cars.

Maybe he was leading the law to Conners, and the law was circling, circling, tighter and tighter.

The same kind of whimper caught in Conners' throat, and once again he felt like a little boy.

He licked dry lips.

He needed his standard beer-and-shot. Needed them real bad.

He had just turned back to his work, when he heard a heavy car door *chunking* shut behind him on the driveway below.

He had to smile. He was getting to be a real paranoid bastard, no doubt about it.

Was he going to jump every time he heard a car pass on the road, or a car door open and slam shut behind him?

He went back to work, getting the saw lined up properly, starting to put some muscle in it.

Then he heard the foreman talking to somebody below. On the drive, near where the car would be.

He couldn't help it if he turned around and took a look, could he?

Wasn't that just a person's natural inclination?

So he turned around and there the guy stood.

The fat one. With the fringe of white hair. In the camel-colored sport jacket.

The one who'd broken into his trailer.

He was talking to Clete the foreman and both men were looking up here.

And that's when Steve Conners did it, acting as casual as he could about it.

He set down the saw. And stood up. And stretched like he was good and relaxed. And then walked across the newly-poured floor to the big red thermos of water that everybody shared.

By now, the fat guy was walking up to the house.

Steve still didn't run.

He walked calmly to the far side of the foundation and then stepped into the tall, chafing weeds on the edges of the construction site.

Steve got over to the grass, which was as high as his shoulder, and that's when he gave in to his fear and panic.

That's when he took off running as fast as he could.

The fat man started shouting his name.

The words sounded like gunshots on the quiet afternoon.

Steve just kept running into the deep woods.

'Damned barbed wire,' Harvey Quinn said. 'I warn the boy every time he takes Chester here out for a ride.'

Like many farmers hereabouts, Quinn kept a horse as a pet, in this case a handsome sorrel who was getting on in years but was still a sound and healthy animal.

The Quinn boy always took him up to the fenced land in the hills and let him run too close to the barbed wire. This time, Chester had gotten some pretty severe lacerations.

'Gonna be all right, Dr Tyler?'

'Going to be fine, Harvey.'

Quinn, a stout man with red hair showing more and more gray these days, stroked the animal's back.

They were in the shadowy barn that smelled of damp hay and horseshit. The boy, a sixteen-year-old who was even bigger than his father, worked nearby on a John Deere tractor engine.

Finished suturing the lacerations, Lynn reached into her black bag and took out a hypodermic needle and some serum. 'May as well do this while I'm out here. Equine infectious anemia.'

'God, has it been a year already?' Quinn said, digging in the pocket of his bib overalls for his pipe.

'Afraid it has been, Harvey.' She smiled. 'We're not getting any younger, I guess.'

He snorted. 'Hell, you don't look no different than you did back when—' And then he caught himself and looked embarrassed. 'Well, you know, when you was in high school.'

When my father murdered that girl and was executed, she thought. It was something never far from the minds of the townspeople, not when Lynn was around anyway. But she could deal with it because their memories had not touched her sons. The townspeople had left the boys strictly alone where their grandfather was concerned. They might always look with a troubled eye on Lynn but not her boys.

'You want to steady him?' Lynn said.

'Sure.'

Unlit pipe in the corner of his mouth, the big farmer stroked the neck of his animal and did a little soothing sweet-talking while Lynn gave Chester his booster shot.

'There we are, Chester,' Lynn said when she was finished, packing up her bags and giving the horse a little nuzzle with her nose. Chester had a good-natured dignity to him that Lynn loved.

On the way back to her truck, Quinn said, 'You know back there in the barn, when I talked about when you was in high school? I didn't mean to bring up no bad memories.'

She smiled. 'I know you didn't, Harvey.'

'It just kinda came out.'

'I understand.'

'Folks around here – we're damned proud of you.'

She touched his arm affectionately. 'I appreciate you saying that.'

'You hung in there and – well, you're one hell of a vet.'

She put her black bag on the front seat and then crawled in behind the wheel.

Quinn came up to the door. 'We're proud of that son of yours, too. Best athlete we ever had.'

She always felt guilty when people told her how proud they were of Michael because this always implicitly slighted Ben. She knew they didn't mean to do this – but sometimes it was as if she had only one son, the one everybody talked about.

'Thanks.'

Quinn banged on the door. 'This old puppy's lasted you a long, long time, Doc.'

She laughed. 'Just like Chester.'

She drove off, honking goodbye when she reached the gravel road.

Steve Conners came out of the woods a hundred yards west of the trestle bridge where as a boy he used to catch pike and bass and drum sturgeon.

He wished he was a boy now.

He wished he had his life to live all over again.

He wished he hadn't done what he'd done.

He was getting a good run down the gravel, glad to be free of grasping weeds and low-hanging branches and sudden holes that made you stumble and bang your head, when he saw the car rounding the bend ahead of him.

The light green Dodge.

The fat man's rental car.

Bastard'd caught up with him again.

Steve Conners did the only thing he could do.

He turned an abrupt right, stumbling as he did so, and headed back for the deep woods.

The fat man started honking at him.

Bastard; fat bastard.

He ran.

Weyrich let Conners go.

He'd rightly figured that Conners would run in the direction of his trailer, so he'd spotted him on the road here.

But now Conners was back in the woods and God only knew where he'd run this time.

Weyrich had some people to interview, anyway. He might as well do them now. Conners would turn up again. And then Weyrich would nail his ass good and tight.

At one time on the river, or so Ben had read, colorful canoes made of birchbark were used in races. These were the canoes of the Indians who'd inhabited this land thousands of years before the white settlers came. When the canoes were painted in certain ways, in certain colors, that meant they were to be used for a water sport, such as racing. Indians lined both banks of the deep, swift river to watch. When the canoes were painted in other ways, and in other colors, that meant they were to be used for war. Warring tribes sometimes fought from canoe to canoe with bows and arrows.

Ben loved the river and associated it with his brother Michael. From Ben's earliest days, Michael had brought him here and shown him how to use the battered old aluminum canoe and its oars. Ben had always felt protected by Michael, and privileged to be part of his world.

The stretch of river they loved especially was a mile up from the roaring, crashing Falls. Here the water ran narrow and fast, its earthen terracotta color contrasting with the white of birch and the black of hardwoods lining the shores. Water moccasins slithered ashore; duck and pheasant touched down in the early autumn, just prior to migration; wolf and coyote and deer and wild dog and bear stood in the trees watching the white man just as they'd once watched the red man. In the summer, the trees in full bloom, Ben could paddle down the river and forget all about civilization, feeling at one with the Indians who had roamed these woods centuries earlier.

And then there was the game they always played.

'You up for it today?' Michael said.

Being 'up for it' meant that you'd get soaking wet and have to remain that way until you got back home. But even more so, being 'up for it' meant that Ben would have to once more conquer one of his worst fears: going over the Falls and being smashed against the ragged rocks below. He still had the nightmare once or twice a week.

'I guess so,' Ben said.

'You don't have to.'

'I know.'

'It scares me, too.'

'It does?' Ben said.

'Sure.'

They were paddling down the center of the river, caught in the current, which made their paddling much easier.

They were headed for the dam.

'You just saying that?' Ben sat behind Michael, so he couldn't see his face.

'Saying what?'

'About being scared?'

'No. I'm not. Honest.'

'You ever have nightmares about it?'

'Sure.'

'Bull.'

'No bull. Honest.'

Sometimes Michael just pretended about things so he wouldn't make Ben feel bad. He still insisted, for instance, that he was just as shy about meeting girls as Ben was, but Ben had seen him in action and knew better. He still insisted that he got just as tired as Ben when

38

they played basketball or touch football but Ben knew that Michael could go on for hours. And he still insisted that he was just as afraid of things such as the Falls as Ben was.

This was why Ben loved him so much. He'd spent years imitating Michael, combing his hair the same way, buying the same kind of clothes, listening to the same tapes, saying the same things in the same way – but unfortunately it all just came out dorky. Even when he stood in front of the full-length mirror in the bedroom they'd shared growing up, even when he half-closed his eyes and imagined it was Michael's reflection he saw there – even then, he was just a bad, dorky imitation of his older brother.

And Michael didn't care. That was the astonishing thing. He'd always included Ben, taken him along to basketball games, movies, even just kind of hanging out on Saturday afternoons when the high school kids went to movies out at the Cineplex and then drove up and down Main looking at girls until suppertime. That's why, even though Ben was never in favor with kids his own age, nobody ever picked on him in any demonstrable way. Because they knew about his older brother, and knew that the older brother would take them apart if they ever hurt Ben in any way.

Michael was not only Ben's brother, he was also the best friend he'd ever had.

'I did a shitty thing to you today, kiddo,' Michael said over his shoulder. 'Saying what I did about Alison.'

'I wish you two liked each other better.'

'She's a fine girl, kiddo.'

'You really mean that?'

'I just want you to have the best is all, Ben. I just want you to have the best.'

'Alison *is* the best. Like you and Mom are the best.' And Elizabeth, Ben thought, images of her death returning.

Michael said, 'You slept with her yet?'

'I don't like to talk about that stuff, Michael. It's sort of private, I mean.'

'I was just going to give you the old condom speech Mom is always giving me.'

Ben laughed. 'Oh, right, the old condom speech.'

'But she's right, you know.'

'Mom?'

'Uh-huh. I mean, I don't know where some of my girlfriends have been. And you don't know where Alison has been.'

'I don't think she's ever slept around much.'

'Yeah, but you don't know that for sure, just like she doesn't know for sure about you.'

'Yeah, all my thousands of conquests.'

'You have any condoms?'

'I'm planning to buy some.'

Actually, Ben had gone into a couple of different stores planning to buy some but both times the clerks were people he knew. And he just couldn't get the word out. *Condom.*

'Well, I've got a couple extra in my billfold. Why don't I give you those?'

'Hey, I'd appreciate that.'

The roaring became louder now, making it difficult to be heard. The Falls were coming up fast. This was where they needed to turn around if they were not going to play their game.

'You want to do it?' Michael shouted over his shoulder.

Ben's entire body clenched. His stomach and bowels felt queasy. The Falls really scared him. 'I guess not, Michael. Will that make you mad?'

'Hell no, kiddo,' Michael shouted. 'I'll take you to shore.'

They had to paddle against the current to reach the shore.

Ben jumped out on the sand. 'You sure you want to try it? The Falls sound pretty mean today.'

Michael grinned. 'That's when they're fun, kiddo.' He nodded downriver. 'See you in a little while.' He patted the aluminum canoe that had been battered by going over the Falls so many times. 'Sure you don't want to go along?'

Ben knew he should say yes. It would really please Michael. But all he said was, 'Maybe next time, all right?'

'Sure, kiddo,' Michael said, a shadow of disappointment moving across his eyes. 'See you in a little bit, then.'

Ben felt ashamed of himself. 'It's just that I'm not a good swimmer.' Which was true. Despite Michael's best efforts, Ben had just never really learned how to master swimming.

'It's all right, kiddo. Really. See you in a few minutes.'

40

There was a narrow worn path through the woods that ran parallel to the Falls. Ben took it now, hurrying so that he could stand at the bottom and watch the canoe come shooting down the splashing water. The Falls was a 200-meter drop.

He should have gone with Michael. All the stuff Michael had done for him over the years, Ben owed him that. But the Falls terrified him. Absolutely terrified him.

When he reached the bottom of the path, he stood on a small rock promontory far enough from the Falls that he could see the water break and bubble at the very top and then fall away splashing to the river below. It wasn't a very big waterfall but it was a perilous one. Local parents had used it as the bogeyman for years. Every few years, some kid got too brave or too foolish and died playing around it.

Blue sky. A hawk gliding down the sky. The narrow rushing river. The birch and hardwoods on either bank. And then the Falls themselves. The air sparkling with drops of water; a foamy bubbling pool at the bottom of the Falls. You couldn't ask for much more from life, especially since Alison liked canoeing as much as he did. They came out here a lot; and sometimes she even came out here by herself. She didn't like the game of taking the canoe right up to the edge of the Falls but she loved staying upriver.

Then he saw the canoe at the top of the tumbling water.

The canoe paused momentarily, as if its bottom had snagged on something.

And then Ben saw Michael standing up inside it. Usually, Michael bailed out a good five yards before reaching the waterfall itself. He'd built clamps inside the canoe to hold the paddles so they wouldn't get lost when it went over the water. After securing the clamps, he then jumped out. It was difficult, swimming against a current this frenzied, but he was a good swimmer and always made it to shore. Meanwhile, the canoe went on over the Falls.

But today Michael had stayed with the canoe right to the very end. Michael loved to show off for Ben, but this time he had waited too long and got in trouble.

'Jump! Jump!' Ben called out to him. But his voice was lost in the fury of the cascading water.

Michael wasn't going to make it this time.

Ben knew this with an awful certainty.

41

Dead. Michael would soon be dead.

Ben started running back up the path, to the place where he'd come ashore.

Through the low-hanging branches, he saw the edge of the waterfall. The canoe was still hung up there on something. This had never happened before. The canoe always went over fast – too fast, if anything.

The canoe was empty.

Michael was gone.

Ben had an image of his brother crying out for help, unheard in the roar of water.

And then drowning.

Even great swimmers drowned sometimes.

Ben felt the way he had earlier today with Elizabeth – that death was about to claim another life of someone he loved very deeply.

'Michael! Michael!' he shouted.

He knew this wouldn't do any good but at least it gave him the feeling he was accomplishing something.

Finally, he came to the point where he'd jumped from the canoe ten minutes ago.

He looked out over the clay-colored water as it rushed toward the fall line downriver.

Nothing. No sight of Michael whatsoever.

A cry caught in Ben's throat.

His premonition of disaster was coming true.

Just the way he'd known last night, when he'd gone to bed, that Elizabeth would not be any better in the morning and that she would have to be put to sleep ... now he knew that Michael was in terrible trouble.

'Michael!'

Should he run for help? But what if Michael suddenly appeared out there and needed him?

Ben's mind was a chaos of fear and indecision. And that was when he heard the sound. Human sound. Male sound. Michael.

Ben's eyes again scanned the rushing surface of the river. Not until his third pass across the far shore did he see the top of Michael's head. Ben would have mistaken it for the top of a rock if Michael hadn't been calling out.

Michael seemed to be clinging to something near the far shore. Then his head disappeared again.

He couldn't swim very well.

The thought lasted only a moment but it was enough to paralyze Ben just as he started into the water.

Couldn't swim.

What if he tried to save Michael and drowned in the process?

What if they both drowned?

One would be bad enough for their mother; but two of them...

And then his head cleared. And he knew exactly what he must do.

This was his brother Michael's life he was considering here. Michael, the closest and truest friend he'd ever had.

Ben dove in, the water chalky-tasting in his mouth, blinding in his eyes. He had bad sinuses and his nasal passages started closing at once.

He did everything Michael had carefully instructed him not to do. He flung his arms wildly through the water, he didn't use his legs properly to propel himself, he kept his mouth open and ingested enough water to make him sick.

And yet somehow, after a few minutes of sinking, of splashing, of feeling stark panic at the prospect of his own drowning ... somehow he managed to reach his brother.

Michael was no longer shouting for help.

His head bobbed up and down on the surface. His eyes were shut tight. He made no sound whatsoever.

He clung to a very heavy fallen tree branch. There'd been a small tornado a few weeks earlier and the branch was obviously one of the dead.

When Ben touched him, he had the sense that life had already left his brother's body.

The panic again.

He imagined his mother's face when she heard about poor dead Michael.

And then Michael gasped and his eyes came open and he shouted Ben's name.

Only now could Ben see the big red bruise on the left side of Michael's head. Michael had apparently struck something when he'd bailed out of the canoe.

Ben got his arm around Michael's chest and shouted, 'I'm not going to be real good at this, Michael, but I'm going to get you to shore. I promise.'

Michael's eyes were glazed with fatigue. He could barely speak. In little more than a mumble, he said, 'Thanks, kiddo.'

Then Ben started the long trek back to the shore, forcing himself to concentrate, to use a combination of the flutter kick and the breaststroke to pull his brother to safety.

Several yards from shore, Michael said, 'You saved my life, kiddo. You saved my life.'

And then Michael, apparently regaining his faculties, gave his little brother a hug.

4

For a woman who had sixty-three children, Lynn Tyler was a damned good-looking woman.

Late this afternoon, her progeny consisted not only of two human boys, but lambs, dogs, cats, hawks, goats, rabbits, a possum named Marie and a raccoon named Conan.

She had spent the last hour doing the work that Ben usually did – walking dogs, cleaning cages, checking food bowls and making out a schedule of appointments for this afternoon.

After the death of her husband, Lynn had turned to her animals for comfort. Her father had murdered someone, and her husband had died young. She'd learned that you just couldn't count on human relationships. There were several town men her age who'd tried dating her but none had gotten past the fourth evening. She simply preferred her own life with her sons and her animals. A shame, the townspeople said, a pretty woman like that.

Her only other passion was gardening. She loved her hand tools, trowel and dibble and cultivator and weeder, and loved the aromas of the garden as night fell, the stars flung wide and wild across the deep blue of sky.

She was in the shed, just getting her gardening tools out, when she heard a car in the drive. She walked over to the door and leaned against the frame and watched as a big man climbed out of a light green Dodge.

For his size, he moved quickly and well. There was a vaguely officious air about him, as if he were used to being in charge. Only his clothes seemed out of place, jacket and pants too heavy for the heat.

He saw her in the doorway and said, 'Would you be Mrs Tyler?'

'I would.'

'I wondered if we could talk a few minutes.'

'Sure. As long as I know what it's about.'

Up close, he smelled of heat and English Leather. She remembered her husband liking that scent, too. She felt a moment of great loss, his funeral and the bleak gray endless days following his death coming back to her with shocking force.

'You have a son named Michael, I believe.'

'Just who are you, mister?' Her words carried an edge now. Mention of her son had made her uneasy, fearful and protective at the same time. Her animals reacted the same way when their own young were threatened. And there was definitely something threatening about this man with the soft jowly face and the hard dark eyes.

'I'm a detective.'

'You work for Chief Rhys, you mean?'

'Private.'

She wanted to laugh. To her, private detectives were the province of bad TV shows and lurid novels. Now one was standing in front of her and he didn't look or sound anything like his counterparts on the screen.

'Is Michael in some kind of trouble?'

'No, ma'am. Not Michael. But a friend of his may be.'

'Which friend?'

'A young man named Steve Conners.'

'Oh,' she said, saying it with a sense of confirmation. She'd never liked Steve, nor trusted him, nor wanted Michael to be friends with him. Steve had gotten into a great deal of trouble in high school, enough trouble that he'd spent a year and a half in reform school. Michael had always defended the boy, not only to her but to his school friends, who never understood why he hung out with Conners, either.

'How does a glass of lemonade sound to you, Mr—'

He put out a hand. He had a firm but not excessive grip. He wasn't trying to prove that he was the big strong man and she the weak little woman.

'David Weyrich is my name, ma'am.'

'Well, then, Mr Weyrich, let's go have a glass of lemonade.'

Even little kids could tell you stories about, 'Smiley's.' The tavern had originally been built back in the thirties to serve the men who worked at the nearby grain factory. But soon enough respectable workingmen drifted elsewhere because 'Smiley's' was too vicious a place to drink in for long. In 1936 a mulatto was castrated out in the back parking lot; in 1949 a white man had his eye scooped out with a fishing knife; and in 1963 an adulterous couple was doused with gasoline and set afire by the woman's husband. This was right inside the tavern. Maybe the violence here wasn't quite so spectacular these days but it never let up. Broken noses, jaws, fists; contusions, concussions, lacerations. A steady stream of bloody predators and victims were taken from 'Smiley's' in an ambulance to the nearby county hospital. The windows of the tavern had long ago been bricked up to save the glass from being smashed out every night. And all decent people had long ago fled. Now 'Smiley's' belonged to bikers and biker gangs and people who took belligerent pride in being riff-raff.

Steve Conners was one of the latter. He was a romancer, a bedazzler, but he was still riff-raff.

Late that afternoon, while Lynn talked with Weyrich, Conners came through the back door of 'Smiley's.' Nothing could prepare you for the odors that jumped on you – urine, cigarettes, marijuana, stale beer, and four decades of puke in the toilet and on the rotted linoleum floor. Not to mention blood, whiskey, rat droppings and disinfectant so strong it brought tears to the eye.

The bartender, a beefy man who wore enough tattoos to open an art gallery, smirked when he saw Conners. Steve couldn't hold his liquor well and he was always starting fights in here and getting the crap kicked out of him. He felt tough when he drank. But he wasn't tough. Not ever.

The tavern was one big room with a long bar on the west wall and nine booths on the other. In the middle was a shuffleboard table, a bumper pool table and two pin-ball machines back to back. Way over in the corner was an empty space that the more romantic used for dancing, which usually meant two really drunk people grinding their pelvises into each other while crazed horny bikers cheered them on.

A family kind of place, 'Smiley's' was.

Conners picked burrs and thistles from his shirt as he stepped up to the bar. 'Beer-and-shot.'

'You look like shit,' the bartender said.

'Yeah? Well so do you.'

Conners drank three beers and three shots in twenty-five minutes. During this time he walked back to the pay phone six times, dropped in the money and then waited for a connection. It always rang busy. Each time, Conners got angrier and angrier. Sonofabitch. Who the hell was tying up the line, anyway?

Workers started to drift in. Most of them were employed at the meat-packing plant. They smelled of sweat and blood. A couple of them nudged each other when they saw Conners down at the end of the bar. He was sort of a joke around here. But he wasn't drunk enough to hassle them. Not yet.

The jukebox thundered on. The bumper pool table was suddenly surrounded by four guys with cues. The pin-ball machines started banging and bonging. One of the girls painted on the face of the machine had breasts that lit up when you scored 500. More workers came in. Conners was largely forgotten.

All he did was drink and walk back to the phone every six or seven minutes. Still busy. He couldn't believe it. One time he slammed the phone real hard and when he came back to his beer, the bartender said, 'You slam that god damn phone again like that, I'm going to put it up your ass. You understand me?'

Conners wanted to say something but decided not to.

He just stood there knocking back beers and shots. They didn't have much effect on him.

There was only one reality now.

They'd found out about him.

What he'd done.

It was all over for him now. All frigging over.

He capsized beneath a wave of self-pity. He wasn't a bad guy, really. Sure he had a police record. Sure he'd hurt some people. But he wasn't really bad. But now they were going to treat him as if he were the worst kind of human being who walked the earth.

He didn't know what to do.

He wanted to cry; he wanted to smash in somebody's face; he wanted to run and never stop running.

He had to get through that frigging phone line. He had to.

'I don't think you're telling me the truth, Mr Weyrich,' Lynn said half an hour after she'd served Weyrich his first glass of lemonade. They'd now had two each, sitting in the kitchen with the tabby cat sleeping next to the lemonade pitcher. The refrigerator thrummed and the box fan in the window whirred. She hated air conditioning and never used it unless she had to.

'Then I'm doing my job.'

'You are?'

'Of course. That's how police and investigators do their job.'

'By lying?'

'Absolutely.'

'You sound proud of it.'

'I am proud of it.'

'I'll stick to animals,' Lynn said.

'Beg pardon?'

'I guess that's why I love animals so much. You can have a very honest, straightforward relationship with an animal.'

'And you can't with a human being?'

'Not very often.'

For the first time, she saw a little wry humanity in his dark eyes. He said, 'You know something?'

'What?'

'You may just be right.'

She laughed. 'You're doing it right now, aren't you?'

'Doing what?'

'Lying. Or at least evading. I asked you a direct question. I said, "Why're you investigating Steve Conners?" And you said, "I think he was involved in a bank robbery." And I said, "You're lying." And you haven't given me a straight answer yet.'

'That's what you want, a straight answer?'

'Yes.'

'A year ago, he killed a girl up in the state capitol.'

She didn't know what to say.

'What girl?'

Weyrich nodded at the lemonade pitcher. 'You think your cat would be real offended if I leaned over her and poured myself a little more lemonade?'

'She doesn't take offense very easily, Mr Weyrich,' Lynn said.

Then he told her about the girl.

49

* * *

Conners went into the men's room and threw up. He didn't know what else to do. The phone was still busy. *He didn't know what else to do.*

When he came out, he went over to the phone and tried once again. The familiar busy signal stabbed into his ear.

He went back to the bar and had another beer and whiskey. He was just about to order another round when he looked down the bar to the front door that had just opened up.

There, silhouetted in the last of the day's light, stood the man who had broken into his trailer.

Conners eyed the back door, ready to move. The bartender was watching his panic with true delight. He'd look at the stranger filling the doorway and then he'd look back at Conners.

The man came into the bar, the door closing behind him. He was still in shadow.

Conners made his move.

He edged away from the bar and started walking slowly toward the back door.

The guy was fat and middle-aged. Conners wouldn't have any trouble outrunning him.

By now, some of the other customers had become aware of the drama, too, the way the big guy kept coming forward, the way Conners kept moving backward, just like a saloon fight in the Old West.

Then the big man stepped up to the bar and Conners got his first real look at him and it wasn't the man in the light green Dodge at all.

This was a truck driver named Verne who stopped in here when he wasn't pushing his eighteen-wheeler through the lower Southern states.

Conners sighed, shook his head and stumbled over to the bar.

He got another round and walked back to the phone again.

Busy.

'I guess this Conners is pretty good with the ladies,' Weyrich said, stroking the cat who lay on the table next to his glass of lemonade.

After telling her about the dead girl, Weyrich had asked her questions about Conners, had she seen him much in the past months, was he behaving differently these days, had her son Michael mentioned anything about Conners acting funny. And so on.

Lynn nodded. 'He always has been good with the ladies. Even back in first grade, he was a heartbreaker.'

'That's how this started.'

'The girl dying, you mean?'

'Right. He used to drive over to the state capitol and see her. It's only thirty-five minutes from here. That's not bad.'

'I just can't imagine him killing anybody,' Lynn said. 'I mean, I don't have much respect for him, and I'd say he's capable of just about anything, but murder—'

'The way she was all cut up – the coroner estimated she'd been stabbed more than seventy times – this was an act of frenzy. He was probably insane at the time he did it.'

'Why would he kill her?'

Weyrich shrugged. 'She dumped him.'

'Oh.'

'She was a convent girl – had a real style about her. He got badly hooked.'

'Why would she go out with somebody like Conners in the first place?'

'My fatal flaw theory.'

'I don't understand.'

He stroked the cat a few more times. The cat started her motor running. 'Half the murders I've investigated – and I used to be a Chicago homicide detective – half the murders I've looked into have involved somebody's fatal flaw. In this case, it was because the girl – Dana Alberg, her name was – really liked to slum. Hit all the worst discos, got involved with people who did a lot of drugs, and maybe even dealt a little on the side. That was her fatal flaw – the fact that she liked lowlifes.'

'The police aren't aware of all this?'

He sipped some lemonade. 'They knew she was seeing some out-of-town boys but they were never able to confirm any of them by name.'

'But you were?'

'Yes, but it took me a while. In the six months before her murder, she'd seen seven boys from out of town, all within driving distance of the state capitol. I had to check each one of them out. It was a process of elimination. Eventually I wound up here this afternoon.'

'You seem so sure of yourself.'

He laughed. 'That's something else an investigator has to do, in addition to lying I mean. He has to seem certain of himself at all times.'

'I'm glad you told me that.'

'You were probably starting to think I was a pretty arrogant s.o.b., huh? Don't worry, it's all part of the show.'

He pushed his glass back toward the pitcher.

'More?' she asked.

He shook his head. 'Wish I could. But now I've got to go interview a few more people.'

'But you said that Conners ran away. How will you catch him now?'

Weyrich shrugged. 'I'm sure he didn't go far. Not unless he hopped a freight or something.'

'I can introduce you to the local Chief of Police. He's a very nice guy and he'd be glad to help you.'

Weyrich stood up, smoothing his shirt out over his girth, then straightening his woolen sport coat.

'Isn't that a little heavy for this weather?'

'Haven't had time to get out to Sears and buy me a new one.'

'Oh.'

'I buy them all at Sears because that way I don't have to worry about getting stuff on them. I'm a spiller.'

'A spiller?'

'I spill stuff. All the time.'

She smiled. 'So do I.'

'Do you have trouble with ballpoint pens, too?' he said.

'How they leak and get blue ink all over your fingers?'

'Fingers, hell. I always get the stuff all over my coats and shirts. That's why I buy cheap ones.'

He put out his hand and they shook and she walked him to the back door. She'd enjoyed having him here. Not in any romantic way, of course, just a simple, human way. He reminded her of a favorite uncle.

'I'll tell Michael you were here.'

52

'I'll probably try and give him a call tonight,' Weyrich said. 'Right after my supper.'

She watched him walk out to his car. He looked lonely somehow, so big yet carrying a real sense of isolation with him, too. Maybe that was why she liked him. Maybe she sensed a kinship. She felt that same isolation.

When he was gone, she went back inside and sat down at the table and started stroking the cat just as Weyrich had. She thought a little bit about what she'd make Ben for supper. And then she remembered that he wasn't coming home. He was eating at Alison's tonight. She smiled. He was really growing up.

'Finally got through, huh?' the bartender said when Conners came back from the phone for the fortieth or fiftieth or sixtieth time.

'Yeah. Finally.'

'Chicks.'

'Huh?'

'That's your problem, man. That's why guys always want to punch your face in. You're too slick with the chicks. For your own good.' He'd been nice for a minute but now he was slipping back into his familiar hostility.

But Conners wasn't paying much attention.

He was thinking about what had just been said.

About what was going to happen in just a few hours.

'Gimme another round.'

As the bartender went away, Conners sensed somebody staring at him.

Chick. Down the bar. Standing next to the biker who was obviously her boyfriend. She was watching him. Very tight T-shirt. Even from here you could see the shadows of her nipples through the fabric.

But this was no time to try and score some chick.

Way too much at stake.

Still, as he started swilling down his next round, he couldn't help but cast a vagrant eye on the biker's chick who was watching him.

The danger was part of the fun.

Flirting with somebody whose boyfriend could tear you apart.

Made the sex all the sweeter, once you finally connected.

Then the biker turned around to see just exactly what his girlfriend was looking at all the time.

He saw Conners.

And Conners saw him.

This was no time for a hassle, he reminded himself. Had to be relatively sober and in one piece to pull everything together for tonight.

Conners turned away and started staring at his drink.

Just a couple of hours now; just a couple of hours.

5

Ben felt kind of strange being alone in Alison's small and very old apartment. Sort of like an intruder. He was careful not to move anything from its appointed place, or to appear to be snooping. Maybe somebody was spying on him. He would not want to give the spy the wrong impression.

The ceilings ran twelve feet and the woodworking was carved with intricate oak clusters. There were sliding doors in the large living room. Long ago this had been a parlor. Alison had half the ground floor. There was a curious impersonality about the place. No photos of any loved ones, no mementos of high school or college. Just heavy dark used furniture and the day dying in here now – sunheat cooling and shadows gathering and the faint melancholy laughter of children playing outside. He wondered if he and Alison would get married sometime and have children of their own. He wanted to. He loved her so damned much. He was crazy about her and he meant the word literally. Crazy.

He took one of the beers from the refrigerator and turned on the TV and sat down on the couch that smelled of dust. The T-shirt and jeans he wore were a little big. He'd changed at Michael's because it was in town here. Michael kept thanking him for saving him. Michael was doing fine now.

He drank the beer and watched the news. Very little of it made sense to him. People were so damned hateful to each other. Most animals hurt each other only for the sake of survival. Humans hurt each other for the sake of pride and hatred. Made no sense at all.

Half an hour later, the network news over, he still had half a can of beer. Alcoholism was probably not anything he'd have to worry about. That was when the phone rang.

He started to get up but then had a terror of answering it. What if Alison had some boyfriend he didn't know anything about?

But that was stupid. She didn't. He was sure of it.

Just as he was reaching for the phone, the answering machine kicked on.

A female voice, thirty perhaps, started leaving its message.

At first, he wasn't sure who was speaking, or why she'd called. But then both things came clear and he stood there shocked and stunned.

Alison had lied to him.

Lied.

Today was his day for sorrow. First putting little Elizabeth to sleep, then Michael's brush with death, and now learning that Alison wasn't telling him the truth.

Why would she have made all this stuff up?

But now he knew that she would never be his, not really; he would lose her, just as he'd dreaded he would.

He wanted to run into the forest with the other animals and live with them in the caves and streams and hills and hollows of the land, and never see another human being again.

Weyrich ate dinner in the restaurant attached to his motel. The food wasn't bad – Swiss steak and mashed potatoes and braised carrots and a piece of apple pie – and the atmosphere was friendly. Lots of farmers with sun-baked faces and arms; lots of dumpling-plump wives with sweet middle-aged smiles and an air of relaxation now that the chores were done for the day. The jukebox even had a couple of Elvis Golden Oldies on it, *Surrender* and *Don't* – songs that took him back to the Chicago of his youth, doing the box-step in the gymnasium darkness of his prom. That was the night he'd secretly given himself the name The Strike-Out King. He'd taken Shirley Carella to the prom, a girl everybody knew was A Sure Thing. He'd even managed to have his older cousin get him a pint of real Old Grandad. He'd taken Shirley to the party afterward and gotten her good and liquored up and then taken her out to the family car he was driving and started to push his hand down the front of her low-cut prom gown and— And then she'd thrown up all over him. All over his rented tux. All over his old man's leather seats. Too much booze,

Sure Thing Shirley said. Take me home. Right now. And thus was born the Strike-Out King.

After dinner, Weyrich walked back to his room. Teenagers were just now starting their nightly trek up and down the main drag. The air smelled of exhaust fumes and cigarettes and apple blossoms.

The phone was ringing when he reached his room. He quickly let himself inside and trotted to the phone, out of breath from the burst of speed.

The caller hung up just as Weyrich raised the receiver to his ear. Great.

He went into the bathroom and got ready for the night shift. Three more people he wanted to contact about Steve Conners.

He washed his face and hands, slapped on some more English Leather, and then started combing his fringe of monk's hair.

The phone rang again.

He went out and picked it up. 'Weyrich.'

Nothing.

Weyrich hated mysterious phone calls. He always gave the caller two chances and then hung up. 'Weyrich,' he said again.

Nothing.

He was just hanging up when a male voice said, 'I know you're looking for me, Mr Weyrich.'

Weyrich brought the receiver back to his ear. 'Is this Steve Conners?'

'Uh-huh.'

'Then you're right, I *am* looking for you.'

'I didn't do what you think I did.'

'You didn't, huh?'

'No, and I can prove it.'

'And how can you do that, Mr Conners?'

A pause again.

'We need to talk. In person, I mean,' Conners said.

'Where?'

'I know you know how to find my trailer.'

'What exactly are we going to talk about, Mr Conners?'

'I have some information.'

'About what?'

57

'Who really killed her.'

'I see.'

Weyrich's body tensed. Little punk. He wished Conners was in front of him right now. At first, he'd been reluctant to accept Conners' invitation. Could easily be a trap. But now all that mattered was finding out what had really happened. He'd take any risk necessary.

'What time?'

'Hour all right?'

'Hour would be fine.'

'You bring the law, I won't talk.'

'I'm private, Mr Conners.'

'You could still call them up.'

'Don't worry, Mr Conners. I'll come alone.' I want all the fun for myself, you little prick, Weyrich thought.

'Hour, then?'

'Hour,' Weyrich said and hung up.

He went back to the bathroom, finished cleaning up and then came out and sat down in the chair, thumb on the channel surfer, and watched some MTV. He hated the music, especially the rap music, but the girls were incredible. They showed more skin on home TV than you used to see in the strip shows of his youth. Who said America wasn't the greatest country of all?

He cleaned his Smith & Wesson 9mm. This was always a religious experience for him. This was the only hand gun that was really the equivalent of a small rifle. He even used bullets that were second-generation hollow points. They were illegal, of course, not that he gave a particular shit. They could penetrate anything you put in front of them.

After he was finished with his gun, he sat back and watched the young girls on MTV.

This was indeed a great country.

When the phone rang, Ben knew it would be Alison and he was afraid of what he'd say when he heard her voice.

Liar.

You liar.

But when he picked up the receiver, a kind of weariness came over

him, and instead of anger all he felt was a vast blinding pain and
sadness.

'Hello.'

'God, Ben are you all right?'

'I'm all right.'

'God, you sound awful.'

'I'm fine.'

He could tell she was pausing to get a better sense of his
mood.

'You know where I'm calling from?'

'No,' he said.

'Baskin-Robbins.'

'Oh.'

This was always their special treat. A Baskin-Robbins cone every
night. He tried to sound enthusiastic, couldn't.

'Ben?'

'Uh-huh?'

'Did something happen?'

'No.'

Pause.

'God, Ben, you're scaring me. You really are.'

He wanted to fake enthusiasm but he couldn't. He felt worse than
he had at any time since his father had died. He wanted to be in the
woods with the animals, hiding in the forest of night.

'I'll see you when you get here.'

'This is really pissing me off, Ben. You're not being honest with
me.'

And then his anger broke, just a flash of it like jagged summer
lightning. 'And you have been honest with me, I suppose?' he
shouted into the receiver.

And then slammed it down.

He tried to stop himself from crying.

But it was impossible.

People had slyly warned him. Why would a girl like that be
interested in a boy like him?

She was too good to be true.

And that was exactly the point.

She wasn't true at all.

* * *

Conners fortified himself with beer. No more whiskey for now. He'd be too drunk to do what he needed to do.

Just as he'd been instructed to, he turned on the small table lamp next to the couch. This way, when Weyrich pulled up, he'd see that somebody was home.

Maybe think it wasn't a trap after all.

Conners took another pull on his beer and belched loudly. He used to get slapped for belching that way at dinner hour in the reform school. Same for farting at the table. Guard would come by and slap him on the back of the head. Now Conners could belch and fart all he wanted to, loud as he wanted to, and nobody could stop him. Freedom was a wonderful thing.

He fortified himself with some more beer.

And waited for Weyrich to show up.

At this point, Weyrich was a half mile from Conners' trailer, the light green Dodge raising gravel dust that glowed in the light of the full Midwestern moon. The night was alive with unseen dogs and coyotes and jays and owls whose cries echoed off the piney hills. A shining ribbon of fast-running creek ran parallel to the road. The corn was just starting to come up in the fields and the air was rich with the scent of good black soil.

He had his Smith & Wesson 9mm on the seat right next to him. He was taking no chances. He was no fast draw. The shoulder rig he used slowed him down.

When he saw the trailer, with its light on, he knew he was walking into a trap for sure.

Only reason somebody would go to the trouble of turning on a lamp was to make you think it wasn't a trap.

And if they wanted you to think it wasn't, it was.

It wasn't easy being a private investigator.

Sometimes you had to think backwards to figure out what was really going on.

'It feels funny, Dr Lynn.'
 'His heartbeat?'
 'Uh-huh.'

'Eva, how can you tell it feels funny?'

'I put my head to his chest.'

'And you're counting the beats?'

'Uh-huh.'

'Well, does he look all right?'

'Uh-huh.'

'And has he been eating all right?'

'Uh-huh.'

'And he hasn't been throwing up?'

'Huh-uh.'

'And he's been playing his usual way?'

'Uh-huh.'

'And he hasn't been making any unusual sounds – you know, weird meows or anything?'

'Huh-uh.'

'Then you know what, Eva?'

'What, Dr Lynn?'

'He's probably fine.'

'But Dr Lynn—'

'You can bring him over if you want.'

'You'll let me in?'

Eva sounded like a little girl. She was a sixty-eight-year-old who'd lost her husband last year to bone cancer and had since found her only comfort in her dead husband's Russian blue cat. Zeb, as the husband had called the cat, was a healthy, strapping tom who had just passed his ninth birthday and probably had five more to go before anything serious started happening to him. He was about as healthy a specimen as you could find. But Eva worried about him constantly, was on the phone with Lynn, usually at night, three or four times a week. Tonight's call had probably been prompted by an article in one of Eva's myriad cat magazines about feline heart attacks.

'Of course I'll let you in.'

'Then you really think it can wait till morning, till I bring him in?'

'Eva, I don't think you need to bring him in at all. But the morning would be plenty of time, yes.'

'Are you mad at me?'

'No, Eva. No, I'm not.'

'I don't mean any offense, Dr Lynn, but sometimes you sound a little mad.'

'Then if I do, Eva, I apologize. Sincerely.'

'God bless you, Dr Lynn.'

'And God bless you, too, Eva.'

'I'll see you in the morning, then, Doctor, God willing that Zeb makes it through the night.'

'Yes, Eva, God willing,' Lynn said, smiled, and hung up. Poor Eva. Lynn really did like her; but she also lost patience with her sometimes. And that wasn't very professional. A client paid not only for diagnosis and medicine, a client also paid for patience and genuine concern.

She was just about to leave the office and go back to the farmhouse and watch some television (there was a 1964 James Garner movie on cable) when the phone rang again.

She sighed. She was tired and just wanted to relax. She hoped it wasn't Eva again. Sometimes the woman called right back with one symptom she'd forgotten to mention.

'Dr Tyler.'

'Mom?'

She knew instantly something was wrong. Something in the voice.

'Hi, Ben.'

'I wondered what time you were going to bed tonight?'

'Probably the usual. Right after the ten o'clock news. Why?'

Pause. 'I guess I need to talk to you about something.'

'You don't sound good, Ben. Did something happen?'

'I really can't talk right now.'

'Where are you?'

'At Alison's.'

'Is she there?'

'No. But I still can't talk. I mean, she could walk in at any time.'

'Ben—'

'I'd appreciate it if you'd wait up.'

'I'll be happy to wait up.'

'I'll be there as close to the News as I can be.'

'I don't even get a hint?'

'I'll just talk to you when I get there. Thanks, Mom.'

Then he was gone.

She hung up, turned off the lights and then locked the place up. She'd bedded down all the animals for the night.

Alison.

Inevitable, she thought, as she had thought all along. As much as she loved Ben and was proud of him, Alison had always struck her as a little fast and sleek for somebody like Ben. She was nice, gentle, kind, Alison was, but she was also a little too knowing for a town this size and a boy as tender-hearted as Ben.

Or was Lynn simply being overly-protective? Every relationship had bad moments; maybe Ben and Alison were simply having one of theirs.

She went in the house, washed up, got the TV going and then promptly lost interest.

All she could think about was Ben, and the sadness of his voice on the phone.

Trap.

Conners must really have thought he was dealing with a moron.

It was a trap sure as hell and there was no way Weyrich was going to pull his car right up to the trailer.

Weyrich went thundering right on past the Airstream, down the dusty road a quarter mile, and pulled his car into a copse of birch trees.

He didn't really feel like walking a whole hell of a lot but he didn't have much choice.

He climbed through the barbed-wire fence and started walking toward the trailer. Luckily, the windbreak of trees hid him in shadow.

He saw no human shape silhouetted against the cheap white curtains of the living-room window. He heard no music, either.

Just the light, brighter as he got closer.

He had his 9mm in his hand.

He was no dummy.

He was winded pretty fast, and covered with a thick glaze of sweat. He'd take a long cool shower when he got back to his motel room. After he turned Conners over to the law, that was.

He was now ten yards from the trailer, breathing hard, feeling chill sweat in his armpits.

For a long moment, he was suddenly aware of the night's beauty, of soft silken shadow, of cows in nearby pasture land, of a gliding hawk silhouetted against the moon.

Then he saw the shape moving away from the dark side of the trailer. A shape that was at first shadow and then human.

Weyrich raised his gun but it was too late.

The man shot Weyrich four times in the chest.

'I know you don't want to come back here, Alison, but you're not leaving me much choice. Do you know how crazy this is? You could be in a lot of danger, honey. A whole lot. I mean, what if you *do* find the man who killed your friend? Then what'll you do?'

This was where Ben shut off the phone machine.

'What the hell's going on here, Alison?'

'The ice cream's melting, Ben. Couldn't I at least put it away?'

'I don't care about the god damned ice cream.'

He hadn't been able to restrain himself.

Soon as she'd come through the door, nervous as hell, clutching the ice cream to her, he'd grabbed her by the wrist and sat her down in a straight-backed chair next to the phone machine.

All he could think of was that she had lied to him.

All he could think of was that she had been using him somehow, and was going to dump him.

He didn't know what to do with his fear and his grief. He felt he might actually be losing his mind. Not even thoughts of the forest helped now. Nothing helped now.

'Who's the woman on the phone?'

'My sister.'

'What did she mean about your friend being murdered?'

'Ben, can't you please calm down? You scare me. I've never seen you like this.' She reached over and tried to take his hand but he yanked it away. 'I'm not your enemy, Ben.'

'You lied to me.'

'I had to.'

'Why?'

'Because—' She stopped herself, bowed her head.

He felt sorry for her, then; and knew that he still loved her and would always love her. He wanted to take her in his arms but somehow he couldn't make himself do it. He just kept thinking about all the lies she'd told him. He just kept thinking that she was no longer going to be his.

She sat there in her prim white blouse, looking oddly old-fashioned, woman immemorial, and she broke his god damned heart.

And then the anger was gone. And he felt drained, exhausted, and he went over and sat down on the couch and started to speak and then said nothing. Because there was nothing to say.

She said, quietly, 'I'm sorry about the lies, Ben.'

Neither spoke for a time. There were just the old sounds of this old apartment in this old house, and the frantic noise of traffic out on the street, teenagers horny for excitement of any kind.

'I shouldn't have lied,' she said.

He said nothing.

'I shouldn't have lied and I sincerely apologize.'

'There. Now everything's all fixed up again, isn't it?'

'Please don't be sarcastic, Ben. I hate that.'

He said, having to say it, terrified of how she might respond, 'Did you lie about being in love with me?'

Her head bowed again. She said nothing.

'Oh, great,' he said. 'Just fucking great.' And then he was up and pacing around in a kind of frenzy. He would never feel good or whole or safe again as long as he lived. Never.

'Of course I'm in love with you, Ben. But right now I don't think you believe that.'

He went to the window and looked out but saw nothing. His grief had blinded him.

He had never been good with girls, had always been afraid to fall in love, and now he knew why. Because he didn't know how to do it, and because loving somebody was death when they said goodbye.

He fought his tears but it was no good. He wanted to run out the door but he seemed paralyzed suddenly.

'Ben.'

'I don't want to talk.'

'I love you.'

'Right.'

'God dammit, Ben, listen to me!'

'I already have listened to you.'

'I'm just as confused as you are.'

'Everything you told me has been a lie, right?'

'Not everything.'

'Did you grow up in Chicago?'

'No.'

'Did you go to a girls' school in Vermont?'

'No.'

'Were you a virgin when you slept with me that first time?'

'Probably.'

And he couldn't help it. He laughed. '"Probably"? What kind of bullshit is that? "Probably"?'

And then she couldn't help it, either. She laughed, too. 'I know how pathetic it sounds.'

'Very pathetic.'

'I mean, "probably" being a virgin.'

'I don't even know what that means.'

'It means the one time that Rick Daily got me up in his bedroom senior year of high school, I was so drunk I don't remember what happened. But I tend to think nothing did.'

He looked at her. 'It doesn't matter to me if you're a virgin or not. I don't have any right to even know. But it's the fact that you lied to me. I didn't even ask you. You *told* me you were a virgin.'

'I just wanted to make it special.'

'It would have been special anyway – at least for me – whether you were a virgin or not. Hell, I was in love with you the first time I saw you. So everything was special. Don't you know that?'

'I know,' she sighed. She looked up at him. 'May I come over there and give you a hug?'

'I really feel like shit.'

'I really feel like shit, too. That's why I want to come over there and give you a hug.'

'You really think it's a good idea?' he said.

'I think it's a great idea.'

'"Probably" I'm a virgin. God.'

She didn't wait any longer. She came over and slid her arms around him and gave him a hug.

He didn't hug her back. Not at first. He just stood there feeling sorry for himself. Then he realized that he was being a jerk and he hugged her back.

'"Probably",' he said

And they laughed together.

And then he said, 'So did you figure out who the murderer is yet?'

And then she told him: she was the daughter of very rich parents who'd been killed in a small plane accident when she was eight. She'd been raised by her older sister, Jean, whose voice he'd heard on the answering machine. Jean was a socialite who shuttled Alison back and forth between private schools and the family mansion outside Chicago. Later, in college, Alison met a girl named Dana Albergo who was just as much an outsider as Alison herself. Sophomore year they got an apartment in the city. But Dana insisted on living on the edge of a ghetto because it was more 'real.' Only then did Alison realize how much Dana liked wild boys, drugs and sex. (Dana always had the same screaming nightmare – being chased through the dark woods by somebody trying to kill her.) Alison tried to get Dana to change, but it was no use. Then Dana was murdered. Alison was convinced the killer was somebody Dana knew so she took some of her inheritance money and hired a Chicago private detective named Weyrich to look into Dana's death. Weyrich traced a young man named Conners to Black River Falls. Alison decided to come to Black River Falls and see for herself. Then she met Ben and everything became complicated once again. Now Weyrich was out here once more, helping her. Closing in. Then, just now, Alison told Ben who she suspected of being the killer.

'No way,' he said. 'No way.'

Conners stayed inside until the sound of the four barked gunshots had faded into the night like fireflies.

The radio played a Vince Gill song as Conners came down the steps of the trailer. He wore no shirt. His torso was covered with tattoos.

Michael Tyler stood over Weyrich's body, looking down at the dead man.

'God damn, man, you have to shoot him four times? This shit makes me nervous, man.'

'Just help me here and shut up.'

'What the hell we gonna do with him?' Conners said.

Michael looked around at the night, as if the answer might be in the dark-edged clouds racing the moon.

'You go grab his feet and we'll carry him over to my car,' Michael said.

'Your car?'

'The trunk, asshole.'

'Oh.'

Conners was, as usual these days, drunk and unable to understand the simplest directions.

Michael started to bend over, as if he were going to pick up Weyrich by the shoulders, but instead he reached down and took the Smith & Wesson 9mm from the ground where it lay next to Weyrich's hand.

It happened fast, then, faster than it had with Weyrich.

'Hey, shit, man!' Conners cried when he saw what was about to happen.

He dropped the dead man's feet and started backing up toward the trailer, his arms and fingers uselessly covering his face.

Michael put three bullets into Conners' chest.

'You're crazy.'

'I hope so.'

'Michael could never kill anybody.'

'They were always together – Michael and Conners, I mean. Michael at least had to know about it.'

'No way.'

They were on the bed. The window was open. They could smell June flowers on the night. The moon sat full and silver just above the peaked roof of a nearby garage. A cat waited, silhouetted on the peak, his tail curled in the air.

Ordinarily they would be making love at a time like this, but after she'd told him of Weyrich's suspicions about his brother Michael at least knowing about Dana's murder, Ben just wasn't interested in sex.

'Now do you see why I couldn't tell you the truth?' she said. 'I knew how angry you'd be about Michael maybe being involved.'

'You're really wrong about Michael. You really are.'

She leaned over and kissed him tenderly on the mouth and then she put her head on his chest and said, 'I hope I'm wrong about him, Ben. I really do hope I'm wrong about him.'

* * *

It took a few minutes to set up but when he was done, Michael had arranged the bodies so that it appeared as if they'd both fired on each other. And both died in the process.

Perfect.

A lot of people in town knew that Weyrich had been looking for Conners.

So it wouldn't be hard to believe that they'd had this kind of confrontation.

Michael hurried away through the woods that started on the edge of the pastureland to the east, the same woods where he'd killed his first victim, a hobo, when he was fourteen years old.

Later on, they did make love, but it was quick and oddly unsatisfying, neither of them making any kind of spiritual connection with the other, and when they were done, he left.

A wind came up and smelled of rain and he thought of poor little Elizabeth this morning, trembling at the last beneath the needle, and then he thought of what Alison had said, about Michael and all, and he felt a terrible irrational fear that what she said might be true.

But no. It was impossible.

Yet—

Then all he could think about was his mother, all she had had to go through with her father and the murder he'd committed.

What if her eldest son was a murderer, too?

TWO

1

'How's Michael taking it?' Etta Charles asked as she checked Lynn out at the hardware store.

'Oh, pretty well,' Lynn said. 'I guess he's in shock like the rest of us and all.'

Etta, who had her gray hair done in angry little curls, leaned her fleshy face forward and said, 'Personally, it didn't surprise me.'

'Oh?'

'That whole Conners family is trash, if you ask me. No wonder the boy turned out that way, is it?'

Did Etta ever talk about Lynn's family the same way? Lynn wondered. She could easily imagine it: *You know that Lynn, so standoffish and all? Don't have no call to feel any better than the rest of us, not with that father of hers a cold-blooded killer...*

Etta was about to say more but fortunately, on this sunny morning three days following the shoot-out that still had the whole town talking, several customers suddenly appeared behind Lynn and forced the woman into silence. There was work to be done.

Lynn was buying a gallon of white paint and a new brush for work Ben would be doing on the exterior of the office's waiting area. The walls were now a dull and dirty and depressing yellow.

After Etta handed Lynn back her Visa card, she said, 'Bet they don't get a half dozen people at the funeral this morning. Sam at the funeral home said it was the least amount of visitors at the wake he'd ever seen.'

If she kept it up, Lynn thought ironically, Etta was going to do the impossible: make Lynn feel sorry for Steve Conners.

As Etta put the paint brush in a sack, Lynn glanced around the store. Usually she loved browsing here. She liked the smell of newly sawn lumber from the yard out back, and the way all the tools looked new and purposeful, and all the sample doors and windows looked ready to be used. Maybe that's what she liked most about hardware stores – they implied new and optimistic beginnings: fixing up something old, or building something brand new from scratch. Then Etta said, half-whispering, 'Between you and me, that Steve's sister is just a tramp, too.' And all of Lynn's good feelings about the hardware store vanished.

She was glad to be out the door and on the street again, thinking about what it had been like to be a young girl in this small town, riding her bike 'downtown' as the locals always called it, sitting in the darkness of the State theater to see such stars as Elvis and The Beatles, looking dreamily at all the new autumn outfits in The House of Glamor, going through a few years of having a new secret love at least once a week and then – and then it all ending with her father murdering that girl.

'Morning, Lynn.'

Chief John Rhys, a rangy man with graying hair and an appealing if not handsome face, came out of Ernie's coffee shop and fell into step beside her.

'Morning,' she said.

He nodded at the gallon of paint in her right hand. 'My least favorite job in the whole world.'

'One of mine, too. Fortunately, I've got Ben.'

He smiled. 'What would we do if we couldn't exploit our children?' Rhys had six kids of his own.

She liked the pace of the town, people stopping to talk, cars moving slowly, merchants sweeping off their sidewalks or rolling down their awnings.

They'd reached the Bronco. Lynn put the paint and brush on the passenger seat then turned back to Rhys.

'That son of yours is probably mad at me by now,' he said.

'Michael?'

Rhys nodded. 'I've had to bug him a lot ever since – well, since it happened. Conners, I mean.'

'I'm sure he doesn't mind.'

'He was the only person who knew the deceased well. So he's the only one I can talk to.'

'This is a terrible thing to say, but I wish Michael hadn't known him as well as he did.'

'Conners was trouble, no doubt about that.'

'Michael just always felt sorry for him. You know, how the kids picked on him, growing up the way he did.' The Conners were the closest thing to rednecks the quiet town had ever known, and the town hadn't liked it a bit.

'Well, unfortunately, not even Michael could straighten him out.' Rhys checked his wristwatch. 'Well, time for the city council meeting. You know how much fun they are.'

'Does the mayor still fall asleep?'

'Every time,' Rhys grinned.

'Maybe one of you should bring an accordion or something,' Lynn said. 'Try to keep him awake that way.'

'Nice to see you,' Rhys said.

His mention of Michael made her swing the Bronco around in a U-turn and head to the east end of town. Michael would be opening up just about now. Ben was watching the office. She could afford to stop in and see Michael a few minutes.

When she pulled up, she saw Michael outside with a long-handled squeegee and a bucket of water. He was washing the front windows of the small, square, cement-block building he'd bought with his bank loan. There'd been a time when Michael had spent most of his free time shining up his 1984 Chevrolet this way. But now he was a man and it was his business that got the attention. Watching him, she felt an almost guilty pride. She'd rarely had to worry about Michael. She loved him in a way that was pure, clean, uncomplicated. He'd always been outgoing, self-confident, personable, successful in everything he tried. She'd taken a fine shiny pride in his accomplishments over the years. But she'd had to love Ben in a different and more difficult way – watching him fail at sports, and fail at school relationships, and stay in his room with his science-fiction novels and the menagerie of pets he'd had down the years. She hadn't always been patient with Ben, hadn't always been understanding – hard as she'd tried – hadn't always been accepting of his failures. She'd even wondered to herself at times why Ben couldn't be more like his brother ... and then she'd really felt guilty.

Michael turned as she pulled in. He waved and leaned his squeegee against the wall and came over to the Bronco, handsome face squinting in the sun. In his blue button-down shirt, conservative blue tie, blue pleated slacks and cordovan loafers with tassels, he managed to look businesslike and informal at the same time.

'Hi, Mom.'

'Morning.'

He gestured at the paint can on the front seat. 'Ben going to paint the office, huh?'

'Tomorrow morning he starts.'

He stood back and admired the Bronco. 'How's she running?'

Lynn laughed. '"She's" running just fine.'

'You have any trouble, you take her directly to Stan.'

'I appreciate that.'

She always let Michael buy her major purchases. He knew everybody and was able to get big discounts. The Bronco had been no exception. His golfing buddy was Stan Turner, the local Ford dealer, and he'd gotten Stan to give her a demonstrator with only 150 miles on it – and knock off thirty per cent in the process.

'You should take her out on the highway, see what she'll do top end,' Michael said, teasing her.

'Oh, yes. And as soon as I started going over the speed limit, Chief Rhys would appear out of nowhere and give me a ticket.' Then she remembered what Rhys had said a few minutes ago. 'He thinks he's upset you, by the way.'

'Rhys?'

'Uh-huh.'

Michael shrugged. 'Well, I guess I'm a little tired of answering his questions. But if he thinks I can help—'

'That's what I told him.'

'The funeral's this morning.' He watched her face for a reaction. 'I'll be there.'

'I'm going to surprise you and tell you that I'm glad you will be.'

'Mom, you hated him!'

She sighed. 'I guess I did. But he deserves some people at his funeral.'

He leaned in and kissed her on the cheek. 'You're an old softie. That's your trouble.'

Then he leaned back and his expression changed. He looked troubled. 'You notice anything different about Ben these days?'

She thought a moment. 'No, I guess not. Why?'

'I've seen him a couple of times the last few days and he acts – funny. I don't know how else to describe it.'

Both of them watched as Michael's assistant taped up a big poster of Clint Eastwood on the inside of the display window.

'He seems fine to me,' she said.

'It's her.'

'Her?'

'His girlfriend, Alison. She doesn't like me and I think she's trying to get Ben not to like me, either.'

'Oh Michael, I'm sure she wouldn't do anything like that. She knows how much Ben loves you.'

'She strikes me as pretty devious.'

'Alison? She seems so quiet and sweet.'

'Just watch her sometime, Mom. Watch her closely.'

Lynn laughed but she was troubled by the intensity of Michael's distrust of Alison. 'You think she's maybe a secret Martian or something, Michael?'

'She's devious,' he repeated, not smiling. 'And she wants to drive Ben and me apart. I can see that in everything she does. She knows how to operate below the surface where nobody knows exactly what's going on.'

He was about to say more but his assistant came to the front door, opened it and leaned out. 'Telephone for you, Michael.'

'That's all right, honey,' Lynn said, putting the Bronco in gear. 'I need to get back to the office anyway.'

He leaned in and kissed her again. 'You're the best, Mom. You really are. Sorry I got sort of nasty about Alison.'

'Maybe it's time I had a good old-fashioned family dinner so all four of us could get better acquainted. The three of us and Alison.'

'Swiss steak?'

'You bet.'

'And chocolate pie?'

'And chocolate pie.'

These had been Michael's absolute favorites since he was a small boy.

'You name the time and I'll be there,' Michael said.

'I'll see what I can do,' Lynn said.

As she watched him walk into the store, she was struck as always by the grace and precision of his movements. No wonder he'd been such a good athlete.

She drove back to the office, thinking of what Michael had said about Ben acting strangely lately.

Had she missed something?

As Lynn was driving back to the office, Alison was at the small dock that rented rowboats and canoes. Because her job at the library required only thirty hours a week, she had plenty of time for her new passion: fishing.

She wondered what her very proper and very formal mother, whose memory she loved and still mourned, would make of her youngest daughter – the one on whom they'd lavished ballet and classical music lessons – taking her rod and spinning reel and fishing for trout and walleye and pike.

'Morning,' Old Bob said.

That's how she thought of him. Old Bob. Grizzled whiskers. Grease-stained work clothes. And a cheek full of chewing tobacco. And no teeth.

At the end of the dock was a small cabin that smelled sourly of bait and gasoline. If you could stand the stench, you could go inside and find a fascinating collection of bait, lures, reels, rods and such oddball items as frogboxes for use in the tiny area of swamp to the south. She'd managed to stay in there once for a little while. One of the things she'd noticed was a calendar of a 'naughty' gal, her dress blowing up around her shapely hips. The calendar was dated 1963. Old Bob didn't clean this place out too often. Somewhere, in a tiny room behind all the clutter, was the bed where he slept.

Piled up against the exterior cabin were two stacks of boats – canoes and rowboats. This was how Old Bob made his living, renting out craft to locals and vacationers. There were nice rental cabins in the bluffs above the river, and the locals were long accustomed to renting from Bob instead of buying their own.

'Suppose you want your regular one?'

Alison grinned. 'Yeah, I suppose I do.'

He went over and took down the Grumman 13-foot rowing-camper. Alison had read about river craft and decided that this, with its flat-bottomed design and classic proportions, was a safe craft. She always wore a bright orange life preserver, too.

She helped Bob carry the boat down to the water and put it in. She speared her arms through the straps of her life preserver and then strapped herself in.

'Got somethin' for ya,' Old Bob said; he trotted off to the cabin, then trotted right back, carrying a small tin can.

He knelt on the edge of the water-rotted dock and handed her the can.

She peered inside.

Who could have guessed, even six months ago, that Alison might actually be happy to gape at the sight of a couple dozen slimy, slithery, dirt-covered nightcrawlers?

'Wow,' she breathed.

'Got 'em last night,' Old Bob said. 'After the rain.'

'Thanks a lot.'

He grinned toothlessly and then spat a stream of brown tobacco juice off the dock. Someday, just as she'd gotten used to night-crawlers, she'd probably get used to Old Bob's tobacco spitting.

'You have yourself a good time today.'

'Don't worry, Bob. I plan to.' She was always afraid she'd slip and call him 'Old Bob'. He probably wouldn't like that much – and she wouldn't blame him.

He gave her a jaunty little salute and then pushed her boat away from the dock.

In the next hour, she rowed slowly toward the Falls, stopping every twenty minutes or so to check out a given area for its fishing prospects. Old Bob had taught her about water temperature and water flow, and what kind of fish she'd find in fast water, and what kind she'd likely find in water that was more still.

Ben had taught her how to use the rod and reel she'd bought from Old Bob. In fact, if Ben hadn't taken her fishing in April, she never would have discovered it. But from the very first time, the tranquility of the surroundings, and the sport of trying to catch fish (all of which she threw back) fascinated her. Now, even when Ben was working and couldn't accompany her, Alison felt comfortable going alone.

On one of her stops downriver, she decided to try some of the casting Ben had taught her.

She did pretty good with the backhand cast but her sidearm cast was as clumsy as ever. Then she tried the underhand cast, and did a little better with that one, but when she cast into the wind she was glad she was alone and nobody could see her. That last cast had been pathetic.

After a time, oaring herself slowly downriver, she could feel the current quicken and strengthen, like an invisible hand suddenly clutching the boat from below and guiding it through the clay-colored water.

She was nearing the Falls.

The Falls terrified her.

The day Ben described the game that he and Michael played, going as close to the edge as possible and jumping free with only moments to spare, she'd started trembling. The force and fury of the water smashing a human body against the rocks below—

She oared back upriver, away from the pull of the Falls, and then got set to bait her hook, open a can of Diet Pepsi and relax.

The nightcrawlers were cold and slimy as she dug for a particularly plump one.

Then the bait was on the hook and she stood up. She tried the sidearm cast – she really needed the practice – and this time it wasn't too bad at all.

Then it was time to sit down, relax and reward herself with the Diet Pepsi.

She wished Ben were with her. She wished they were getting along the way they used to. She wished she'd never told him that she suspected his brother had helped murder her best friend...

Dana Albergo had been one of those girls who loves to slum around. Over their two years together at St Mary's College, where the nuns running the place had once allegedly trained with the Gestapo, Dana had dragged her shy and frightened friend to any number of truly horrifying places. The black rhythm and blues bar where Alison had actually seen a man stabbed in the shoulder. The transvestite bar where a lesbian had tried to pick both girls up. The disco where a huge drug deal went down, and where a girl sank to her knees and did a boy right on the floor. The country western bar where a brawl resulted in every single window being smashed out by a flying bar stool or beer bottle.

Dana was no better at men than her mother had been. She always gave body and heart to losers. At the beginning of a love affair, when her fever was highest, Dana disappeared. Went to classes then took off right away for the city where she could spend all her time with her new beau. There were many new beaus. Early in their relationship, Dana had always told Alison everything about her latest honey. Even all the details about sex, who was good at this, who was better at that. Alison had been both shocked and spellbound by it all. But gradually, thinking of all the chances Dana was taking – there was AIDS, to be sure, but also Dana chose fairly violent young men to fall in love with – Alison started to disapprove out loud, to try and dissuade her friend from living the way she did. Eventually, Dana stopped confiding in her.

Alison would never have seen Steve Conners and Michael Tyler if, late last May, she hadn't been invited to the same party where Dana was. The party was held by a 'townie,' a girl who took classes at St Mary's but lived at home with her parents. Dana went to be polite but she was drunk and stoned by the time she got there, and toting two hunky guys with her. Steve and Michael. They didn't stay long, just enough to display their contempt for such hopelessly dweeby people. Dana barely spoke to Alison and didn't introduce her friends. Alison wouldn't have known anything about them if she hadn't left the party early and noticed the license plate on the sports car they were in. A county about thirty-five minutes away. In effect, a suburb of the state capitol.

Two nights later, Dana was found murdered in the apartment they shared.

Alison had a breakdown. Not right away, and nothing dramatic. Just a steady depression that eroded her desire to do anything. She blamed herself for Dana's murder. She should have done a better job of protecting her. If she hadn't driven upstate to see her sister Jean that night, it wouldn't have happened. Dana had been the only person she'd felt close to. Certainly Alison didn't feel close to Jean.

The police investigation went nowhere. She told them about the two young men she'd seen at the party but they didn't seem particularly interested, probably because she'd been so shrill about their shortcomings.

And then she stopped eating. And then she stopped going to class. And then she stopped returning Jean's calls. And then she woke up one day in a mental hospital, being given massive doses of psycho-babble and electro-shock. Sometime during this bleak and mournful time, she managed to contact the family lawyer and tell him to hire a private investigator to track down the two boys she'd seen Dana with.

After the mental hospital, after trying uselessly to live under the same roof with her relentless sister Jean, Alison decided to come out here to Black River Falls and look up the two boys the private investigator had led her to.

Then Weyrich came out here a few days ago and cleared up the case for her. He'd had a shoot-out with Steve Conners and both had died.

Apparently, according to the notebook Chief Rhys had found on Weyrich, the private investigator believed he had identified the young man responsible for the death of Dana: Steve Conners.

Case closed.

Unfortunately, by the time Alison knew all this, she had already told Ben that she thought his brother was a murderer.

Since she hadn't seen Ben the past few days, she sensed that she might well have destroyed their relationship. He'd canceled two dates they'd arranged, and wasn't returning her phone calls. There was something she needed to tell him.

She'd even written him a letter telling him how sorry she was, explaining that she'd been wrong about his brother and that clearly Weyrich's notebook – which was referred to in all the news accounts – proved that Steve Conners had acted alone.

But he was not his old self, and might never be again. She felt as sick about Ben as she'd once felt about Dana. The two most important relationships in her life – gone.

Alison fished for two hours, catching a walleye and a pike, throwing them both back. Then she just sat in the boat for a time, listening to the forest on either shore, the cry of birds, the bark of dogs. So lazy and peaceful. She needed to relax this way. But she was thrown out of paradise by a noisy, powerful outboard craft bearing three men swilling beer and listening to a loud country western radio. One of them called something to her she couldn't hear. The other two laughed.

Her beautiful day on the water – hawks sliding down the air, a gentle doe standing next to a birch and watching her – had ended.

She reeled in her line and started rowing back toward the dock and Old Bob, feeling more isolated than she had at any time since the death of her parents.

One of them had a glass eye. Another a club foot. A third a badly burned cheek. Geeks and freaks, the Conners clan, shanty Irish the lot of them, the women gone to pale fleshiness by age twenty, the men losing all semblance of youth by age twenty-five, looking bent and furtive and malicious. They wore cheap bright K-Mart clothes, most of which had gone out of fashion fifteen years ago. These were the clothes they wore to weddings and funerals. One guy had on a pair of white plastic shoes and kept buffing them on the back of his red polyester pants as the priest muttered his indifferent farewell to Stephen Conners. A few of them, that part of the clan that lived up in the hills, still had outhouses and practiced incest regularly. Steve had told Michael all about it.

Poor people with dignity you could feel sorry for: their economic condition was not their own fault. But there was a meanness and a stupidity to these people that they seemed to cultivate deliberately. Steve had dropped out of high school in tenth grade, Michael remembered, and his mother had been happy about it. Somebody to drive her back and forth to work, and run her errands. She hadn't been even slightly interested in him getting an education.

The mourners were on the windward side of the steep cemetery hill, twenty of them at most. Two bored workers stood by to lower the coffin, coughing up phlegm with their sharp incessant cigarette coughs.

The whole spectacle robbed the blue sky and sunny day of its majesty. These were creatures of the night, these Conners, and should not inflict themselves on the human eye during the day.

Steve's mother was, as usual, drunk.

She stood swaying and sobbing across from the priest, lurid in the red mini-skirt and transparent blouse and pearl-colored push-up bra

83

she often wore to taverns. She'd been a looker once years ago, but it had been beaten and sexed and whiskied out of her. She was thirty-eight and looked fifty.

He wanted to be away from here. The feeling was becoming urgent.

'Dust to dust, earth to earth,' the priest said as he sprinkled holy water across the wooden casket.

And then he said a bit more and then it was over.

He turned to go but she caught up with him, as he knew she would.

Steve's mother.

'Oh, honey, I appreciate it so much,' she said drunkenly, wearily. 'You're the only one of his friends who showed up.'

She smelled of bad perfume. Her crumpled white handkerchief was green and puffy with snot.

Friends.

He noted the plural, when in fact Steve had had only one friend and that was Michael himself.

She hugged him, or that's probably what it looked like to the casual observer. Actually, she ground her pelvis into him and rubbed her breasts against his chest.

Her smell was overpowering, a mixture of sweat and sleep and whiskey and perfume.

'You come see me, hon, all right? And we'll talk about Steve and the old days, all right, hon?'

But he knew what she wanted, what she'd wanted since he was fifteen. To make love to her. *No way.*

He had just eased himself out from under her grasp when she turned suddenly away and began vomiting violently all over the piece of fake grass the funeral home always laid down next to the coffin.

One of her sisters said, 'Aw, fuck, I tole you you was drinkin' too much.' And then went begrudgingly over and held her until she was done throwing up.

Michael got out of there. Fast.

In the early afternoon, after lunch, Michael drove out to the farm. Ben's strange attitude bothered him. Had he done something to make his little brother angry? He sensed not. He sensed that it was that little bitch Alison who had come between them somehow. But how?

He walked into his mother's office to find the waiting area empty. A sign on the inner door said SURGERY. He knocked once on the door and said, 'Hi, everybody. I'll be over at the house when you're done.'

'Hi, honey,' his mother called back. 'It'll be another half hour or so.'

Ben usually said something. But – nothing.

'You in there, Ben?'

'Yeah.'

Definitely not the old Ben; the response was reluctant somehow.

'How you doing?'

'Oh, fine.'

'I brought you a couple sci-fi videos. Brand new.'

'Thanks.'

Dull voice; not bright the way it usually was.

Little bitch. Michael could picture her. She had a fetching face, that was for sure, not a beauty but wryly seductive in a sweet, quiet way.

He imagined slashing that face with a knife, making it ugly for ever, slashing and hacking until nobody would want to look at it again.

Little bitch.

He'd cut up a few of them. He was certainly willing to cut up another one.

'See you guys in a while, then.'

'Ben,' Lynn said, as she was finishing up, 'is everything all right between you and your brother?'

He spoke too quickly. 'Sure. Why?'

'You just seem – different – when you see him now. At least, he thinks you do.'

'He said that, you mean?'

'Yes. He's worried that you're mad at him or something.'

Ben shook his head. 'Why would I be mad?'

But she could see it in his shifting glance, hear it in the slight edge in his voice. Something was wrong.

'Maybe you should go talk to him.'

'Now?'

'When we're done here. He said he'll be at the house.'

'Yeah, I guess I could.'

The morning had been busier than expected so they hadn't been able to get to neutering the big St Bernard until early this afternoon. Ben had done all his usual assisting – prepping the animal by shaving him and scrubbing him; connecting him to the IV anaesthetic; intubating him by putting the tube down his throat; hooking him up to the gas machine, and then – as surgery began – constantly checking the animal's pulse, eye reflexes, the color of membranes in both mouth and eye. Neutering required Lynn to use her scalpel between the dog's penis and scrotum. And now that they were finishing up, Ben would keep on monitoring the St Bernard and then gradually take him off the machine as he regained consciousness. Ben would then put the animal in the small recovery room, watch him for a few more minutes, and then they'd be able to go over to the house and see Michael.

'You know how much he loves you, don't you?' Lynn said.

Ben nodded, finished up with the dog.

When she was done, and washing up, she said, 'He thinks this has something to do with Alison.'

He spoke too quickly again. 'Huh-uh. Nothing to do with her at all.'

He came over, waiting his turn at the sink to scrub up after the surgery.

She dried her hands on paper towels, leaned against the wall as he soaped up his hands and held them under the hot water.

'You really need to be honest with him, honey. I think his feelings are hurt.'

He stared down at his hands a moment, then looked up at her. 'I'll talk to him, Mom.'

'I'd appreciate that. Get it out in the open, whatever it is.'

'Yeah,' Ben said. 'That's a good idea.'

Michael spent twenty minutes just wandering through the old house where he'd passed the first nineteen years of his life. He had glimpses of himself at various ages – the seven-year-old who played basketball until his parents absolutely dragged him inside; the ten-year-old who was told he could start on the junior high basketball team; the fifteen-year-old who took the senior team to State; and then the nineteen-year-old who'd broken his leg playing touch football, for God's sake, but somehow, even after three operations, the leg wouldn't heal properly and – no more career.

Other images, too: the fourteen-year-old boy who'd stayed in his room for three days, pretending to be sick, after smashing in the head of that hobo with a brick. The sixteen-year-old who'd trapped the twelve-year-old girl in the storm sewer and then forced her to drown; the twenty-year-old who had, on three different occasions, driven to strange towns and slashed up the faces of three beautiful women. And when he was done slashing them, he killed them. Then there was dear Dana, who had confided to Steve Conners that she thought Michael was clinically insane – as if she knew anything about insanity, clinical or otherwise. She'd been a slut was all, a slut who needed to be slashed and killed. Steve had been scared to do it at first but it had been fun. No doubt about it. And Steve had finally gotten caught up in it all. And then they took turns raping her, and then took turns cutting her up. No telling which of them had actually killed her. They'd each stabbed her a good twenty times apiece. Then they learned that a private detective named Weyrich was looking for Steve. The cops had never made the connection but somehow the private detective had discovered that Dana had been dating this out-of-towner named Steve. The investigator had shown up here in town again and—

And case closed.

Chief Rhys was satisfied that Steve had killed Dana and Weyrich.

And now, with Steve having been put in the ground today, the case was closed...

Michael drifted upstairs.

There was a soft breeze through the landing window and he thought of being a kid again and lying on his bed in his underwear reading *Spiderman* and *Batman*. Kids had it knocked – too bad they didn't ever realize it when they were still kids. They just couldn't wait to grow up – and growing up wasn't near as much fun as they imagined.

There were five doors on the upper floor. The big bedroom, which Mom and Dad had used; the bathroom; the spare room that Mom had fixed up into a kind of den; and the boys' bedrooms.

Ben's room was closest so he went in there and right away he was smiling. Instead of pictures of models or rock stars, Ben's wall was filled with snapshots of various animals he'd raised over the years. Ben and his animals. God, Ben was such a sweet kid. Or had been until he'd met Alison.

The room was small, containing a single bed with a red spread, a desk and goose-necked lamp, a four-row bookcase packed with sci-fi novels, a set of barbells that Michael had given Ben for his fourteenth birthday, and a bureau on top of which sat three framed photographs – Mom, Dad, Michael.

Sweet kid. God, he really was.

Michael walked over to the window, took in the sun-scented breeze, looked out over acres and acres of fertile soil, of corn just beginning to grow, of alfalfa and soybeans, too.

You couldn't ask for a better life than one in the country.

He decided to go visit his room.

He had just turned away from the window, just started leaving the room, when he saw the envelope sitting in the center of Ben's desk.

Buff blue. Small. A female hand in ballpoint.

Alison.

No doubt about it.

He picked up the envelope, held it to his nose. Perfumed. Little bitch. Took every chance she could to be seductive.

He looked at the postmark. Yesterday.

He wondered why she'd write his brother a letter, when she was right in the same town.

He'd better read it.

It might have something to do with why Ben was acting so weird around him.

Just as he started to extract the letter, he heard them come in downstairs.

Damn.

His first thought was to stick the envelope in his pocket and walk out with it.

But from the way the top of the envelope looked slightly worn, he could tell that Ben had read this letter many times. And would probably read it again.

No way he wanted to get caught stealing the kid's mail.

He put the envelope back on the desk and hurried downstairs.

Before they'd come inside, Lynn had told Ben to be friendly with his brother so Michael would know that everything was all right between them.

Now he wasn't sure how to act. How did he usually act around Michael? Big smile? Hearty clap on the shoulder? No, that was never Ben's style.

All he could think of was to say, 'Hi, Michael, how's it going?'

He wasn't sure Michael had ever looked at him this closely before. It was as if Michael were examining him rather than simply looking at him.

'Great, Ben. How about you?'

'Oh, pretty good.'

The conversation was so strained it sounded like dialogue from an old family sit-com.

'Been boating lately?'

Ben shook his head. 'Haven't had time. Busy.'

Icy smile. 'Alison, probably, huh?'

Ben glanced at his mother.

Lynn said, anxiously, 'Ben and Alison have decided to take a little break from each other.'

'Oh?' Michael said.

Ben shrugged, trying to seem casual about it. 'We just figured things were going kind of fast. You know. We're pretty young and all.'

The pain had to be evident in his voice; just had to be. Ben hadn't slept much in three nights, and walked around constantly on the verge of tears. Nobody had ever warned him about love being like this. Love was fun and love was sex and love was little spats that you kissed and made up about. Love wasn't a girl you loved telling you that your brother was a murderer.

Michael's eyes were on Ben again. Ben walked into the kitchen, opened up the refrigerator, took out a Pepsi.

'I'll have one of those, kiddo,' Michael said.

Ben took another can of pop out and handed it to his brother.

Michael leaned against the sink. Ben went over and sat down at the table. His knees trembled a lot these past few days. He was afraid sometime he'd just fall down. He kept hearing Alison's voice and smelling her hair and seeing her smile.

'Any time you're ready, I am.'

'Ready?' Ben said.

'Women.'

'Oh.'

Lynn came in and went over to the Mr Coffee.

'I just offered to line him up and he didn't seem very interested,' Michael said. 'And I'm talking fabulous babes.'

Lynn smiled. 'I'm not sure "fabulous babes" is what he's got on his mind right now. I think he'd probably rather work it out with Alison.'

'Not the only fish in the sea, kiddo. Take my word for it.'

Ben wasn't sure what to say to any of this. He sensed that Michael was as uneasy with him as he was with Michael. He was sure that his mother had also prompted Michael into being 'extra nice' to him, too. Maybe that accounted for the slightly desperate edge in Michael's dialogue. Trying too hard.

Ben drank some of his Pepsi and listened as Michael and his mother talked briefly about the profit picture at the video store. 'Profit picture' was a phrase Michael seemed to love. He was especially happy with the way CD-ROMs and video games were going, he said.

Ben had a few rocky moments again, Alison coming back to him in stray words and gestures. God, he loved her so much.

But as he watched his brother now, he realized how crazy her accusation was. Michael was no killer. He was a handsome, bright, clever young man who liked people and was genuinely liked by them in return.

Ben was scarcely aware of crossing the kitchen and throwing his arms around Michael and hugging him.

'Hey, kiddo,' Michael said as they held each other. 'You beat me to it. That's what I was going to do before I left here today.'

'I sure appreciate everything you've done for me, Michael,' Ben said.

He had passed through the barrier of the past few days. His old spontaneous love and affection for his brother was back again. Alison and her crazy ideas.

When Ben walked back to the table, he noticed that his mother had tears in her eyes. Happy tears. They were a happy family again.

'Think I'll go upstairs and use the john,' Michael said. 'And then head back.'

'Use the one down here if you want,' Lynn said.

'I have sentimental memories about the one upstairs,' Michael grinned, and leaned over and gave her a kiss.

When he was gone, Lynn said, 'Thanks, honey.'

'For what?'

'For being such a darned nice young man. And you know what?'

'What?'

'I'll bet you and Alison work this out.'

He hadn't, of course, told her the truth about why he wasn't seeing Alison at the moment. After what she'd gone through with her father, all her years of shame and embarrassment, there was no way he could even bring the subject up. 'Alison thinks that Michael murdered that girl in the state capitol.' Yeah: he could just hear himself saying that.

'I sure hope so,' he said.

'Why don't you go see her tonight?'

'Maybe I will.'

'She's probably just as miserable as you are.'

He laughed. 'I sure hope she is.'

Fast.

Had to work fast.

Up the stairs. Straight to Ben's room.

Straight to the desk and the letter.

Froze.

Was that somebody coming up the stairs?

He trembled. What if it was Ben? How could he explain being in here?

He remained frozen. Listening.

Nothing. Nerves was all.

Open the envelope. Take out the letter.

Read it.

* * *

'I think I'll go change clothes,' Ben said.

'Change clothes?'

He nodded. 'Yeah. Maybe I'll go to the library.'

She smiled. Alison at the library. 'Oh.'

He went over and kissed her on the cheek. 'You know, all things considered, you're a pretty good mom.'

'All things considered, huh?' she said, swatting him on the bottom.

He walked out of the kitchen, down the hall to the stairs.

Dear Ben,

It's probably redundant to tell you that I love you but I really do. You're all I think about. You're the only person in the whole world I want to be with. I didn't understand that until we had that argument the other night.

I never should have said what I did about Michael. He's your brother and you love him and now I realize that he isn't a killer. The only thing I based it on were a couple of notes I got from Dana right before she died. The private detective, Weyrich, said that they were incriminating and that he wanted me to give them to him. But I couldn't. They were Dana's last words to me. I still have them with me.

Anyway, afterwards, Chief Rhys told the press about Weyrich's notebooks, and everything that Weyrich had learned – that Steve Conners was the killer and not your brother. I just wasn't thinking clearly.

I hope you'll forgive me. I love you so much, Ben. I hope we can pick up where we left off. Please let me hear from you soon.

Love,

Alison

Bitch.

Little bitch.

Then – noise on the steps.

This time there was no doubt about it.

Quick.

The letter back in the envelope.

The envelope back on the desk.

Quick.

Get out of here.

When Ben reached the top of the stairs, he saw that Michael was just leaving the bedroom. Ben's bedroom.

At least that was how it appeared, all in a kind of flash and blur.

He wondered why Michael would have been in his room.

Then Michael was in the bathroom. Door closed.

Why would Michael have been in his room?

Ben went in and changed clothes.

Then he went over and picked up the buff blue envelope on the desk and held it to his nose.

Pretty sappy, but he couldn't help it. Loved to inhale the perfume.

He was going to see her.

Now she knew the truth.

Michael was no murderer.

And they were going to be all right again, he was sure of it now, Alison and Ben, for ever.

He had just put the envelope back on the desk when Michael came in.

Then he wondered again: why had Michael been in his room?

'You find it, kiddo?'

'Find it?'

The big Michael grin. Sincere now. Not pasted on the way it had been at first this afternoon.

'See your pillow there on the bed?'

'Yeah,' Ben said.

'Pick it up.'

'Huh?'

'Go ahead, kiddo. Pick it up. See what's underneath.'

Ben went over and picked up the pillow that rested on top of the cover.

A twenty-dollar bill lay there.

'What's that for?'

'For you being such a great kid, kiddo.'

'Jeeze, Michael, you don't have to do that.'

Michael came over and slid his arm around him. 'Don't have to, kiddo. But I *want* to.'

Ben felt guiltier than ever. First that he'd even *listened* to Alison speculate that Michael was a murderer. Second that he had been so suspicious about Michael being in his room.

Twenty dollars.

That was just like Michael.

Ben gave him another brotherly hug, and they walked downstairs together, their mother delighted that they were getting along again.

2

'Mind if I walk with you?'

'I'd like that.'

'I got your letter.'

'I thought maybe you'd have called about it last night.'

'I wanted to.'

'What stopped you?'

'Well,' Ben said, 'I'm not sure.'

'Oh.'

'I was still kind of angry, I guess.'

'I don't blame you.'

'And sort of hurt.'

'I'd have been hurt, too.'

'You would've?'

'Sure. It was a stupid, awful thing I did, Ben, accusing your brother like that.'

They walked through the summer afternoon of butterflies and kids on rollerblades and skateboards and old men in the town square playing checkers and horseshoes. She wore a crisply starched baby blue blouse and jeans and sandals. She had cute little feet.

Alison always took her break right at two o'clock and always went the same place, to Emerson's Rexall Pharmacy where they still had a real Coke fountain circa 1920.

'You know how many times I read your letter?' Ben said as they walked.

'How many?'

'At least twenty.'

'Twenty? Are you kidding?'

'At least twenty, I said.'

'God.'

'And I smelled it even more.'

'I love that smell.'

'It's great.'

'So how come you read my letter so many times?'

'Because I missed you.'

'That's sweet.'

'I really felt like hell.'

'So did I.'

'I really love you.'

'I know. And I really love you,' Alison said.

She slid her hand in his. He got embarrassed about public hand-holding sometimes but not today. Today he felt proud and bold.

'Hey,' he said.

'What?'

'You're turning away from Emerson's.'

'I know.'

'How come? That's where you always go.'

'Not today.'

'Why not?'

'I'd like to go sit by the river.'

'You don't have that long a break.'

'I don't need a long break for what I want to do.'

He gave her a weird look. She was acting funny. He wondered why.

'You going to give me a hint?' he said, as they reached the walk that eventually wound down by the river bank.

'About what?'

'About "what you want to do."'

'Oh.'

'It's going to be bad news, isn't it?'

She was going to leave town. He was sure of it. She was going to tell him that she loved him but that she had to leave town. And maybe someday they'd get together again. The sort of thing girls always said to spare the boy's feelings.

'I guess that depends on your point of view,' she said. 'Whether it's bad news or not.'

'God.'

'What?'

'I'm scared.'

'I'm sorry, Ben. I mean, I can tell you now and get it over with if you want me to.'

'Are you going to leave town?'

'Not unless you ask me to.'

'Did you find somebody else?'

'God, Ben, that's a terrible thing to say.' She smiled. 'After all, you're talking to somebody who was "probably" a virgin when you first slept with her.'

He wanted to laugh but he couldn't. He was too nervous.

'You're going to break my heart, aren't you?'

And then she took his hand and moved it gently to her stomach and said, in her quiet way, 'I'm pregnant, Ben.'

People were kicked, stabbed, slashed, shot, burned, hanged, electrocuted. And boy wasn't it fun.

Being summer and all, the video store's largest customer base was teenagers, and teenagers loved violent movies.

'You got that one where they cut the guy's tongue out and make him eat it?' a nine-year-old boy with freckles and two missing teeth asked Michael late that afternoon.

'That one's rented,' Michael smiled, 'but how about the one where they cut the guy's eyes out and make him swallow them?'

'Neat-o!' the kid said. 'I'll take it!'

Michael smiled, and went to the wall slots to retrieve the masterpiece he'd just described. Most American directors today were imitating the Japanese director John Woo. Unfortunately, they had neither his style nor his ingenuity, nor his ability to give action movies the emotional underpinnings of grand opera. The trouble was, he couldn't get many of his teenage customers to give Woo a try. He'd show them a few minutes of, say, *The Killer* but then they'd start saying where are the girls? That was one thing Woo didn't do much of in his films. Very little tits and ass. In Woo movies, women had brains, integrity and dignity. What the hell was wrong with the guy, anyway? Michael had read all this in one of his film magazines. He didn't have time to view all his rental films so he read about them. He enjoyed quoting from them and sounding smart. Not a lot of guys in a little town like this could give you five minutes on John Woo.

'They really rip his eyes out?' the kid said when Michael handed him the video box.

'Uh-huh.'

'And make him swallow them?'

'Uh-huh.'

'You know where that is on the counter?'

'The counter?'

'Yeah, you know, so I can go right to it.'

'Don't you want to see the whole movie?'

'I just like the neat parts.'

'I see.'

'So you don't know where it is on the counter?'

'Afraid not.'

'Well, I'll fast-forward through it, then.'

'Good idea.'

The kid had given him a wrinkled five-dollar bill. Michael gave him three ones in return.

The rest of the afternoon went slowly. UPS dropped off two large boxes of new videos. Michael and his assistant catalogued them and shelved them and hung up some of the point-of-purchase material, the best being a life-size stand-up cut-out of Sylvester Stallone lunging at customers with a knife.

He tried not to think about the note Alison had written Ben. Little bitch. What if she was lying? What if she didn't really believe Chief Rhys' final report, based on Weyrich's notebook, that Conners had acted alone? And what about the letters she'd kept from Dana? Were they really as incriminating as she'd made them sound?

The letters.

No doubt about it, he'd have to get a look at them somehow.

Just before five, a small group of customers arrived at once. One of them was Chief Rhys.

Rhys went to the back of the store, the Western section, and picked up two John Wayne movies.

Michael waited for him at the cash register, smiling. Rhys was a regular in here.

'Let me guess,' Michael said as the chief of police approached the cash register. '*She Wore a Yellow Ribbon* and *True Grit*.'

''Fraid you lose, Michael,' Rhys laughed.

'One more guess?'

'All right.'

'*The Searchers* and *The Quiet Man.*'

The Chief shook his head. 'And here I thought you were going to win that convertible.'

'Didn't win anything, huh?' Michael said.

'Sorry.'

The Chief put his film boxes on the counter. *Flying Leathernecks* and *The Shootist*. Rhys rented a lot of John Wayne movies. His wife joked about it. She rented her own movies, she said, and Rhys rented his. That was the funny thing. Rhys was a quiet guy, more like a businessman than a cop. No swagger, no brag. Michael would never have figured him for such an obsessive John Wayne fan.

Michael went and got the movies and brought them back.

Rhys said, 'You know what's funny?'

'Funny?' Michael said as he rang up the movies.

'Yes. About Conners.'

Michael tensed. 'Conners?'

'Yes. That he never let on to anybody. Not even you.'

'Yeah, that kind of surprised me, too.'

'Most people who commit murder, they always end up telling somebody. Or they at least act funny. Start doing things they wouldn't ordinarily do. I had a case once where this guy who'd been a real slob suddenly started taking care of himself and his house and lawn. Got real fixated on it. And that made his neighbors suspicious. Somebody mentioned it to me so I just had a hunch that maybe the guy was worth checking out. I found the murder weapon buried in the floor of his garage. This garden trowel. Still bloody and everything.' Rhys paused. He stared down at his John Wayne movies then slowly raised his eyes to meet Michael's. 'But you say he acted normally – Conners, I mean?'

'As far as I could tell.'

Michael began to wonder if this was such a casual visit after all. Had the Chief simply stopped in to pick up a couple of John Wayne movies – or did he have some other motive?

Neither Rhys' face nor manner told Michael anything.

This might just be a casual conversation, after all.

On the other hand . . .

'Well, I guess it's over now, so it doesn't make much difference, does it?' And Rhys' eyes once again met Michael's.

Michael was well aware that the Chief had said, '*I guess* it's over.' Did that mean that it really wasn't over?

Did that mean that the Chief had some suspicions about Michael?

Three customers came up to the register.

'Well, looks like you're getting busy, Michael. I'll head home for supper. Take care of yourself.'

'You, too,' Michael said.

He wondered if his face reflected any of the anxiety he'd felt there at the last. Not until a few minutes ago had he realized how formidable Rhys could be when he was asking you questions.

Did Rhys really know something?

And then the thought: had Alison secretly contacted Rhys and shown him Dana's letters?

'Is everything all right, honey?'

'Uh, yeah, pretty much,' Ben said.

'You sound – different.'

'I'm fine, Mom. Really.'

He'd called to tell her that he was going to stay in town the rest of the afternoon, and then meet Alison when she got off work at the library.

'Well, don't I get a hint?'

'A hint?'

'About Alison.'

'Oh.' He couldn't help it. He was still in shock from Alison's news. A baby. He was going to be a father. It was astonishing to him, unreal.

'Well?'

'Well, she was glad to see me, I guess.'

'And?'

'And I was glad to see her.'

Mom laughed. 'You'd make a great spy. Nobody could ever get any information out of you.'

'I guess I'll know more tonight.'

He'd thought of telling her, about the baby and all, but somehow he couldn't imagine himself saying the words.

'I'm sorry if I'm being a pest.'

'You're not being a pest.'

'I'm just curious.'

'I know. And I don't mind.'

'Tell Alison hello for me.'

'All right, Mom. See you later tonight.'

'Have a good time.'

'I will. Bye.'

Just about six, he was walking along the street a block from the library when he heard a motorcycle come roaring up behind him at the curb.

Michael on his Harley.

He looked cool on his Harley, dark hair all windblown, tan muscled arms thick in his yellow polo shirt.

But then, Michael always looked cool.

God, if only Ben could look like that for one day. Just one day.

'Hey, kiddo,' Michael said when Ben walked over.

The big black machine smelled of oil and dust and sunlight. Michael kept giving it some gas to keep it running well.

'You ever going to let me borrow this?' Ben said.

'Soon as you let me give you a couple lessons.'

'Yeah, I guess that'd be a pretty neat idea, huh?' It felt good feeling good about his brother again.

'Hey, I almost forgot, kiddo,' Michael said, and leaned back so he could stuff his hand deep inside his pocket. He pulled out a twenty and a five and handed them to Ben.

'What's this for?'

'So you and Alison can have a nice dinner tomorrow. Take her to The Grove. You know, somewhere nice.'

'But I thought—'

Michael leaned forward and clasped the back of Ben's neck in the palm of his hand. 'Kiddo, I ran my mouth and I shouldn't have. Alison is a great girl. She really is.' The famous Michael smile. 'So she isn't crazy about me. There had to be some girl somewhere who wasn't.' He tapped the bills he'd just given Ben. 'Be sure and tell her that big brother gave you the money, all right?'

'You really don't need to—'

'Don't need to. But want to.' The smile. 'I'd give you a kiss, kiddo. But people'd start talking about us.'

And then he leaned back, gave the big black Harley some power and zoomed away.

Ben finished the rest of his walk to the library trying to cope with everything he'd learned today. Not only were he and Alison seeing each other again, they were going to have a child. And now Michael was trying to be nice to her so they'd get along better.

Life was amazing sometimes, all its unexpected twists and turns, sometimes in just a matter of a few hours.

He walked the rest of the way to the library, whistling.

3

The little girl was terrified of Lynn, kept clinging to her mother's side as they came through the front door of the office.

Becky Harper was the niece of the young woman Lynn's father had murdered. As long as there had been two veterinarians in town, she'd never had to use Lynn's services. But Doc Pelham had retired last year and now Becky had no choice. This was her very first visit here.

She'd called Lynn twenty minutes ago and asked if she could bring the family dog out right away. The dog had run under the car as Becky had been backing out of the driveway. She'd driven over the dog's right paw.

Becky and her seven-year-old daughter Lisa both had the same dark hair worn short. And both had huge somber blue eyes. But Lisa was slender and Becky was at least twenty pounds overweight. Both wore western-style shirts and jeans.

'What's his name?' Lynn said, as she took the dog from Becky's arms.

'Rudy,' said Lisa.

'He's a handsome little tyke,' Lynn said. Rudy was a chubby little mutt with dark sad eyes and a small sweet face that showed some beagle heritage. He cried constantly now, and held his white-spotted right paw out at an awkward and tender angle.

'Is he gonna die?' Lisa said.

'I don't think so, honey,' Lynn said. 'But why don't we take him in the examining room and see exactly what's wrong with him?'

Lynn opened the door and took Rudy in and set him on the examining table. She was just starting the exam when Lisa said, 'My mom says your pa was a bad man.'

'Lisa!' Becky said, grabbing the girl by the wrist and shaking her. 'You be quiet.'

Lynn tried to proceed as if nothing had been said. But the girl's words had stunned her. All sorts of terrible memories came back. Of the town snubbing her for several years. Of watching her mother slowly sink into death. And of seeing a newspaper photo of the victim. She'd looked young and pretty and intelligent. And somehow that picture had brought home the savagery of what her father had done. Taken a young and precious life. After seeing that photograph, she had never been able to forgive him. Love him, yes. Remain loyal, visit him in prison, yes. But never forgive him. To her, her father would always be a monster. Always.

'I'm sorry, Dr Tyler.'

'That's all right,' Lynn said, continuing with her examination.

But she knew that the girl had only been expressing what Becky had told her, that Lynn's father had done something dark and terrible.

And how could Lynn dispute that?

After getting off work at the library, Alison went home and got sick.

Ben had heard of morning sickness but he'd never heard of 6:38-p.m.-sickness.

Yet there she was. Alison. In the bathroom. Being sick.

He sat in the living room with his butt planted on the couch. 'Rocky and Bullwinkle' was on. Yosemite Sam and Bullwinkle were his two favorite cartoon characters and they always made him laugh out loud.

The small apartment seemed melancholy with dusk in the windows, the dying day a cacophony of birdsong and kids playing the last of their games and teenagers already starting the trek up and down the main drag.

Then he thought he could smell something burning. Paper, it smelled like.

Alison came back and sat down next to him and put her face close to his and exhaled and said, 'Is my breath all right?'

'Yeah. Great.'

'Really?'

'Really.'

'Good, because I've been getting sick a lot. All day and all night. So I got this killer mouthwash.'

'God. Will you be all right, being sick and all?'

She kissed him on the cheek. 'Thanks for worrying but I'll be fine. Some girls get sick more often than others. I'm one of them, I guess.'

'You feel like going out?'

'Not really.'

'Michael gave us twenty-five dollars.'

'I know and I really appreciate it, but – could we wait a day or so?'

'Sure.'

'Maybe I'll feel better. If we go out, I want to enjoy the food.'

He took her hand. 'Anything you want to do is fine with me.'

She turned at an angle, so she was facing him. 'I want you to go look in the toilet bowl.'

'Boy, that sounds romantic.'

'Really.'

'You're serious?'

She nodded.

'How come?'

'You'll see.'

'You get weirder all the time, you know that?'

She smiled. 'Just go look in the toilet bowl.'

So he went in and peered into the toilet bowl and came back and sat down.

'I thought I smelled something burning,' he said.

'You see what was in the toilet bowl?'

'Uh-huh. Pieces of burned paper.'

'Dana's letters.'

'The ones that mentioned Michael?'

'Right.' This time, she took his hand. 'If I'm going to be part of the family, I want to start off with a clean slate.'

'You really believe that Michael didn't have anything to do with Dana's murder?'

'I really believe it. That's why I burned the letters. I'm putting it all behind me.' She guided his hand to the small swell of her stomach. 'We've got other things to be concerned about.'

Then she paused and said, 'And one more thing.'

'I know.'

'You do?'

'Uh-huh. You want to know when I'm going to tell my mother.'

'Well, I guess I was kind of wondering.'

'In the next couple of days. When the time's right.'

'I'd rather have to face your mother than face my sister.'

'Is she going to take it bad?'

'Bad? Are you crazy? She'll start screaming and crying and swearing at me. She'll want me to get an abortion, for one thing.'

He said, 'I guess you could.'

'Yes, I could.' She looked at him. 'Do you want me to?'

'To be honest, I've had the thought a couple of times.'

'To be honest, so have I.'

'And?'

'And,' she said, 'I don't want to. Do you want me to?'

'A couple of times I did. I mean, when I was still getting used to the idea and all.'

'But not now?'

He smiled. Touched her stomach. 'Not now. Now I'm curious about what our kid's going to look like.'

They kissed gently, tenderly.

'There's one more thing,' she said, when she was still in his arms.

'What?'

'You know this afternoon when you said you might have to drop out of school?'

'Uh-huh.'

'I don't want any argument now.'

'Argument about what?'

'My trust fund. I'm going to help you finish school.'

'Aw, Alison, I don't know if I—'

'Not for your sake, Ben. For "our" sake. For the three of us.'

'Well, I guess I can't argue about that.'

'And when you get done with college, then I'm going to go. I need a degree, too.'

'God, this is just incredible. I'm going to be a father. I just keep saying that to myself.'

He kissed her and then held her for a long moment. Precious. She was so precious to him. And the child inside her ... He couldn't help touching her abdomen every once in a while. All the tenderness he felt for animals was quadrupled whenever he thought of the life she carried in her womb...

She eased his arm from her shoulder and stood up slowly and said, 'Now, if you'll excuse me.'

'Where're you going?'

'To be sick again, believe it or not.'

Then she was gone, and the bathroom door was closing again.

He sat back and closed his eyes and thought of how much he loved Alison. And now the prospect of fatherhood wasn't all that frightening, either.

Now he sort of looked forward to the idea of being a father, weird as that was.

Even at his young age.

Lynn took two X-rays of Rudy's right front paw. She wanted to double-check herself. The fracture was such that she couldn't be sure without a second picture.

Finished, she went back into the room where Becky and Lisa waited, petting Rudy and talking to him as he lay sprawled on the examining table.

Rudy looked up at Lynn with his big sad eyes. He looked nervous and she felt sorry for him. Visiting the vet was a traumatic experience for many animals.

'Good news,' Lynn said. 'At least as good as it could be. It's a clean break. Right between the paw and the elbow. So we can put a splint on it.'

'No surgery?' Becky said, obviously relieved.

'That's only when we need to put a pin in the break.' Lynn leaned down and patted Rudy on the head. He made a faint, whimpering sound. 'You're sure a good boy, Rudy.'

'Can we stay and watch you put the splint on?' Lisa said.

She no longer sounded afraid of Lynn.

'Sure, honey. You stay just where you are and you'll be able to see everything.'

Lynn went into the other room again for a few minutes, returning with everything she needed to splint Rudy's leg.

Rudy was good the whole time. Lisa kept petting him and talking to him as Lynn did her work. At one point, his eyes ran with tears. She daubed the tears with a Kleenex.

When she was finished, Lynn bent over and kissed Rudy on the head. 'Thank you, Rudy.'

Lisa giggled and looked up at her mom.

Her mother smiled back.

'Can Rudy go out to the car now, Doctor?' Becky asked.

'Sure.'

'Honey, why don't you take him out to the car?' Becky said to Lisa.

'Can we get him a Dairy Queen?'

Becky laughed. 'I'm not sure that the doctor would approve.'

'A lot of animals love Dairy Queens,' Lynn said. 'My son Ben has a cat –' and then she remembered putting Elizabeth to sleep '– had a cat. She loved Dairy Queens. She always sat on the seat between us and Ben would hold the cone down to her and she'd lick it until she was full and then she'd go right to sleep.' At the time, they didn't know that her sudden exhaustion was a symptom of leukemia. Lynn felt a sharp sorrow for the loss of sweet little Elizabeth, and for Ben's sorrow, too.

'You take Rudy out to the car, honey.'

'All right, Mom.'

Lynn lifted Rudy up and set him down in Lisa's arms. He was still getting used to his splint and moved his broken paw carefully.

'What do you say to the doctor, honey?'

'Thank you, Doctor.'

'You're welcome.' Lynn petted Rudy a final time. 'I'll need to see him in four to six weeks and we'll do another X-ray. But I think he'll heal fine.'

Lynn held the doors for Lisa so she could get Rudy out to the car without banging into doorframes.

When Lynn walked back to the waiting room, Becky was lighting a cigarette. So few of Lynn's clients smoked that she'd never bothered with a NO SMOKING sign. She supposed she could survive somebody smoking a single cigarette.

'Will this bother you?' Becky said, holding up her cigarette.

'No problem.'

'Thanks.' She inhaled deeply, then exhaled. 'I was a little nervous coming here tonight.'

'I sensed that.'

'Your family—'

Lynn nodded. 'I understand. My father and all.'

'Right. Your father and all.'

Lynn took a deep breath, held it, then let it out slowly. 'I hate him for what he did to her, Becky. I hope you understand that.'

'My mother raised us to think of you people as—'

She didn't have to finish the sentence.

'You people' had said it all.

'I appreciate your business, Becky, and I'm looking forward to seeing you again.'

'I'm sorry that Lisa said that about your father – about him being a bad man.'

'It's all right. He *was* a bad man. Not completely. But he was certainly bad when he killed your aunt. And he paid the price he should have.'

Murder had become the one act for which Lynn had no tolerance. The TV was filled with criminals who always had excuses for killing other people – they came from a bad background; they needed money for drugs; they didn't really mean to kill anybody . . . but she had little or no sympathy for them.

She had seen what murder does to the family of the victim and to the family of the killer.

There was no excuse for it.

She felt the same way about people who were cruel to animals. No tolerance. No sympathy. The harshest of penalties.

'I just wanted to apologize for what Lisa said,' Becky said.

'I appreciate it.'

Becky hurried to change the subject. 'So you think four to six weeks?'

'Right.'

'You don't think he'll need another splint?'

'Probably not. He's young. He should heal fine.'

Becky came up and touched Lynn's arm. 'Thanks a lot.'

'Thank you, Becky. It took some courage coming over here.'

She walked the woman out to the car and then stood there watching as the car retreated into the darkness. When Becky got to the end of the long drive, she honked. Lynn waved.

She stood there a long time, enjoying the night and the smell of the flowers she'd planted around the house, and the sound of the horses in the high pasture to the east.

She thought of Becky, too, and how difficult it must have been for her to come over here tonight.

She was proud of both of them, both Becky and herself, for how they'd handled it.

Maybe the town would someday forget all about the murder.

Maybe someday.

4

Somebody came into the bathroom.

Michael was in the shower, soaping his chest, when he saw through the opaque glass stall door the vague shape of a human being open the bathroom door and come inside.

Michael froze.

The sound of the shower was deafening suddenly; and Michael naked, wet, his eyes still stinging from soap, felt young and defenseless and vulnerable.

The shape had not moved, simply stood there, apparently staring at the shower door. This was a large bathroom and so the intruder stood so far away, Michael could make out no detail. The intruder was wearing dark clothes. That was all Michael knew for sure.

A weapon.

That's what Michael needed.

His eyes searched the stall but found nothing more deadly than a bar of soap.

'Hello?' he said, finally.

But his voice was soft, shaky.

'Hello?' he said, shouting now. There was anger in his voice. He needed to sound angry to discourage his visitor.

But the intruder said nothing.

Stood there.

'Hello?' Michael said again.

Had one of Steve Conners' relatives figured out what had really happened and come here to take his vengeance?

The shape was still an unmoving inkblot.

The sound of the shower again.

Roaring, steady.

Steam; Michael's flesh puckered from being under the water so long. He loved long showers. They relaxed him. But now—

Michael huddled in the back of the stall, self-conscious about being naked, scared that his intruder had some sort of weapon. Michael feared few people – if they were unarmed. But if they had a knife or worse, a gun...

The intruder made a series of sudden quick movements. What was going on?

White.

The intruder was wearing dark clothes but now the opaque darkness, following the sudden quick movements, had become white.

By the time Michael had figured out what was happening, the shower door was opening and Denise Fletcher, naked, was stepping into the shower with him.

He wanted to slap her, or at least scream at her, for scaring him this way but she didn't give him time.

Her mouth found his before he could utter a word, and her wet sleek body pressed into his, her bountiful breasts against his chest stirring him immediately.

She leaned him back against the shower wall, parted her legs, and took him up into her.

Paul Fletcher sat in the alley behind Michael's house on the edge of town, watching.

He'd given Denise a three-minute head start, then raced out to the used Ford he'd brought home from the car lot this afternoon – Denise never having seen the blue Ford before – and followed her.

Suspicions confirmed.

For the past six months, he'd suspected that she was seeing Michael Tyler but he'd never been able to catch her, probably because he'd been busy with a couple affairs of his own. He saw nothing ironic about his rage and feeling of betrayal. Men having affairs was one thing; women having affairs was another. And there was the matter of being humiliated. This was a small town and eventually everybody knew everybody else's business. This meant sitting in Rotary Club, in Lions Club, in Junior Achievement, and in one of the front rows of Grace Methodist Church knowing that everybody there knew that your wife was balling somebody else. This was a pretty sad comment on Paul Fletcher, at least the way he saw it. Was he not the Buick dealer? Was he not handsome? Was his dad not the richest man in the valley? Was not Paul himself the number one choice for master of ceremonies every year at the Country Club stag party?

But now he'd be a figure of pity and scorn.

People would forget about all the chicks he'd balled on the side. All they'd remember was that this was a guy who couldn't keep his wife from straying. They'd forget all about his dad being rich, and all about Paul's Buick dealership (it was his now, anyway, even if he did originally inherit it from his dad), and they'd forget about his master of ceremonies gig every year. They'd just see this pathetic wife-betrayed guy for whom everybody felt pity and contempt in equal parts.

Paul Fletcher pounded the steering wheel so hard and so fast that it began to vibrate.

Bitch.

She got him ready to go a second time with no trouble at all.

This time it was Denise who leaned back against the wall.

Much as he was tired of her personally, Michael had to admit that he was anything but tired of her physically.

She was erotic in an open, simple way that only enhanced her sexy body. No coyness. No games. Just a hearty tireless lust, and a quiet, knowing manner.

He even suspected that she didn't like him a whole lot more than he liked her. But used him in much the same way that he used her.

She was getting back at Paul for being unfaithful – and Michael was the beneficiary.

She tilted her head, closed her eyes, her face beading with silver drops of water.

Michael was inside her, then, and they found a slow, luxurious rhythm to get lost in.

In just two minutes, sitting out back in his used Ford, Paul went through jealousy, grief, rage, lust (knowing somebody else was screwing his wife made her just all that much more desirable), self-pity, hatred, love, melancholy, and shame.

Especially shame.

What was that word he could never remember?

Cock-something?

No; it was a weirder word.

Cuck-something.

Cuckold!

That was it.

Cuckold!

That's how people would see him – and him the god damn Buick dealer – even if they didn't know what it meant.

And look who she was balling.

The Tyler family wasn't respectable and hadn't been since the time the father killed that girl he was having an affair with.

Lynn Tyler had not been invited to join any of the ladies' groups, especially not the Country Club auxiliary which any woman who was anybody belonged to, and her two boys had never really found acceptance, either.

Michael was the town's supreme athlete, to be sure. But despite all the records he'd set, all the times he'd taken the team to State, all the girls who'd had crushes on him, and all the boys who'd wanted to be his friend – well, as Paul's dad often said at Sunday dinner, 'They just don't belong in Black River Falls. If that Tyler woman had any self-respect, she would've moved from here a long time ago.'

And if his dad said it, it must be true because his dad was not only the richest man in the valley, he was also the first choice for speaker every year at the Milburn Bible College commencement, the college faculty obviously knowing a wise man when they saw one.

And now Paul's wife was opening her legs to one of the white-trash Tylers.

Bitch.

How could she do this to him?

He pounded his steering wheel some more.

Michael was in the bedroom, putting on a clean shirt and chinos, when she attacked him again.

A) He didn't think he had the physical wherewithal to go a third round right now.

B) He knew he had to get over to Alison's. He'd given Ben the money for dinner tonight to get him out of the apartment. That way Michael could sneak in. He had to get a look at the letters Dana had written Alison.

But he didn't count on the stealth and cunning and ingenuity of Denise.

She came into the room silent as the nightshadows gathering in the corners, and snuck up behind him and slid her silken hands down the front of his chinos.

She was something, she was.

She eased him over to the bed and took him again, and he had absolutely no choice in the matter.

No choice at all.

The funny thing was, it just sort of snuck up on him. He was sitting out there pounding the steering wheel, wanting to strangle her, when this image came to him of Denise doing it with another guy, not Tyler necessarily, just some other guy, and he got turned on.

God, getting turned on by something like that. It was terrible.

'You know what I want to do?'

'What do you want to do?'

'I'd like to videotape us,' Denise said.

'Oh, yeah?' Michael said.

'Yeah. Doing it, I mean.'

'Wow.'

'And then you know what I'd like to do?'

'What?'

'Then I'd like to send it to him.'

'To Paul?'

'Yeah.'

'God.'

'You know, just nice and anonymous and all.'

'He'd kill you with it if you ever got divorced later on.'

'I don't care. It'd be worth it – just to see his face.'

'I've got to go.'

'Oh, c'mon, you can do it one more time. I know you can.'

He grinned. 'Are you crazy? You wore me out.'

'I can help,' she said, sliding her hand on to his thigh.

He had to get to Alison's while there was still time.

Had to.

He got up from the couch.

'I really have to go, Denise. Honest.'

'Oh, c'mon, Michael, I can help, I really can—'

He lifted her up from the couch, kissed her, and gave her a gentle push toward the back screen door.

She pouted and looked sexy as hell doing it.

'All right, I'll go,' she said. 'But you owe me one.'

That got him laughing out loud.

Paul Fletcher watched as his wife slipped out the back door and ran to her car, which she'd parked on the far side of Tyler's garage.

Bitch.

Even if the thought of her with another guy turned him on, he still wanted to kill her.

Michael finished getting ready and then left the house quickly.

Had to get to Alison's.

Had to see the letters Dana had written her.

Had to.

He hurried.

5

Michael drove past Alison's apartment house slowly so he could see in the downstairs window.

The lights were on.

And then he saw Ben carrying two cans of Pepsi in from another part of the apartment, presumably the kitchen.

There was no way Michael was going to get in the apartment tonight. No way.

He drove home and got on his Harley and went out on the highway and ate some bugs.

The Midwestern night was moonlight-perfect as he chased up and down the asphalt roads between the cornfields.

He wanted to make himself feel better about not getting into Alison's.

He had to get in there. Had to.

Had to.

6

'So he didn't act funny?'

'Not that I noticed, anyway.'

'Didn't seem depressed?'

'No.'

'Didn't drink more than usual?'

'No.'

'Didn't hint about something he might have done?'

'No,' Michael said. And then he sighed. 'Chief Rhys, you've already asked me all this stuff.'

'Hey, don't get hot, Michael, I'm just doing my job.'

'I thought it was all wrapped up. He killed the girl and then the private eye came out here and he and Steve got into a gunfight and killed each other.'

'I just want to be sure.'

'I thought you *were* sure.'

'Pretty sure.'

'Pretty sure? What else could've happened?'

Rhys laughed. 'Maybe I should quit renting all those videos from you.'

Michael smiled, too. 'Yeah, all those John Wayne and Sherlock Holmes videos are rotting your brain.'

'You ever see *Murder By Decree*?'

'Huh-uh.'

Chief Rhys looked around inside the video store, as if trying to locate it among the 8,000 titles Michael had in stock. Rhys had shown up twenty minutes ago, picked up some videos and then started talking to Michael. This was a sunny late morning two days following the shower visit by Denise. Rhys and Michael were alone in the store.

'You know what it's about?'

119

'Guess not.'

'Jack the Ripper is actually a relative of Queen Victoria. That's the deal, see?'

'Wow. I can see why you'd like it.'

'It's a really incredible movie.'

'I'll take it home tonight.'

Chief Rhys looked right at him. 'You know what I still can't understand?'

'What?'

'What we were talking about the other day. You know – that he didn't tell you.'

'Steve, you mean?'

'Right.'

'You kill a girl the way he did, why would you tell anybody?'

'Most killers do.'

'They tell people?'

'Sure. All the time.'

'That doesn't make any sense.'

'It's part of the pathology. Either they want to brag about it or they're so guilty, they can't keep it to themselves.'

'Well, Steve sure as hell didn't tell me about killing any girl. I mean, I think I'd remember something like that.'

Chief Rhys smiled. 'Yes, I guess you would.' He shook his head. 'It just seems a little strange.'

'What does?'

'The whole thing. Weyrich and Conners killing each other that way, for one thing.'

'Oh.'

'That doesn't happen very often. Usually one person shoots another. But to have two people die...' He shook his head again. 'Just seems pretty strange is all.'

As he spoke, he looked directly at Michael. There was no hint of accusation in his brown eyes. He was simply watching Michael for a reaction.

The famous Michael grin. 'Those videos really are rotting your brain, Chief. Maybe I should refuse to rent them to you unless you bring a note from your mother.'

He knows I killed them, Michael thought.

He knows.

'What're you getting today?' Michael said, the grin still on his face.

Chief Rhys held up two video boxes, as if he was displaying them on a TV commercial.

'*Abbott and Costello Meet Frankenstein* and *Ma and Pa Kettle Go To Town*,' the Chief said. 'I wanted to get something my youngest boy could watch.'

'I saw him on the street the other day and barely recognized him. How old is he now?'

'Eight.'

'Wow. He's going to be a big one.'

'Yeah, and fortunately he's got his mother's looks and brains. She's the genetically superior one in our family.' Then he said, 'Sort of like you and Steve.'

'Me and Steve?'

'Umm-hmm. Most people could never figure out why you hung around with him. I know he was your friend, but he wasn't a real neat guy.'

'He wasn't as bad as people thought,' Michael said. 'Till the end and all, anyway. With the girl and the private eye, I mean.'

Just as Michael was about to say more, the door opened up and four people came in. This was typical of the traffic flow here. Nobody, or almost nobody, and then a small crowd.

Michael rang up Chief Rhys' tapes, slipped them into a plastic bag and handed them over.

'Hope your boy likes them,' Michael said.

'Hope so, too,' the Chief said. 'Then I'll have a good excuse to rent some more Ma and Pa Kettle movies. My wife can't stand them.'

He hefted the plastic bag and said goodbye. 'Well, if you think of anything about Steve, you let me know.'

'I sure will.'

Michael watched the Chief go out the door.

He thought, again: he knows.

He knows I killed them.

7

Alison could feel the current getting stronger, faster and she asked Ben to stop here. She didn't want to go anywhere near the Falls. Too scary.

They had been out in Ben's canoe for the past hour, their first real chance to be together since she'd told him, two days ago, that she was pregnant. She'd had a library meeting the night before last, then, just as he was leaving to go to her place last night, he and his mother were summoned to a farm where a horse had been badly injured falling down a small ravine. They'd worked on the animal till early this morning.

'I'm going to make supper tonight.'

'I didn't know you could cook,' Alison said.

They sat in the canoe, their fishing lines out. The water surface was still except for the occasional jumping fish or frog. A deer watched them from the east shore. Two crows sat crying atop the birch trees. The day smelled of lazy summer heat and river mud. A mist of hot air gave the trees on the shore a touch of the prehistoric – easy to imagine dinosaurs lumbering through here, pausing to drink gallons of water from the river. Easy for Ben to imagine, anyway.

'Spaghetti. That's the only thing I know how to cook but I do it real good,' he said.

'You're making me hungry.'

'Really?'

'Uh-huh. I get sick so much, I can't hold down a lot of food and—. Say, I just thought of something.'

'What?'

'Where're we going to eat this dinner?'

'I figured we'd eat at my place,' Ben said.

'And invite your mom?'

'Sure. She lives there, remember?'

She stared at him. 'You didn't tell her, did you?'

Ben turned his face, so she couldn't see him, pretended this great sudden interest in his fishing line.

'The other night at my place, you called her and told her to wait up for you. That you wanted to tell her something. But you didn't tell her, did you?'

'I guess not.'

'You guess not.'

'I just figured it'd be easier with you there. You know, sitting next to me and all.'

'You're kind of putting her on the spot.'

'I am?'

'Sure. What if she wants to get mad at you for me being pregnant. There isn't much she can say in front of me. She'll just have to be polite.'

'I guess you're right.'

She leaned forward and touched his arm. 'On the other hand, it would be kind of nice to be sitting there with you. So she can see how happy we are.'

He kissed her on the mouth. 'I really am happy, Alison.'

'Not scared?'

'Well.'

'Scared *and* happy. That's how *I* feel,' she said.

'I guess I feel more the other way around.'

'Huh?'

'Happy and scared.'

She laughed. 'Oh, I see.' She unconsciously tugged on the red silk scarf she wore around her neck like a kerchief.

Ben pointed to it. 'That belonged to Dana, right?'

'Yes.'

'How come you're wearing it today?'

'It's her birthday.'

'Oh, I'm sorry.'

'It's all right. But the scarf reminds me of her. I don't ever want to forget her.'

In the next half hour, the canoe started to drift downriver again.

Alison and Ben stopped it, turned the craft closer to shore.

'It really scares you,' he said.

'I have nightmares about it. The Falls, I mean.'

He kissed her again. 'You know what I did this morning?'

'What?'

'Went over to Morheim's.'

'God, really?' She was excited.

'Really.'

Morheim's was the name of Black River Falls' one and only jewelry store.

'Did you see anything you liked?'

'Yeah. One thing especially.'

'What was it?'

'Like you couldn't guess.'

'We can't afford anything fancy.'

'It isn't fancy. But it's pretty. And Mr Morheim said we could pay him twenty dollars a month until it was paid off.'

They fished some more and then he looked up at the sky and said, 'It's almost three.'

'You can really tell by looking at the sun?'

'Uh-huh. Where it sits in the sky.'

'Teach me how to do that, will you?'

So he taught her, and when they were done they tethered the canoe to shore and got it tied down and covered with canvas, and then they went off to the grocery store to get the things they needed to make spaghetti.

Halfway through their shopping, she got sick and had to use the rest room.

When she came out, she was very pale and unsteady and the sight of her this way just made Ben love her all the more. Sometimes when he looked at her, she just broke his heart, she was so little and vulnerable and sweet.

He really did make good spaghetti.

The trick, as least as a master chef like himself saw it, was in:

A) The variety of spices you used in the sauce.

B) How long you let the sauce simmer.

The most important ingredient was not the tomato sauce, nor the oregano, nor the green peppers. What mattered most was the fresh mushrooms you sliced into the sauce.

He had learned all this from an article in his *Boy Scout* magazine. They were big on self-sufficiency and so they were always instructing boys how to take care of themselves, cooking included. So Ben had given the spaghetti a try. His first few attempts weren't exactly award-winning. In fact, the first few times, neither Michael nor his mother seemed able or willing to gag down much of Ben's bubbling and boiling concoction. But eventually, Ben got good at it. Now he made spaghetti six or seven times a year, and his mother always seemed glad he did.

Alison set the dining-room table.

'Your mom won't want me to, but this is supposed to be a treat for her. OK?'

'Sure.'

Alison found a good white linen tablecloth and some nice drinking glasses and some beautiful white china that Lynn kept on the top shelf in one of the kitchen cabinets.

When she came in from the living room, she saw him standing at the stove, stirring the sauce.

'You look like a mad scientist,' she said.

'I'm fixing things up good for bad little girls,' he said in a really terrible Boris Karloff impersonation.

She came over and stood next to him. He kissed her and then patted her stomach. 'Our kid's going to be President of the United States someday,' he said.

'Yes, she will be,' Alison said.

'You really think it's a girl?'

'Uh-huh.'

'How come?'

'I just do is all.'

'I hope she looks like you.'

'You're not exactly ugly, Ben,' she said.

Then he said, ever the egotist, 'Sure I am.'

The terrible thing was, he was serious.

Lynn finished up late in the afternoon. She made her final rounds in the back of the office, checking all the animals boarding here, then washed up and walked over to the house.

The smell of spaghetti greeted her as soon as she reached the back porch. It was like an old friend paying a surprise visit.

When she walked into the kitchen, Ben looked over from the stove and said, 'Hi, Mom.'

'Hi, honey.'

'Hi, Lynn,' Alison said from the dining room.

'Hi, Alison,' Lynn said.

'Go check out the dining-room table,' Ben said.

'The sauce smells great, honey,' Lynn said, kissing him on the side of the head on her way to the dining room.

With the daylight dying in the window, with a soft breeze carrying the scent of flowers and newly mown grass through the open window, the dining room was a spectacle indeed. Her best china; even her silver candlesticks; and best linen tablecloth.

'Oh, Alison, this looks great,' Lynn said.

Alison grinned. She wasn't a beauty but she had the clean freckled good looks that appealed to Midwestern tastes. Lynn gave her a little hug.

'What's the occasion?'

For just a moment, Alison looked troubled. 'Uh, I'll let Ben tell you that.' Then she smiled. 'But I think you'll be happy.'

'Is there anything I can do? To help you, I mean?'

Alison nodded to the chair at the head of the table. 'You can sit down and get ready for a great meal.'

Lynn laughed. 'I'm bushed and that sounds wonderful.'

'Would you like a little wine? I bought a bottle of Burgundy.'

'That might hit the spot,' Lynn said. She'd never been a drinker but red wine with Italian food was always good.

'Well, as Ben likes to say,' Alison said, 'this is pretty expensive stuff so we have to hold it down to no more than a half gallon for each person.'

Lynn laughed. 'That sounds like something Ben would say.'

'Be right back with your wine.'

As she sat there looking out the window, Lynn wondered if the occasion for the special dinner might have something to do with Ben's phone call the other night. He'd been upset about something but wouldn't tell her what. He'd asked her to wait up so that they could talk but when he got home he was vague, evasive. He didn't tell her what was on his mind.

Now this spaghetti dinner.

Lynn wondered what was going on.

After saying grace, at Alison's suggestion, they dug in.

'This is your best yet, honey,' Lynn said after three forksful.

'It's really great, Ben,' Alison said.

Lynn noted the way that Alison gently touched Ben's hand. She was so happy that he'd found Alison. She felt so many fears for Ben – at least one of those fears, his loneliness, had been put to rest. She really liked Alison and hoped she'd stay around for ever.

There was garlic bread and a small plate of extra olives, both black and green, and two different kinds of grated cheese.

Dinner topics included Alison trying to get more hours at the library, some of Ben's ideas for rearranging the back of the office, the new Clint Eastwood picture Alison and Ben were going to see this weekend, a magazine article Lynn had read on preparing Italian food the healthy way, and then Ben telling Alison all about the trouble they'd had getting the injured horse up from the ravine the other night.

They were all a little smitten with the candlelight that flickered in the dusk, all a little taken with the soft summer breeze that turned the white lace curtains into frolicking ghosts, when Ben said: 'I, uh, we, uh, need to tell you something, Mom.'

Here it was.

Lynn prepared herself for virtually every eventuality.

'All right, honey. These old ears are ready.'

Ben usually had a difficult time saying things straight out. He used an awful lot of pauses and 'uhs' when he was telling you something difficult for him to say.

But now he said: 'Alison's pregnant and we're going to get married.'

'Oh, my Lord,' Lynn said, and turned her attention to Alison. 'How far along are you?'

'Just about two months,' Alison said cautiously. 'Are you mad at us, Lynn?'

'Mad at you? Mad at you? Are you crazy?'

She then got up from her chair, went over and kissed and hugged Alison, and then went over and kissed and hugged Ben.

All the time she did this, she choked on her own tears. She hadn't been this happy since her husband's presence had graced her days.

There would be new life in her life, new life in this house.

God had truly smiled upon her.

After finishing up at the video store, letting one of the teenagers run the place for the night, Michael drove past Alison's. The lights were off in her ground-floor apartment. Maybe tonight would be the night. Then he noticed the people at the grill in back. They were frying burgers on a gas grill and sitting at a picnic table. They were near the alley. No way he could sneak up the back entrance.

He decided to drive out to the farm. He hadn't talked to his mother in a few days and he knew how lonely she got sometimes.

But she wasn't lonely tonight.

Both the old truck and the new one were in the drive. And so was Alison's car.

Even before he reached the back door, he could hear her laughing, his mother laughing.

He went inside, walked through the kitchen, and entered the dining room.

Silver candleholders. The linen tablecloth. The best china. Something special must be going on.

Then he noticed his mother, sipping wine from her glass, her eyes sparkling. He smiled. His mother was at least a little bit drunk. He couldn't ever remember seeing such a thing.

From the doorway, Michael said, 'You're all under arrest.'

When they saw him, they laughed even harder. Ben and Alison weren't feeling any pain, either. She smiled when she saw him, smiled as if she genuinely liked him.

He went in and sat down and poured himself a cup of coffee.

'Want a little vino?' Ben said.

'"Vino," eh?' Michael smiled.

'That's what the college kids call it,' Ben said.

'Oh, I see,' Michael said. He hoisted his coffee cup to his mouth.

'No, I'd better stick to coffee. Somebody around here's got to stay sober.'

'Hey,' Lynn said. 'I resent that.'

'Boy,' Michael said, winking at Ben, 'I never thought I'd live long enough to see our own mother swacked.'

'Swacked!' Lynn said. 'What kind of word is that?'

'It's Latin for drunk out of your mind,' Michael said.

'Out of my—' Lynn said. But couldn't finish the sentence because she was giggling too hard.

'C'mon, Uncle Michael. Have a little bit of vino. C'mon.'

When Alison said this, he looked at her carefully. Her eyes were as friendly as her voice. The old suspiciousness seemed to be gone. Only after a moment did he realize that she'd called him 'Uncle.'

'Thanks, Alison,' he said, making his voice as warm as possible, 'but I'll stick to coffee.'

'Maybe if we tell him, he'll have a little vino,' Ben said.

This was like a college frat house party, Michael thought, where the freshmen insisted that everybody who walked through the door get absolutely smashed.

Except that this party involved his mom.

He found himself smiling like the rest of them now. They all looked so cute, slurring their words and laughing.

'You tell him,' Ben said to Alison.

'No, you tell him,' Alison said.

'I'll tell him,' Lynn said.

'Tell me what?'

'No, maybe it'd be better if you told him, Ben,' Lynn said.

'Gee, people, will one of you please tell me what's going on around here?'

Alison giggled. 'Ben's pregnant.'

And then he knew what was going on here, what they were all so drunkenly giggly about. Alison was pregnant.

And he didn't like it at all.

He wasn't sure why, but now when he looked at her, so prim and smug and female sitting there, he loathed her, felt an anger he could barely control.

She must have seen what was in his eyes because her face quit smiling and she looked at him with a kind of frightening recognition,

130

as if for the very first time she knew who and what he really was.

'Isn't that wonderful, Michael?'

He made a joke of it. 'That Ben's pregnant?'

'Oh, you joker,' Lynn said.

Michael looked again at Alison. 'Congratulations, when's the kid due?'

'Next January.'

Their eyes held. He was trying to simulate happiness but she knew him now, knew him truly, and he would never again inspire anything but fear and disgust in her eyes.

'Thank you,' she said. Polite but cool.

'And congratulations to you, too, kiddo,' Michael said, turning to his brother.

'Thanks,' Ben said. 'I just can't believe it.'

Lynn had tears in her eyes. 'I can't, either. I'm finally going to be a grandmother.'

Michael said, 'I guess I will have some of that wine, after all.'

'Oh, great,' Ben said, and poured his brother a small glass. 'We have a house rule here tonight.'

'Oh yeah, and what's that?' Michael said.

'No more than half a gallon per person.'

Then he laughed his kid laugh and smiled his kid smile and Michael suddenly felt sorry for him, poor dopey kid getting caught up in the clutches of a scheming little bitch like Alison. She'd probably gotten pregnant on purpose, just so she could trap him. She was probably screwing somebody else on the side. That's how they were. All of them.

But what he found most sickening was the thought of the baby. He wasn't sure why.

'A toast,' he said, raising his glass. 'To my brother and his beautiful Alison.'

'Oh, that's so sweet,' Lynn said, tearing up again.

Even Ben was moved, startled by the warmth of Michael's words, and the drama of sweeping his glass up into the air for the salute.

But Alison knew better. Her eyes never left Michael's face. She knew what was going on here, and he was happy she did. But if she said anything to either Ben or Lynn about him – about how he'd acted kind of funny tonight – they'd just see her for the paranoid troublemaker she was.

Good sweet Michael.

So happy that he was going to be an uncle.

How could anybody possibly say a word against good sweet Michael?

The evening rolled on, the three of them switching to coffee and starting to sober up, all four of them helping with the dishes, carrying them from dining room to sink, scraping them off in the garbage, putting the dining room right again.

After the dishes, Lynn and Ben had to go over to the office to check on a couple of the boarders, specifically a raccoon and a possum.

Leaving Michael and Alison alone in the kitchen.

He leaned against the refrigerator, watching her dry waterspots off the good drinking glasses.

'I'm very happy for you two,' he said.

Her eyes shifted from the glass she held in her hand. 'No, you're not.'

'What the hell's that supposed to mean?'

'You don't like me.'

'Why don't I like you?'

She dried the glass. 'The way you looked at me tonight when Ben told you I was pregnant.' She set the dried glass down and picked up a wet one from the sink. As she dried it, she said, 'I guess there isn't anything I can do about you not liking me, Michael. But I do want to be a part of this family, I really do. So I hope you'll let me.'

Lynn and Ben saved him from responding to this. They came through the back door, smelling vaguely medicinal. The office put a stench on you. Michael had always hated the office, the poor sick endlessly needy animals. He liked only strong and healthy beings.

Ben hugged Alison and said, 'My big brother been giving you a hard time?'

She shook her head. 'No, he's been very sweet, actually.' She stared directly at Michael as she said this.

He smiled, too. 'That's how I usually am, right, Mom? Sweet, that is.'

Ten minutes later, Michael was in his car, heading back to town.

All he could think of was Dana's letters. He had to break into Alison's apartment and get them. Had to. She could tell he hated her. It was only a matter of time before she went to Rhys and told him what she knew.

Only a matter of time.

8

Over the next five days, Michael tried three times to get into Alison's apartment but he had no clear opportunity to get in and out without being seen.

He even followed her around, seeing where she went, what she did, so that he could gauge how long her trips usually lasted.

She liked antiques, and spent considerable hours within the dusty walls of Black River Falls' two antique stores. She liked clothes, so she spent almost as much time walking around the shopping center. And, most surprising of all, she liked fishing, so she spent long hours on the river. No reason women couldn't like fishing as much as men, but he'd just never seen one who took to it quite this way. Three different times, he stood on shore, hidden behind trees, watching her. She couldn't cast worth a damn but that didn't slow her down at all. Not at all. Each time she went, her skiff drifted downstream toward the Falls. He sensed her panic when this happened. She oared upstream immediately. The Falls terrified her.

On a rainy Friday night, Michael followed Alison home from the library. He watched as she went inside, turned on several lights in the gloom, and then moved in silhouette about her small apartment. Michael saw all this from the alley in back of her house.

Deciding that she was probably going to be home for some time, he put his car in gear and started to pull away when headlights made a golden bar of his rearview mirror and somebody honked loudly at him.

Somebody had recognized him.

Here behind Alison's house.

The headlights died; a vehicle door slammed; footsteps crunched gravel.

135

'Hi, Michael.'

He turned and saw Ben standing next to the car.

'Hey, kiddo, how you doing?'

'Great. But I'm kind of surprised to see you here.' There was just a hint of concern in Ben's voice. Why was his brother sitting in the dark alley behind Alison's house, anyway?

Michael lied smoothly. 'Looking for you, kiddo.' He reached over on the seat and picked up two new videos he'd planned to watch tonight. 'Thought I'd drop these off for you and Alison.'

He handed Ben the tapes.

'John Woo is one of them,' Michael said. 'Then there's the new Van Damme movie.'

'Hey, great. Thanks a lot, Michael. These'll help.'

'Help?'

Ben looked embarrassed. 'Oh, I'm sorry, that kind of slipped out.'

'What kind of slipped out, kiddo?'

Ben hesitated. 'Well, it's about you and Alison, I guess.'

'Oh? What about me and Alison?'

'Well, she doesn't think you like her very much.'

'I see.' Then, deciding he had to be more positive about this, he said: 'That's kind of funny.'

'What is?'

'I always got the feeling that Alison didn't like *me* very much.' He saw a way to make his lie even better. 'That's why I was sitting in the alley here, in fact. Waiting for you to show up so I wouldn't have to go inside and see Alison. I don't want to upset her or anything, her being pregnant and all. I really do like her, kiddo.'

Ben laughed. 'Wow. You two. Someday I'm just going to sit you down and make you have a good long talk.'

'That's probably what we need, Ben. A good long talk.'

'I really appreciate the videos.'

'No sweat.'

'And Alison will, too.' Then he nodded to the house. 'I guess I'd better get in there.'

'See you, kiddo.'

'Thanks again, Michael.'

'You bet.'

* * *

'Wasn't that nice of him?'

'Uh, yes, it was.'

Ben had brought the videos in and set them down and started talking about Michael even before he gave Alison a hello kiss.

For Ben there was no one quite like Michael on the entire planet.

But Alison was bothered by the first thing Ben said.

'You say he was sitting in the alley when you pulled up?'

'Yeah,' Ben said, 'he was waiting for me. So he could give me the videos.'

'How did he know you were coming over here?'

'How did he know? We're engaged, Alison. I mean, I spend most of my time here.' He looked at her, troubled. 'Is something wrong?'

'No,' she said. 'I guess for a minute, I just thought it was kind of weird.'

She had to be careful. She had put aside any suspicions she'd had about Michael playing a part in Dana's murder. She had accepted Chief Rhys' explanation that Steve Conners had acted alone. But other things about Michael still bothered her – the fact that he obviously didn't like her, the fact that she feared he would somehow undermine her relationship with Ben and Lynn. And now the creepy knowledge that he had been sitting in her alley with his lights out, watching. She didn't believe his story about wanting to give Ben the videos. No, he'd been sitting out there for some other reason. But why?

Careful, she thought. Careful.

She hadn't had a real family life since her parents had died. And that's what she most wanted now. A family. A center for her being. She loved good, innocent Ben so much – and she loved Lynn, too. She just hoped that she and Michael could find some way to get along for the sake of the family.

But why had he been sitting in her alley, watching?

'So,' Ben said, touching his fingers to her belly, and then giving Alison a sweet kiss on the mouth. 'How's our kid doing?'

She forgot all about Michael.

Lynn was working in her garden, three days later, when Michael's car appeared in the driveway.

She stood wiping sweat from her forehead with the back of her white cotton gardening glove, watching Michael walk toward her with his familiar grin and loping walk.

He gave her a kiss on the cheek and then let her give him the 'tour,' a three-minute inspection of her garden that undoubtedly bored him. But he was a good sport, oohing when she showed him how the tomatoes were coming along, ahhing when he saw the summer flowers, even bending down to sniff a couple of them and tell her how great they smelled.

'Could you stand a little iced tea?' she said.

'I sure could.'

Ben and Alison were off to the county fair this afternoon. The house felt empty and a little hollow to Lynn. But she knew she'd have to get used to it someday. Alison had some money of her own. Eventually, the three of them would get a place of their own and Lynn would have to face life alone. In some ways it would be good – to have absolute freedom, or as much as her veterinary practice allowed anyway – but in other ways the prospect was terrifying.

She filled two tall glasses with iced tea from a refrigerator pitcher covered with frost.

They sat at the kitchen table.

'Everything going all right?' she said.

'Your "Mom" question.'

'Right. My "Mom" question. And I promise, the only one.'

'Everything's going fine.'

She knew how quickly your world could come undone. One moment a man was the father you loved and trusted. The next he was shown to be a murderer. One moment your husband was alive and healthy. The next, an accident had killed him.

So she always asked her 'Mom' question when Michael just showed up this way.

Michael looked around the kitchen. Golden sunlight gave the frilly white curtains and off-white refrigerator and stove a pleasant glow. The kitchen smelled of spices and Irish Cream coffee. One of her dozen farm cats sat in the back window, tail curled up, watching some summer scene in the yard beyond.

'I'll always love this old place,' he said.

'So will I.' She shrugged. 'I'm kind of hoping that when I retire, Ben and Alison will want to take it over.'

A strange look fixed Michael's face a moment, some kind of tight quick displeasure. She couldn't be sure what she was seeing.

His words didn't reflect his expression. 'Yeah, it'd be great if they'd take this place over. With their kid and all.'

'You like Alison, don't you?'

'Sure. Why ask me that?'

'No particular reason. I guess 'cause I just never asked you before.'

'She's a sweetie.'

'Yes, she is,' Lynn said. 'I'm just so happy that Ben met her.'

He reached in the pocket of his short-sleeved white button-down shirt and took two tickets out of his pocket.

'This is how much I like Alison,' he said. 'I know what a Rolling Stones fan Ben is.'

'That's right. I forgot.'

'Well, they're playing over at the capitol tomorrow night and it's sold out. But I managed to get two tickets. I was going to take him myself, but I think Alison should go with him instead.'

'Oh Michael, that's great. They'll be so happy.'

He handed over the tickets and put a fake scowl on his face. 'So I don't want to hear any more about how I don't like Alison.' Then he smiled. 'I like her a lot. It's just that I need to adjust to the fact that my little brother—'

'I know, honey. It all happened so fast and—'

He sipped the last of his iced tea. 'You're still the best iced-tea maker on the planet.'

'Thanks.'

He got up and came around the table and kissed her on the cheek.

'Now I have to start worrying about you.'

'Me? What about?' Michael said.

'Meeting the right girl. Settling down.'

'Aw, Mom. Now you're *really* being a Mom.'

'I guess I am.'

'I'm just not ready.'

She smiled. 'Too many girlfriends – that's your trouble.'

139

He was at the back door, hand on the knob. Always moving. That was Michael. 'I can't help it if I'm incredibly handsome and sexy, can I?'

'It must be a burden.'

'It's a terrible burden. There just isn't enough of me to go around.'

'And I'll bet it's hard to stay humble, too.'

'Oh, no. That's easy. Humility is part of my basic nature.'

'Yes, I can see that.'

He paused and said, 'They still going to get married in a month?'

'That's the plan.'

'Wow,' he said, sounding sentimental. 'My little brother. Married.'

'And a father.'

His face tightened again. This time there was no mistaking it. 'Yes, and a father.'

She wondered what was going through his mind at this moment, the way he'd looked so unhappy just now.

'Tell them to enjoy the concert,' he said.

'I will. And thanks again, honey.'

He got the inside back door opened and now rested his hand on the knob of the screen door.

He was leaving the house, as usual, in stages.

'You going to the fair this year, Mom?'

'I suppose I will.'

'Go and see the male strippers as usual?'

'Yes, and when I'm done there I'll probably go over and check out the bearded lady and then probably put on a little show on the high-wire act.'

'Just the usual "Mom" kind of things.'

She grinned. 'That's me. Just your typical Mom.'

'Well, I love you, typical Mom.'

'And I love you, too, honey. And thanks again for the tickets. They'll go crazy.'

The next night, Michael broke into Alison's apartment. The tickets had been a good idea. He finally had plenty of time to get in and out. No fear of them suddenly coming back home. The state capitol was a good drive from here – and the concert, by the time it was over, would take four or five hours.

'Oh, gosh.'
   'What's wrong?'
   'I'm going to be sick.'
   'I'll pull over.'
   'I'm sorry,' Alison said.
   'What're you sorry for? It isn't your fault.'
   'I know but—'
Then he was pulling over.
Then she was tumbling out of the car.
Then she was leaning over the sun-scorched summer grass, vomiting.

Alison had a desk. That was the logical place to start, right? Most people kept letters in a desk. And letters were what he was looking for. So –
   He started with the desk.
   A wide center drawer – nothing.
   Two left-side drawers – nothing.
   Two right-side drawers – nothing.
   A moment of panic.
   Had she already turned Dana's letters over to Rhys?
   Had to keep looking.
   Had to find them.
   Had to.

'You feeling better?'
   'Uh-huh.'
   'A lot better?'
   'Well.'
   'You sure you want to go?'
   'How many chances are you going to have to see the Stones?'
   'I know, Alison, but you're not going to enjoy it if you're sick all the time.'
   'I'll be fine.'
   'You sure?'

141

'I'll just take an extra dose of the medicine the doctor gave me.'

'So I should keep driving?'

She leaned over and hugged his arm. 'You should keep driving.'
Then: 'Oh, God.'

'What?'

'My breath. When I leaned over and hugged you.'

'What about it?'

'I'll bet it's awful.'

'It's fine.'

She laughed. 'Yeah, I'll bet.'

The second place he looked was in her bedroom: the bureau drawers.

He found: panties, bras, T-shirts, socks, slips, half-slips, nylons, panty liners.

Touching her personal things sickened him.

How could little Ben stand to touch the bitch?

He found nothing.

The panic again: had she already turned them over to Rhys?

'You all right?'

'Fine.'

'You made a funny noise.'

'I did?'

'Uh-huh.'

'I wasn't aware of it.'

'Kind of a gurgle.'

'Oh.'

'Like you were going to be sick or something.'

'I'm fine. Really.'

'Really?'

'Ben, I know how much you want to see this concert.'

'But I don't want to see it at your expense.'

'Oh, Ben.' She smiled. 'I was going to hug you again but then I remembered about my breath.'

'I really should keep driving?'

'You really should keep driving.'

'You're sure?'

'I'm sure.'

'All right, then.'

Finally, he couldn't stop himself, Michael couldn't.

He snicked open his switchblade and started slashing one of her slips.

Breasts. Stomach. Sex.

Slash slash slash.

Cut cut cut.

Stab stab stab.

Bitch.

He imagined the white slip soaked with blood.

Heavy with blood.

Reeking with blood.

Funny, how good blood smelled at the moment of death, especially intermingled with the stench of hot feces.

The first couple of times, the feces had put him off. But the last couple of times, on his various trips, he'd had the time to kneel next to the corpse and smear himself with her feces. Like war paint.

Blood intermingled with feces.

Becoming one with her death.

He had to force himself from reverie back to Alison's old and dark apartment.

Cars on the street.

Heavy footsteps on the ceiling, the apartment upstairs.

The smells of her perfumes mixed with the hot night smells coming through the open window.

The panic again.

Rhys in the video store the other day.

Acting suspicious.

Questioning; questioning. Staring openly at Michael. Assessing him.

He stuffed the knife and the butchered slip into his pocket and resumed his search.

Dana's letters had to be somewhere in this apartment. Had to be.

There was a smaller bureau across the bedroom, between two open windows.

There.

He would find the letters in one of those drawers.

He was sure of it.

'How you doing?'

'Great,' Alison said.

'You made that noise again.'

'That gurgle?'

'Uh-huh.'

'How could you tell? With the radio up so loud?'

'That's the thing.'

'What's the thing?'

'Even with the radio up so loud, I can hear it.'

'The gurgling?'

'Yeah, the gurgling.' He looked over at her. 'You're swallowing it back down, aren't you?'

'Swallowing what back down?'

'The vomit.'

She hesitated. 'Well, I guess I sort of am.'

'Dammit, Alison. I asked you to be honest.'

'I am being honest.'

'No, you're not. You're swallowing it back down and pretending you're fine.'

He looked at the Midwestern night rushing by. Dusk was a gray haze punctuated by a bright slice of quarter moon and a few million stars. The corn was waist-high now. On the slope of a hill, a lone rider rounded up his horses and steered them toward the farm to the east. The night roared past with wind-tunnel intensity, dark and chill and sweet-smelling, utterly beautiful and bedazzling as only Midwestern nights can be.

Then: 'Ben.'

'Yeah?'

'I tried to swallow it back down.'

'Just now, you mean?'

'Yes. And I had a real hard time.' Then: 'I'm sorry.'

'I'm pulling over.'

'I'm sorry.'

'God, Alison, quit saying you're sorry.'

'I know how much you want to see them.'

He got the truck over to the shoulder of the road and set the

144

emergency brake and then got out and ran around to her side of the car and got the door opened up and helped her step down.

And just in time.

Because her feet had barely touched the grass before she was throwing up.

She paused once, in the midst of being sick, to look up at him and say, 'I'm sorry, Ben.'

Then she was sick again.

He stared at the scarf a long time.

Dana's scarf.

Silk the color of autumn red.

She'd worn it often.

He could feel himself getting excited, pressed the scarf to his groin, closed his eyes, luxuriated in remembered images.

The knife hacking and slashing her face until she was as ugly outside as she was inside.

Her cries.

Her useless cries.

Without thinking, he slid the scarf into his pocket. Later. He would use it later. He knew he shouldn't take it, but it brought back such overpowering memories . . .

The drawers.

He'd found her scarf.

Now maybe he'd get lucky and find the letters she'd written Alison.

'You sure?'

'Positive.'

'But maybe I could help you.'

'There isn't anything you can do, Ben. There really isn't. But it's sweet of you to offer.'

'I feel like I'm deserting you.'

'It'll be better if you're not there. I mean, it gets embarrassing, throwing up all the time.'

'What happens when we get married?'

'Then I guess I won't have any choice.' She smiled. 'I guess I'll just have to give you the privilege of letting you watch me throw up.'

'It makes me feel closer to you.'

'When I throw up you feel closer to me?' she said, teasing.

'You know what I mean.'

'Intimacy.'

'Yes. Exactly.'

'What a way to be intimate. Watching somebody barf.'

They were just reaching the town limits now.

BLACK RIVER FALLS
YOUR KIND OF PLACE

'You wanna stop and get some Pepto-Bismol or something?'

'I've got plenty at home. Mostly, I just want to lie down.'

'I'm hurrying.'

'I know you are, Ben. And I appreciate it.'

'I'll call you later.'

'All right.'

'Unless you'd mind.'

'Why would I mind?'

'Well, you might be trying to sleep or something.'

'I'd love to hear from you.'

'Really?'

'Really.'

'Good,' he said, smiling, ''cause I'll really want to talk to you by then.'

Not in the second bureau.

Not in the cedar chest.

Not in the shoe-box where she kept old letters.

Not in the plastic letter-holder on the kitchen counter.

Not in the first bureau, which he was checking for the third time.

Not in the desk, which he was checking for the fourth time.

Not. Anywhere.

Where the hell could Dana's letters be, anyway?

He walked through the apartment, following the narrow beam of his flashlight.

He reached the kitchen, the trembling refrigerator, the waving leaf patterns on the white wall, silhouettes from the street lamp.

Not. Anywhere.

And then he saw it.

It had been here all along.

Each and every time he'd walked into the kitchen.

But he hadn't really noticed it till now.

Really hadn't thought about its implication.

He walked over to the back door and opened it up and there it was.

A small back porch that smelled of yellowing newspapers and faded summer heat.

And there, stacked against the far wall, were three cardboard boxes with big Magic Marker letters on the side of each box:

DANA

Right here.

All along.

Right here.

He set to work.

'G'night.'

'Night, Ben. Thanks for understanding.'

'I wouldn't mind if you wanted to watch *me* throw up.'

'Boy, there's an invitation.'

'You know what I mean.'

'Yes, I know what you mean.'

'Because I love you.'

'You know I love you, Ben. More than I've ever loved anybody.'

'It makes me goofy when I hear stuff like that.'

'It makes me goofy when I say it.'

'Then I guess we're even.'

'I'm afraid my breath is bad.'

'Your breath is fine.'

'No, it's not.'

'Well, maybe it's not fine but I don't care.'

'Now the truth comes out.'

She reached over and kissed him on the cheek. 'There.'

'Wow,' he said.

'Wow what?'

'Even when you give me teensy little kisses like that, I get excited.'

'Maybe you're part dog.'

He barked. 'Yeah, maybe I am.'

She got out of the car. He walked with her to the door. 'You'll call me later?' she said.

'Around ten all right?'

'Around ten would be fine. And I'm sorry about tonight.'

'I'm going to start charging you a dollar every time you apologize.'

She chuckled, waved and went inside.

She watched him walk back to his truck, get in, and drive away.

And that's when she heard the noise on the back porch.

Helen's cat was back. Goliath.

Helen's cat was a big yellow tom that liked to knock things over. He was strong enough to butt through the screen on the bottom of the back door, strong enough to get inside.

He had knocked the boxes over several times before.

Now Goliath was back at it again.

Alison didn't turn on any lights.

She wanted to scare the hell out of him.

She'd wait till she got to the inside back door and then she'd hit the light and then he'd run away screeching.

She reached the kitchen.

Started walking on tiptoe.

Didn't want to alert him in any way.

Moved silently through the darkness.

Put her hand on the doorknob.

Got ready to flip on the light switch, which was on this side of the door.

One. Two –

She could hear him rummaging around back there.

She peeked through the glass square that let her see the back porch.

Three –

She flipped on the light switch.

And there he was.

But he wasn't a cat.

He was a human.

And his name wasn't Goliath.

It was Michael.

She'd caught him just as he was starting to look through the bottom box. The other two sat now in different corners of the back porch. He'd obviously searched through them already.

Michael.

My God, what was he doing here?

What was he looking for?

Their eyes met, held.

He was furious. That was evident from his dark and glaring gaze. Furious. 'You're going to regret ever coming to this town, you bitch.'

Then he stood up, walked over to the screen door. It was latched shut.

He opened the latch and walked out, the door slamming shut on its spring.

She stood there for a very long time.

What did this mean, Michael in her apartment?

What did he want?

Why no attempt at explanation or apology?

But she knew what it meant.

Steve Conners had not acted alone . . .

9

He drove.

Later, he would not remember where he drove.

River. Wind. Forest. Fields. At one point: a deer running fast and scared across the highway, bobtail startling white in the headlights. Empty highway. Silos. Barns. Faster faster now.

Bitch. Little bitch.

Her part of the bargain had been to go to the concert. To give him plenty of time in her apartment.

Not to—

Bitch. Little bitch.

Rock quarry. Herd of semis like elephants lumbering up the hills. Motorcycles coming at him in opposite lane, big noisy fireflies. Faster faster. Around the semis. Over the crest of the hill. Faster faster still.

Bitch. Little bitch.

She would know for sure now, wouldn't she?

There could be only one reason he'd be in her apartment, wouldn't there?

She would tell Ben, for sure for sure.

Bitch little bitch.

'You've still got it in the popcorn department, Mom,' Ben said.

'So it's enough butter?'

'Just right.'

'Great.'

In the Tyler household, the kitchen table had always been the preferred meeting place. Over the years, everything from report cards to dating tips to Michael's sports triumphs had been discussed here. It was the Tyler town hall.

There was a night breeze now, bringing down the scent of the piney

151

hills, as Ben and Lynn sat at the table eating the popcorn she'd fixed for them.

'I guess I just don't understand.'

'She's embarrassed is all, honey,' Lynn said. 'I'd be embarrassed, too.'

'Did you have morning sickness?'

'A little. Not the way Alison does, thank God.'

'When you had it, you didn't make Dad go away, did you?'

'I couldn't. We were living here together. Married.'

'Well, we're engaged and practically married.'

'Honey, it's different with each person. It bothers Alison to be around you when she's having a particularly bad spell. It doesn't mean anything.'

'Really?'

'Not at all.'

'Then how come I feel sort of – lonely?'

'It's natural.'

'It is?'

'Sure,' Lynn said. 'A lot of men feel lonely when their wives are pregnant. The wives can't be as attentive as they once were.'

'God,' Ben said.

'What?'

'That really sounds selfish.'

'What does?'

'How men react. How I'm reacting. Alison's carrying the baby and getting sick all the time and I'm whining about not being able to spend more time with her. I'm being a jerk, aren't I?'

'Well, not a jerk exactly.'

He laughed. 'Not exactly, huh?'

'You're being a typical man who wants a lot of attention from the woman he loves. That's only natural. But it's also only natural that she has other concerns right now.'

'And I should respect her wishes?'

'And you should respect her wishes.'

'Thanks, Mom.'

'For what?'

'For saving me from being a jerk.'

She smiled. 'Honey, you're so far from being a jerk it's—' She

152

patted his hand. 'You're a very sweet kid, Ben. You really are. And that's part of the reason Alison loves you so much.'

'You know, I figured you'd be real mad.'

'About what?'

'Her being pregnant and everything. And us being so young and getting married and all.'

'Well, it's not the way I would have preferred it to happen. But I'm glad you chose to keep the baby and I'm glad you're going to get married and finish school. And then Alison'll go back and finish school. And you have to be sure she does. You owe that to her. She has a right to finish her education, too.'

'I will. I promise.'

They were out of popcorn.

'You want to go with me and see how the Mama cat is doing?' Lynn said.

'Sure.'

On the way out to the barn, walking in the deep summer shadows of the night, Lynn said, 'How you doing about Elizabeth these days?'

'Oh, you know.'

'Still think about her, huh?'

'Yeah.'

She gave him a little hug. 'That's what I told you, Ben. You're a sweet kid. You really are.'

Sometime around ten, he pulled into the drive that ran along his darkened house.

Still so tense, his heart pounded and pounded.

Still so tense, his headache was blinding.

Still so tense, whimpers caught in his throat.

Up the three side steps. Into the house. Darkness. J&B Scotch, his favorite, still on the air from his generous sampling last night. Through the kitchen, shiny in the moonlight, the cleaning woman having been here today. Sweet scent of furniture polish in the living room.

Then: 'Hi.'

He turned around so abruptly, so angrily, that he accidentally swung his right fist into the table lamp and sent it smashing into the wall behind it.

He saw her in the moonlight now, sitting in the leather recliner. She was naked. Her clothes were draped neatly over the ottoman.

'I knew you'd get here eventually. Have a heavy date?'

'Get out of here.'

'You know what I've been doing?'

'I said get out of here.'

'I've been sitting here thinking about you – about us – and doing myself. You should have heard me scream a few minutes ago.'

'This isn't funny, Denise.'

He paced. Blindly, unconsciously. He needed to move, even if it was only within the confines of the dark living room, the shape of the fireplace mantel and the divan and the dry bar only outlines in the gloom.

'Come here, Michael.'

'Forget it.'

'Then if you won't come to me, I'll come to you.'

And she did so, quickly, her hands gliding silkily behind his neck, tugging him to her so that their bodies fitted easily together.

She had an irresistible body, no doubt about that, and despite his wishes, he felt himself stirring vaguely.

'Going to take a little work to get you interested tonight,' she said. 'I like that.'

She guided his hand between her legs. He felt how moist and hot she was, as her pelvis thrust forward against him.

'Nice?'

'Denise, I've got a million things on my mind.'

'You just want a BJ? I'll be happy to give you one.'

'What I want is for you to go home, can't you understand that?'

But then she was unzipping him and her hand, a smooth wriggling fish, found his groin. And then she became truly irresistible.

'Dammit, Denise,' he said.

'Shut up and carry me into your bedroom and fuck me.'

He did just as he was told.

All the time Michael and Denise were inside, Paul Fletcher sat across the street in a black Ford he'd borrowed from a dealer in a nearby small town.

The gun wasn't borrowed, the old Army .45 on the seat. That

belonged to him. His father had carried it in WWII. The other gun, the Smith & Wesson .357 Magnum, he'd bought himself a few years ago.

It was time to go inside, he figured.

He'd followed his wife over here about an hour and a half ago, watched her take out her key and slip inside.

Michael hadn't shown up until fifteen minutes ago. Which meant they were probably getting it on just about now.

He wondered which one of them he would shoot first. Denise. Or Michael.

Probably he'd shoot Michael first and make her watch. He'd make Michael do some real groveling. He wondered what Denise would think of her bad-ass football player when she saw him pleading for his life.

Her, he'd shoot right between the legs. The first shot, anyway. Then he'd move up to the heart. And finally, the face. That sexy, deceitful face of hers.

The car door made a lot of squeaking noise opening. He was glad he sold Buicks.

He supposed he should duck down, sneak up on the house as if he were conducting some kind of military operation.

But right now he didn't give a damn.

All he could think about was some football hero ramming into his wife over and over again and her crying out all the same things she used to cry out to him.

Right now he didn't give a damn about anything else.

He reached the back door. Michael had conveniently left it unlocked.

Paul Fletcher, gun ready, went inside.

The kitten was so tiny, it was more toy than animal, its eyes still closed, its body still curled in the birth position, its black and white fur damp and matted down.

Ben knelt next to the hay where the tabby mother had delivered her and lifted the kitten up with great and abiding reverence, and set it in the center of his palm. The kitten was fuzzy and warm and smelled of her mother's milk.

Lynn, who had been looking in on the raccoon and the possum, came into the corner of the barn where the birth had taken place, and knelt down in the straw next to Ben.

The barn was vast and dark, the only light coming from this empty horse stall, where Ben had hung a Coleman lantern. The two colts in the adjoining stalls snored and murmured in their sleep.

Ben put his nose to the tiny creature and nuzzled her.

Lynn watched him. His tenderness with animals was overwhelming sometimes. He knew how to love, this boy. He might not be the handsomest kid, or the brightest, or the most clever but in a world of people, of angry, resentful, embittered people, Ben knew how to appreciate the gifts God had given all humanity, and how to respect and protect the animals. He knew that man wasn't *homo superior* at all but simply one more species on a nowhere planet in a nowhere galaxy.

'I wish I had a camera,' Lynn said.

'She's damned cute.'

'You both are.'

She saw him blush. He never could accept a compliment. He was just one of those kids who didn't seem to think very much of himself, and compliments only served to reinforce his notion that he wasn't much.

'I wish I could put her in bed with me.'

Lynn smiled. 'A little early for that, hon.'

'I know. But Elizabeth—'

He'd taken Elizabeth in soon after she was born. She'd slept on his pillow. Lynn had come in one morning and found Elizabeth asleep on Ben's chest. She couldn't remember ever seeing anything much sweeter than that.

'I hate to put her back.'

'I know you do, hon.'

He nuzzled her once more then set her gently back at her mother's side, along with five other mewling, half-blind kittens all struggling to survive in an incomprehensible world. They all looked like toys, snuggling up to their mother.

Ben and Lynn stood up.

'They're doing fine.'

'Yeah, they are.' He nodded to the house. 'Guess I'll go back and give Alison a call. See how she's doing.'

'Tell her I'm thinking of her.'
'I will.'
He went back to the house.

Tiptoes.
Kitchen. Dining room. Living room. Hallway.
Bedroom.
Paul Fletcher and his gun waited just outside the bedroom door.
He was sickened by what he heard. Denise was all juicy with
whimpers and sighs and half-screams as Tyler slammed into her and
into her yet again.
Fletcher was afraid he was going to be sick.
He raised the gun.
Turned to the open door.
And started firing.
He didn't hit them but he hit everything else in the room, it
seemed, lamp, mirror, picture frame, cologne bottle, two basketball
trophies, two windows – glass shattering, shards and chunks of it
tumbling in the air and raining down on everything, the shouts and
screams of the lovers lost in the harsh repeated noise of the bullets
blasting from the gun.
That was the .45-caliber Colt.
The second one rode in his belt in back. This was the Smith &
Wesson .357 Magnum.
He took it out now and walked over to the bed where they sat
staring up at him in fear and terror.
'She's pretty good, isn't she?' Fletcher said to Tyler.
Tyler didn't know what to say.
He had covered his privates with an edge of blanket and he looked
young and pathetic now, all his arrogance gone.
There were no lights on. There were none left to turn on. Fletcher
and his gun had taken care of them all.
'I said she's pretty good, isn't she?'
Tyler managed to find his voice. 'Yes.'
Fletcher feinted right, as if he were now going to address his wife,
but then he brought the handle of the Magnum down hard and fast on
the side of Tyler's head.
The sight of Tyler's blood was satisfying indeed.

'He's going to kill us,' Denise said. She was so scared, her voice shook. 'You're going to kill us, aren't you, Paul?'

Once again, Fletcher feinted in the opposite direction from which he would soon move. Denise took this moment to pull the blanket chastely over her ample breasts.

Fletcher turned without warning, entangling his right hand in Denise's hair, and then yanking on it so hard that she screamed. He pulled her hair even harder, dragging her off the bed.

'Oh God, Paul, please don't kill me, please don't kill me,' Denise sobbed over and over.

Fletcher slammed her against the wall, parted her legs with his Magnum, touched the tip of the gun to her sex, which was still moist.

'Oh God, Paul, no, please no,' she said, as he manipulated the gun against her.

'You like cock so much, Denise, you must really like this, huh?'

'Oh Paul, please, I won't do it again, I promise you. I promise, Paul, I really do.'

He jammed the Magnum up her harder.

'You're scum, Denise, you know that?'

'I know that, Paul. I know that.'

'And he's scum, too.'

'Yes, he is, Paul. Yes, he is.'

Fletcher, keeping his second gun in her, turned back to Tyler and said, 'Get over here.'

'Why?'

'Because I said so, you asshole.'

'You're out of bullets with that gun.'

'Oh yeah, jerk-off? Well, I guess there's one way you can find out for sure, right?'

'Just do what he says, Michael. Otherwise he'll kill us. He really will.'

Tyler looked disgusted but he got off the bed and walked over to Fletcher.

Fletcher put the barrel of the .45 against Tyler's temple. 'You take over this one,' he said, nodding to the gun he had between her legs.

'No way.'

Fletcher eased the hammer back on the Colt. 'Take my word for it, asshole. I've got two bullets left.'

158

Tyler sighed, reached down, took over the Magnum that was up Denise.

'Now hold it there nice and steady, asshole.'

'Oh God, Paul, I'm sorry, I'm really sorry,' Denise said.

'Shoot her,' Fletcher said.

'Don't shoot me, Michael, please don't shoot me. Oh, please, don't.'

'I won't,' Tyler said.

'Shoot her, I said.'

But Tyler didn't shoot her.

Fletcher struck him very hard across the back of the skull with the Colt.

'Shoot her now.'

But dazed and bleeding as he was, Tyler said, 'No.'

Denise started whimpering again, muttering 'Please' and 'Oh God' and 'Please' over and over again.

Fletcher moved quickly.

He slammed Tyler back against the wall and pushed the barrel of the .45 into his mouth.

'Which one is it going to be, Denise?' Fletcher said. 'I'm going to kill one of you. Either him or you.'

'God, Paul, you're crazy. I promise you, I won't do it again. I promise.'

Fletcher shoved the barrel deeper into Tyler's mouth. 'Which one, Denise? You call it. If I don't kill him right now, I'm going to turn around and kill you.'

'Paul, please, listen—'

'Which one is it going to be, Denise?'

'Paul, please—'

With his right hand, Fletcher raised the .357 Magnum and pointed it directly at Denise, while keeping the .45-caliber Colt in Tyler's mouth.

'I'm counting to three, Denise.'

'Paul, honey, I—'

'One.'

'He doesn't deserve to die over this, honey—'

'Two.'

'Paul, please, for God's sake—'

'Three—'

'Then shoot him! Shoot Michael!'

Fletcher pulled the trigger of the gun that was inside Tyler's mouth.

Click.

Click.

Click.

Fletcher kept right on clicking his way through the empty chambers. But now the sound of the clicking, empty chambers was joined by Fletcher's laughter.

'You can see she really loves your ass, Tyler. "Shoot Michael, then, honey. Shoot Michael, then."' He had a good time mocking her.

He finished up with precision and speed, bringing his knee up to meet Tyler's uncovered groin, then driving his fists deep into Tyler's ribs and kidney. Tyler was suddenly in too much pain – the groin shot virtually blacked him out – to offer any resistance. Warm blood filled his mouth and came trickling out his nose. He fell to the floor, doubling over.

Fletcher walked across to Denise, slapped her several times, drove a fist into her stomach, and then grabbed her hair and tilted her face back so he could kiss her.

'You ever cheat on me again, I'll kill you, you understand me?'

'Yes, yes, oh God, yes, Paul. I understand; I understand.'

'Now get your clothes and go get in your car and go straight home.'

She was sobbing again. 'I want to go home, Paul. I want to be with you. I really do.'

As she was gathering up her things in the darkness, Fletcher went over and kicked Tyler in the ribs. Three times, in fact.

Good measure.

Then Mr and Mrs Paul Fletcher left Michael Tyler's house for the evening. They'd overstayed their welcome.

His instinct was to kill Paul Fletcher and to do it with his hands rather than a gun. He wanted that kind of personal satisfaction. But if Fletcher was killed there would be an investigation like none this town had ever seen – and Michael would ultimately be implicated.

10

'Hello.'

'Alison?'

'Uh-huh.'

'You sound sort of – weird. Are you all right?'

'You know. Just kind of sick.'

'The vomiting?'

'Uh-huh.'

'Everything else all right?'

God, she really did sound funny.

'Yes.'

'So what're you doing?'

'I was just taking a nap.'

'I'm sorry I woke you up.'

'That's all right. I'm glad to hear from you.'

'Alison?'

'Yes?'

'If something was wrong, you'd tell me, wouldn't you? Wrong with us, I mean?'

'I'd tell you, Ben. But everything's fine with us. It really is.'

'You know how much I love you.'

'You know how much I love you, too, Ben.'

'Well, I guess I'd better let you sleep.'

'That's what I need right now, Ben. Sleep.'

'I'll talk to you tomorrow, then. Now get some sleep.'

She laughed. 'Yes, Doctor.'

But she got very little sleep that night.

For one thing, the vomiting kept up. She'd just lie down, close her eyes, think everything was going to be all right – and then she'd be running to the john, her hand clamped over her mouth.

For another, there was the clear, sharp image of Michael crouched on the back porch, rummaging through Dana's boxes. When he'd finally looked up and seen Alison, he'd looked like a trapped and angry animal. He'd terrified her.

Now, she had to make a decision.

She could go to Chief Rhys and tell him what she'd seen, and tell him that she suspected that Michael had played some part in Dana's murder.

Or—

Or she could do nothing. Forget it. Tell herself that Michael had had nothing to do with the murder. Tell herself that the case was closed. Tell herself that justice had been done.

She loved Ben. She loved Lynn. She loved her life out here, the first real family life she'd ever had. And if the cost she had to pay for that life was—

By dawn, a streaked pearl color in the lower half of the bedroom window, she'd slept off and on for a total of maybe an hour or so.

She lay naked, on her back, her right hand riding the belly that became more pronounced each day. The belly that made her so proud and happy. The belly that made Ben and Lynn so proud and happy, too.

Two hours later, Alison swung her car into a space in front of the barn Lynn used as her office. Today was her day off at the library.

The warming day and the ground fog burning off in the piney hills would usually have slowed her down. She had wasted most of her life in cities. This was so beautiful.

But there was no time for appreciation today.

She had come to a decision and the decision was all she could think about. She was going to present Ben and Lynn with the facts, let them decide her course of action. If they asked her to forget everything, to let Michael go on with his life—

Well, Alison was prepared to abide by that.

She went inside the office. The waiting area was empty.

Behind a closed door, she heard Ben's voice saying, 'Just a second

162

here, little girl, everything'll be fine. Nothing to be afraid of, honey. Nothing at all.'

Alison smiled. He was talking to an animal. He always called them honey and sweetie and darlin'. He loved the animals so much.

Alison sat in a chair in the waiting room until Ben and Lynn came out of surgery forty-five minutes later.

Alison used the time to look through back issues of *Time* and *Newsweek* and to rehearse.

She'd start off by telling them about last night. About Michael crouched on her porch. About Michael running away. And then she'd say: I know he didn't have anything to do with Dana's murder but—. And she'd let them make of 'but' what they wanted to. She'd let them take it from there.

The door opened.

There stood Ben and Lynn both looking surprised to see her.

'Hi,' Ben said. Then he smiled. 'I figured you'd be home getting sick.'

'Now there's a romantic for you,' Lynn said, coming over and taking Alison's hand. 'How're you doing, honey?'

'Better, thanks.'

'I shouldn't have said that,' Ben said, leaning down to kiss her on the cheek.

'It's all right. Actually, I thought it was kind of funny.'

'How about some coffee and a sweet roll?' Lynn said, walking over to the desk and checking her appointment book. 'Over to the house. We've got almost an hour before the next person scheduled.'

'The coffee sounds great. But I'll probably pass on the sweet roll.'

She couldn't tell them.

She tried two or three times but finally couldn't get the words out.

She sat there and let them steer the conversation. They talked about babies, puppies, the weather, a picnic Lynn was planning for the three of them, Ben's classes this fall, the two wedding chapels that Alison and Ben were planning to see this weekend, and how Lynn really felt that Alison was already a part of the family.

Not a single opportunity presented itself to say, 'Oh, yes, and by the way, your oldest son's a cold-blooded killer, Lynn. I just thought I'd mention that.'

Only toward the end, just after she'd broken down and tried a little slice of prune Danish, was there even a vague chance to bring the subject up.

'Say,' Ben said. 'I just realized something.'

'What?' Alison said.

'I forgot to ask you what you're doing out here.'

'She doesn't need a reason to come out here,' Lynn said. 'She can come out here any time she wants. Heck, she can move in if she wants to.'

Lynn reached out and first took Ben's hand and then took Alison's. 'You've made me very happy, you two. I just want you to know that.'

There were tears in her eyes.

Michael is a murderer, Lynn. I can't help it. I just had to tell you.

'I love you both so much,' Lynn said.

No way Alison could say anything about Michael now.

No way.

A few minutes later, the next appointment walking into the office, Alison got in her car and drove back to town.

At home, she opened the phone book, found the number she wanted, and dialed.

'Hello.'

'Michael?'

'Yes.'

'This is Alison.'

Silence.

'We need to talk, Michael.'

'I don't have anything to say to you.'

'Yes, you do. And I have something to say to you. I want you to be in the park by the Civil War memorial at a quarter to twelve today.'

'I can't make it.'

'Do you want me to go to Chief Rhys instead?'

Silence.

'Michael?'

'What?'

'Did you hear what I said?'

'I heard what you said.'

'Well, if you don't want me to go to Chief Rhys, then you'd better be there.'

'I'll see what I can do.'

'We need to protect them, Michael.'

'Protect who?'

'Your mother and your brother.'

'Protect them from what?'

'You know from what, Michael.'

'Like I said, I'll see what I can do.'

'Yeah, you see what you can do, Michael.'

'I got a customer. I've got to go.'

'A quarter to twelve.'

'Right.'

'Otherwise I go to Chief Rhys.'

He slammed the phone down.

11

Ben spent the morning with Lynn in surgery. He had to struggle to keep focused on the various procedures. His mind kept drifting back to Alison's sudden appearance this morning. She'd never just abruptly appeared out here before. He had the sense that she'd wanted to say something but finally decided against it.

The last animal of the morning was a small cat that was being declawed.

Ben always felt sorry for the animals, the mincing way they had to walk for a few weeks after the operation, the way they would always be vulnerable if they were forced to be outdoors. Claws were vital to cats. But cats could be destructive, too, so you couldn't blame the owners for not wanting to have their furniture shredded.

After the animal was in post op, and after Ben had made sure that she was reviving properly, he went back to the surgery room where Lynn was scrubbing up.

She glanced up at him while she put a froth of soap on her hands and said, 'You all right, honey?'

'Yeah, I guess anyway.'

'You "guess" you're all right?'

'Just thinking about Alison.'

'It was nice to see her. I'm glad she surprised us that way. Wish she'd do it more often. I'd really like to help, you know. With her pregnancy.'

There were two sinks. Ben used the second one to start scrubbing. He got the water too hot and had to yank his hand back, scalded. He ran cold water on it. Then gradually increased the stream to warm.

'I do that all the time, too,' Lynn said. She handed him the bar of soap. 'So you weren't happy to see her?'

'Sure I was happy to see her. But she doesn't usually show up like that.'

'You think something was wrong?'

He shrugged. 'I'm not sure. How'd she seem to you?'

Lynn thought a moment. 'Well, a little tense, I guess. Especially at first.'

'Like maybe she wanted to say something?'

'I guess that could've been it.'

'That's how it struck me.'

'Maybe you should ask her.'

'Yeah. Maybe.'

As she finished drying off with paper towels, she patted him on the back. 'I'm sure it's nothing, honey. And anyway, we may be wrong.'

'You mean about why she came out here?'

'Sure. Today's her day off. Maybe she just felt like going for a drive in the country and ended up out here.'

'I hope so.'

'Honey, don't read too much into it. You and I are always doing that. Over-interpreting, I mean.'

In the next room, the phone rang.

Lynn hurried to get it, saying over her shoulder, 'She seemed very happy when she left.'

Ben had to agree with that.

Alison sure had seemed happy as she'd said goodbye this morning – much happier than when she'd first appeared.

Maybe it was her pregnancy.

Maybe this was just how women got when they were carrying babies in their stomachs.

Maybe.

But he spent the rest of the morning wondering about Alison's visit. And if everything was still all right between them.

He still had this awful dread that somebody would take her from him.

She could still change her mind and get an abortion and go back to live with her sister Jean in Chicago, the wealthy life of Lake Shore Drive.

He hoped not.

God, he hoped not.

There was an old Catholic church Alison had always planned on visiting, and this morning, just before she met Michael, seemed an appropriate time.

Beneath a framed faded photograph of the church as it was a century ago, there was a neatly typed card explaining that the church had been built of native stone carried twenty miles to this site. The card also noted that a cardinal from Chicago had come out here to bless the church before the first mass was said.

Alison knelt in one of the back pews, looking at the sunlight stabbing through the stained glass windows that depicted various Biblical scenes. She wondered idly if life back then had been any easier. If the human heart had somehow been less complicated than it was now. But then she remembered what a history teacher of hers had once said – the human mind and spirit had not changed since the time we first learned to walk upright, since the time we became the dominant species on the planet. Man was certainly capable of great beauty – music, art, and that most profound of skills, compassion – but he was also subject to jealousy, rage, unbidden lust, and treachery.

Michael had killed Dana.

She was sure of it now.

Throughout time, there had been men like Michael.

To Alison, the act of murder was unthinkable, of course. To actually take the life of another human being—

No.

Impossible to imagine.

And yet he'd done it.

Then she thought of Lynn, and all the things she'd had to go through with her father.

If Alison went to Chief Rhys, told him her suspicions, Lynn would be destroyed. No doubt about it.

And she could never forgive Alison.

Oh, she might try, for Ben's sake.

But deep down she would always blame Alison for bringing shame once again to the family.

Her father had been a killer; and now her son.

No, Lynn would be unable to forgive Alison, and Alison could understand why she'd feel that way.

Poor Lynn.

Alison knelt there for twenty minutes, smelling the faded incense, looking at the statues of the Blessed Mother and Joseph on either side of the altar, listening to the hacking cough of a sad old woman who knelt up at the communion rail, swaying back and forth in some kind of grief. Perhaps she had a terrible disease, or was close to someone who did. Every few minutes, she would sob, and Alison wanted to go up there and hold her, tell her it would all be all right. Somehow. That's what people always had to tell themselves in order to keep going. That it would all be all right if only they had faith. Somehow; somehow.

Then Alison made a sign of the cross and left the church.

Suddenly, she needed to be outdoors again, amidst the reassuring realities of the summer day, the rich slanting sunlight, the occasional brilliance of the occasional butterfly, and the chant-like laughter of summer children.

This afternoon, she would go fishing on the river. And relax. She needed that. Badly.

Now she needed to go see Michael and get it over with.

'Could you leave it a little longer than last time?'

'You didn't like it last time?'

Chief Rhys had forgotten how sensitive Chet was about the haircuts he gave.

God forbid you even hinted that you were less than pleased with your last haircut. God forbid.

'I liked it just fine, Chet,' Chief Rhys said. 'It's just that I'm going to that family reunion over in Sioux City and I want to be sure that my face doesn't look too round.'

Had to be careful which words you used with Chet, very careful.

Chet calmed down and set to work with his scissors. There were no other customers in the shop, just the sound of the radio tuned to 'Radio Swap-Meet,' a local show where folks traded stuff, and the smells of talc and hair tonic. Sunlight shone on the old linoleum and Rhys had a thought about his father, and how his father used to love to take him to the barbershop, and then to a movie afterward, always a second-run double feature because that was all they could afford. He'd loved his father and got sad when he thought of him dying in the car accident, skidding off the icy highway into a ravine.

Chet said, 'You think about what I said last time?'

'What was that?'

'You know – about Michael Tyler.'

Snip snip snip went the scissors.

'Oh. Right.'

Snip snip snip.

'I didn't mean to imply nothing.'

Snip snip snip.

'I know, Chet.'

'I just meant it was awful funny, them bein' thick as thieves, Michael and Steve Conners I mean, and Michael not knowin' anything about it, Steve murdering that young gal and all.'

'As a matter of fact, Chet, I did.'

'Did what?'

'Think about it. What you said.'

'Oh?'

'Yes, sir. I even asked around about it. But everybody said Michael acted just fine.'

'What's that prove?'

'Nothing, I suppose, but most murderers I've read about usually give themselves away.'

'They do?'

'Yep. Their behavior gets erratic or they start doing things they wouldn't ordinarily do.'

'Like what?'

'Well, you remember that guy named Patterson who killed that waitress and then set her car on fire?'

'Over at Dunkerton that time?'

'Right. But it was still in my jurisdiction because he'd actually killed her on the outskirts of Black River Falls. Anyway, he had a girlfriend and you know what she told me?'

'What?'

'The day after the murder – which she didn't know anything about – he told her they should start taking dance lessons.'

'Dance lessons?'

171

Snip snip snip.

'You know, line dancing, things like that.'

'Yeah? So?'

'And then you know what he told her?'

'What?'

'That they should start seeing a counselor, the way she'd always wanted them to, because they argued so much and everything.'

'And line dancin' and seein' a counselor proved that he was the killer?'

Snip snip snip.

'No,' Chief Rhys said, 'but it proved he was acting awfully funny. And that made some other people suspicious. And when they told me about it, I went and talked to him.'

Snip snip snip.

Rhys said, 'I think I shook up ole Michael, though.'

'Yeah?'

'Yeah. I asked him some questions, kind of trying to make him think I might have a suspicion or two up my sleeve.'

'He go for it?'

'He got a little nervous, I think. But most people do, a cop questioning them like that.'

'But you think he's clean?'

Snip snip snip.

'Yeah, I do. He may've hung around Conners since they were little boys together but that doesn't mean they were the same kind of kid. Far as I'm concerned, Michael's a solid citizen.'

'You know me, Chief,' Chet said. 'I didn't want to start no trouble.'

Chief Rhys almost laughed out loud.

You didn't want to start no trouble.

Right.

Half the gossip that got started in this town got started right in this barbershop.

Chet whispering things in people's ears.

Chet just asking his sly little questions.

Chet was never really happy unless he was subtly undermining somebody else's reputation.

I don't want to start no trouble.

Right.

'Well,' Chet said, 'I guess you heard about Jerry Gurney, huh?'

'No,' Chief Rhys said, knowing that he was about to.

Jerry Gurney was a horse breeder west of town, good family man, churchgoer, decent guy, no saint of course, but a very solid and decent guy.

Rhys wondered how Chet was going to slander the poor guy, which kind of whisper would be aimed at the vital beating heart of Gurney's pride and integrity.

'Well, this is strictly between you and me, of course,' Chet said.

'Of course,' Rhys said. 'Of course.'

12

Alison wanted to be one of the little kids in the wading pool, running through the water yelling and splashing. The water looked clean and smelled fresh. And little kids didn't have to worry about young men who killed young women.

At least a dozen mothers had parked their strollers near the wading pool so they could watch over their children in the water.

Next summer, I'll be one of them, Alison thought. And then: well, maybe two summers from now. When she's old enough.

She wandered over by the refreshment stand, a tiny building of concrete blocks where half a dozen boys had their bikes parked. They were taken with Alison's looks and nudged each other and giggled as she walked past.

I'm pregnant, kids, she wanted to say. Pregnancy was one way of spoiling fantasies.

But she decided to take their interest as flattery. She smiled at them as she passed by, taking the narrow path that led to the pavilion. Out on the open grass a middle-aged man in lurid yellow Bermuda shorts was sailing a Frisbee for his eager collie.

Michael sat inside the pavilion, at a table, alone.

Despite the cool, shadowy interior of the pavilion, he wore very dark sunglasses. He sat erect, unmoving, large hands placed flat on the surface of the picnic table.

He scared her, sitting there so enigmatically like that. She wondered momentarily if she'd done the right thing, coming here, trying to talk with Michael.

But the alternative was going to Chief Rhys.

Which meant involving Ben.

And Lynn.

No, she'd had no choice but to come here.

She walked into the pavilion, her footsteps echoing hollowly off the pitched ceiling.

'Hi,' she said.

He didn't say anything back.

She sat down.

'Aren't you going to say hi?'

'Hi,' he said.

He sat there, unmoving, unreadable in his dark glasses.

'I'm trying to be friendly about this, Michael.'

'Right.'

'I am – whether you believe it or not.'

He wore a crisp white button-down shirt and an expensive gold watch that was partially lost in the thick black hair of his arms.

He looked around the pavilion, apparently making sure they were alone.

'I shouldn't have broken into your apartment. I apologize.'

'I appreciate that.' She paused. 'It had to do with Dana, didn't it?'

He didn't say anything for a time.

A cardinal perched on a nearby table. Its feathers were almost shockingly red. She loved animals nearly as much as Ben did.

'Yes,' Michael said. 'It did.'

'What were you looking for?'

He was silent again.

'Michael, I'm trying to resolve this.'

His dark glasses. His completely erect, unmoving posture. Scary. Definitely.

'Michael,' she said.

'I was looking for letters.'

'What sort of letters?'

'That Dana had written you.'

She couldn't help herself. She laughed.

'What the hell's so funny?'

'I burned those letters nearly two months ago. You were looking for something that didn't exist.'

'Why would you burn them?'

'Because I realized I was wrong.'

'About what?'

'About you.' She paused. 'About you killing Dana. I decided that

Chief Rhys was right, that Conners did it himself. Ben was very upset when I told him about the letters – and that's why I got rid of them. Because I love Ben so much.' Another pause. 'You broke into my apartment for nothing.'

'I didn't kill her.'

'Then why would you break in?'

'Because one day I saw a letter you wrote Ben. About Dana's letters.'

'And you thought I—'

'I thought you might take the letters to Rhys and use them against me.'

'Then I guess you don't understand me very well, do you, Michael?'

'Maybe I don't.'

She touched her belly. 'I'm almost two-and-a-half-months pregnant, Michael. With Ben's baby. Do you have any idea how much I love your brother? Or your mother, for that matter? They're the two best people I've ever known in my life. They're the first real family I've ever had. And I don't want to ruin that, Michael. That's what I came here to tell you.'

Behind the dark glasses. Eyes. Staring.

He said nothing.

'That I want to forget all this. About Dana, I mean.'

'You mean not go to Rhys?'

'I've convinced myself that there's no reason to go to Rhys. I'm going to take you at your word.'

'That I didn't kill Dana?'

'That you didn't kill Dana.'

'And that I broke into your apartment because—'

'Because you were scared. About the letters.'

He smiled.

Sitting there, ominous dark glasses covering a good portion of his upper face, a boyish grin suddenly burst wide across his mouth.

'God,' he said. 'Then it's over?'

'It's over.'

'And you're really not going to Rhys?'

'I'm really not going to Rhys.'

He took his glasses off.

She gave a little start of shock.

She had never seen two black eyes that looked this way – like real wounds rather than simply discolored flesh – reddish-yellow-blue whorls that had both a sinister and comic edge, like the mask of a very mean raccoon.

'God, what happened?'

'I did a stupid thing.' He shook his head. Miserably. 'Married woman.'

'Oh.'

'And her husband finally caught up with us.'

'Oh.'

'That doesn't sound very nice, does it? Sleeping with somebody else's wife?'

'Not really, I guess.' She tried not to sound too prim. She had that tendency sometimes, to be too judgmental of others.

'Maybe it's time I settled down, huh?'

She smiled. 'Doesn't sound like such a bad idea, does it, Michael? There're a lot of women in this Valley who'd like to settle down with you.'

He put the shades back on.

This time they didn't seem ominous.

Now that she knew what they were hiding.

Michael put his hand out. 'Friends?'

She shook with him. 'Friends.'

'Boy, I'm sure glad you made us get together this morning. I feel a lot better.'

'So do I,' she said. 'So do I.'

'I'll walk you to the street.'

'Great,' she said.

They walked back through the young boys taken with her looks, the man in the yellow Bermudas sailing his Frisbee, the young mothers with their strollers next to the wading pool, the tots having a furious good time splashing in the water.

On the sidewalk, he turned and said, 'All right if I give you a small kiss on the cheek, sort of welcome you to the family?'

'I'd like that.'

He kissed her on the cheek.

'Welcome to the family, sister-in-law.'

'This sort of does make it official, doesn't it?'

He laughed. 'Yes, I guess it does. Well, I'd better be getting back to work.'

'Thanks, Michael.'

'Thank you, Alison. Thank you very much.'

He turned and walked away, giving her a jaunty little wave that was almost a salute.

She stood there feeling better than she would have thought possible. Her long, silent struggle with Michael Tyler was finally over.

13

Sometime around one o'clock, Alison fell asleep in the skiff. She was sitting up, actually, when it happened, her fishing line fed out into the clay-colored river, a blue jay parked on the far end of the skiff, taking sun and the light wind shimmering up the water from the Falls.

This was the loneliest stretch of river, a leg whose shoreline was heavy hardwood timber that had not been cut in the past twenty years.

By the time Alison had reached the river today, a great calm had come over her. Everything was going to be all right now. With Ben. With Lynn. With Michael.

And now, almost beatific, she dozed, one with the woods and the water and the wind.

Whoever would have predicted that Alison, who had been in an asylum just eight months ago, could ever have found such peace?

Something jerked her awake and for a long moment she was bewildered, forgetting where she was.

Then she saw the hand that came up on the side of the skiff. She was in the middle of the river but somebody was boarding.

A second hand appeared.

A large, white, rough hand.

And then Michael's face appeared.

He said nothing.

He simply turned the skiff over on its side, throwing Alison into the water.

She tried hard to stay calm but it wasn't easy. She took in huge lungsful of water and immediately felt sick. Her eyes burned from the silty water. And her swimming kicks seemed terrifyingly ineffective.

181

Blind, she was sinking.

And then he was next to her, sharp elbows and quick fists, hooking her inside his arm and swimming her downriver.

She fought with feet and fists, even teeth, but it did no good. His hold was absolute.

Once, she managed to break water and gulp down breath but before she could really redouble her strength, Michael was pulling her down again.

She struggled for what seemed hours and then she got the idea. His groin. Of course. If she could find his groin, she could injure him.

He kept on swimming her downriver, despite all her flailing arms and legs and scratches and bites.

She was beginning to lose consciousness, her head dizzy, her lungs afire.

My God, why was he doing this?

Hadn't he just given her a kiss on the cheek a few hours earlier, and welcomed her to the family?

She broke water again, took in a deep and angry breath, and then raised her left heel and caught him perfectly in the crotch.

She felt his entire body jerk with the pain she'd inflicted; and she felt his hold on her weaken suddenly.

She swam away. Toward the shore.

She wasn't sure if she screamed, or only imagined screaming. She wasn't sure if she was actually getting closer to the shore, or simply wasting a lot of motion.

She looked over her shoulder.

No sign of Michael.

She did the breaststroke, hurrying, hurrying. Soon she would feel soil beneath her feet. Soon she would lose herself in the woods, run to the fishing rental shack and have Old Bob call the police.

She knew the truth about Michael now.

He *had* killed Dana. She was sure of it.

Had to get to shore.

Had to.

And then she felt real exhilaration.

No sign of Michael anywhere.

She was going to make it after all.

She was sure of it.

And then, from below, he grabbed her ankle, twisting it so violently to the right that she was afraid he'd snapped it in half.

She kicked viciously with her other foot but it did no good. He was pulling her under again and she couldn't stop him.

This time, she seemed to go deeper down, splashing, struggling, trying to scream even though she was several feet below the water line.

And he was pulling her.

And only now did she realize where he was taking her. The Falls.

She could feel the current shifting, the water grow chill, run faster.

She was already under the sway of the Falls and knew it.

Panic.

She tried once more to find his groin but this time her kicks did more harm than good, sapping the last of her strength, the last of her oxygen.

And then she had a thought so terrible that it virtually paralyzed her: what if her daughter – she had had a premonition their child was a girl – what if the little girl in her womb knew everything that was going on, and was just as afraid as her mother?

My God.

She struggled some more, and tried a few more times to find his groin with her foot, but it was over now; over.

And then the darkness came, rushing fast and absolute, her senses shutting down like lights going out in a vast dark universe.

All she could hope for was that the little girl in her womb was not aware of any of this.

Please God. Please.

And then there was just the utter silent darkness.

Once she was dead, and offering no resistance, Michael was able to move quickly, taking her but a few feet from the edge of the rushing, roaring Falls, and then setting her free of his arms, and letting her be taken by the current to the Falls, and over.

He needed all his strength not to be carried over himself. The Falls was not satisfied with her alone. It also wanted him.

But he swam upstream until he'd reached the skiff, and then swam it back to the Falls and let it, too, go over, spinning in circles, bumping up against rocks, spinning some more, and then hurtling over the Falls like a crazed bird of some sort.

Tired now, he had an even more difficult time swimming upstream but finally he made it, and when he was in calmer waters, he swam to shore and then ran along the path that took him to the edge of the Falls.

The top of her head, hair streaming like blonde ribbons, bobbed in the churning waters at the bottom of the Falls.

It was done now, and he needed to be away from here quickly.

He ran.

THREE

1

In the week of August 17, a local news photographer ran the following pictures, without the permission of, and indeed much against the will of, the Tyler family.

– Jean, Alison's elegant big-city sister, entering the rather shabby apartment where Alison had lived.

– A sobbing Lynn in the arms of her eldest son Michael; Ben, in the background, looking dazed, as they watch Jean go inside.

– Jean and the Tyler family at the back door of the mortuary where the body had been residing.

– (Still at the mortuary) Jean and Ben holding each other.

– Jean standing by a sleek black hearse as Alison's casket is off-loaded on to a Lear jet white and brilliant in the Midwestern sunlight.

– Jean and Lynn embracing just before Jean goes up the steps into the Lear jet.

– A memorial plaque in the local cemetery reading:

ALISON LAURA COMPTON
August 5, 1976 – July 18, 1996
We Will Always Love You.

– (Another angle of the plaque) The Tyler family, Lynn, Ben, Michael, kneeling in front of the plaque – Ben's face streaked with tears.

– The Tyler family leaving the mortuary for a final time.

– (Under the headline: '*Forging Ahead With Their Lives*,' a photo of Lynn and Ben looking at a dog with a broken leg, the dog just happening to belong to the newspaper photographer – who snapped several shots of Lynn and Ben at work, and then did a brief interview with the reluctant pair about how life was going one month after Alison's tragic accident on Black River Falls.

187

2

September 4

BEN TYLER ARRESTED FOR OMVI

Chief John Rhys told the *Clarion-Ledger* that he had no choice but to arrest Ben Tyler for Operating a Motor Vehicle While Intoxicated.

Tyler was arrested last Thursday night on the Cherokee Road that parallels the river, near the Falls.

Rhys says that the entire town sympathizes with Tyler's tragic loss of his fiancée Alison Compton but that, 'We can't have drunken drivers endangering other people.'

Tyler spent the night in jail, and was then released into the custody of his mother.

September 11

BEN TYLER INJURED IN CAR WRECK

Black River Falls resident Ben Tyler was injured when he lost control of his car on the Cherokee Road this past Tuesday. Chief John Rhys said that Tyler was 'lucky' his injuries weren't more serious. Skid marks, Rhys noted, indicated that Tyler was traveling at a high rate of speed.

Rhys would not speculate on the possible role alcohol played in the mishap.

October 2

BEN TYLER IN SERIOUS CONDITION AFTER
MOTORCYCLE ACCIDENT

Ben Tyler, son of Black River Falls veterinarian Lynn Tyler, was injured when his motorcycle spilled on a newly oiled road.

At press time, Tyler was in stable condition in St Mary's Hospital. This was Tyler's second vehicular accident in less than a month, Tyler having been involved in a car crash on September 11. A few weeks before that, Tyler was arrested for OMVI.

Chief Rhys would not speculate on the possible role alcohol played in the mishap.

3

The Reunion was held every year in late smoky autumn, about the time when jack-o'-lanterns appeared on front porches, and glowing paper skeletons hung from bedroom windows, and little girls begged their mothers to let them wear their witch costumes around the house on the day before Halloween.

The site was the old County Fair grounds. Folks came by car, van, truck, train, plane, and horse to be there, 100,000 of them in a two-day period, which was a lot of folks for a town the size of Black River Falls.

This was the Midwest's largest display of steam-driven machinery, dating from that time, roughly around 1920, when steam had been the chief propellant for threshers, tractors, trucks, electric trolleys, steam trains, and a few score different kinds of industrial engines. In the old days, threshers required crews running to fifteen men who moved from field to field with the steam-huffing threshers, all part of an operation as carefully planned as anything that ever came out of West Point. Many farmers had to rent threshers and had to get their work done quickly before the rental fees broke them.

The steam era was America's last age of innocence, before the cynicism of world wars had set in, before the intractable problems of race and class beset the political dialogue.

A lot of men and women chose to wear the styles of bygone eras for the two-day Thresher festival. You saw sleeve-garters and handlebar mustaches; bustles and bonnets. There was ragtime music, and tents filled with food of all kinds – from hams to pies to sweet potatoes agleam with sugar glazing – and square-dancing contests, and hog-calling contests, and pet shows that ran from garter snakes to a dog that could sing along with *The Star Spangled Banner*.

191

The Thresher Reunion was usually one of Ben's favorite events but this year, despite Lynn's urging, he'd been reluctant to go. Alison's death and his two accidents had made him a public figure, and he hated the stares and the whispers, the unceasing attention his presence brought.

But given the number of children, of grandmas and grandpas, of wives and husbands, Ben was nobody special today. There were too many other things for people to pay attention to.

Lynn, Michael and Ben ate lunch in a big tent where fried chicken and potato salad and pumpkin pie were the specialties.

Lynn noted that Ben's appetite was slowly improving. He'd lost something like twelve pounds in the month following Alison's accident. He'd also started drinking heavily, something he'd done briefly in high school. But now he hadn't had a drink for three weeks and he was starting to eat regularly again.

Michael held court, people, especially local young women, stopping to greet the area's most eligible bachelor. Ben even managed a smile and wink for his mother. They'd long joked about Michael's celebrity status. She always said that Michael should learn to play the guitar and then he could be just like Elvis.

In the early afternoon, they drifted down to the carnival that was set up in the town square. The autumn afternoon vibrated with the motors and music of the carousel and the Ferris wheel and the Tilt-A-Whirl. The air smelled of motor oil and popcorn and cotton candy.

Michael tried a couple of the games. He knocked over three bottles and won a pink teddy bear, which he gave to Lynn. She said, 'Pink? This must be a Martian teddy bear.'

At the rifle booth, Ben shone. He put three shots directly into the tops of three wooden milk bottles. He won a dinner plate that read: *Home Swe t Home*. The other *e* in *Sweet* had faded. Lynn received her second gift for the day.

By the time they reached the parking lot, Lynn had actually heard Ben laugh twice.

'I'm pooped,' she said. They'd been here four hours.

'Pooped? It's only two in the afternoon,' Michael said.

'You're too young to be pooped,' Ben said. And she again noted the festive tone of his voice. She hadn't seen him like this since the accident.

'Flatterer,' Lynn said. 'You know I'm an old lady and I need my rest.'

'Well, I need some action, old lady,' Michael said. Then he gave her a quick sharp look and she sensed what he was going to say next. They'd talked about it several times and decided that today would be a good day to try it. If Ben's mood seemed improved, as it certainly did. 'Hey, I've got it, Ben. You know what we should do?'

'What?'

'Go on the river.'

Ben's face tightened. A vague anger came into his eyes. Since Alison's death, he'd treated the river like a sentient monster, one that had destroyed not only Alison, but Ben, too. They couldn't get him to talk about the river, let alone go on it.

'No, thanks,' Ben said.

'It might not be a bad idea, honey,' Lynn said softly. 'Maybe it's time to go back there. You know what the coroner said. She stood up and fell out of the boat somehow. And then got pulled downstream. The river didn't do it to her, honey.'

Michael slid his arm around Ben's shoulder. 'C'mon. I'll even let you save my life again.'

'I think I'll just go back home and do some reading or something,' Ben said.

Lynn assumed that there was no way he'd change his mind now but good old Michael, who knew just how to play his brother, said, 'You know those sci-fi videos I said were coming in?'

'Uh-huh.'

'Well, they came in.'

'The Warner Brothers' ones from the fifties?' Ben loved fifties 'giant mutation' movies. They were great, giddy fun, so preposterous in premise, so exuberantly crazed in execution.

'Right,' Michael said. 'Including the first movie Clint Eastwood ever made.'

'Is it good?'

'It's very good. There's this big hairy spider and he eats Cleveland.'

Ben laughed again, and the sound pleased Lynn.

'Can I borrow them?'

'Only if you go on the river with me.'

Ben's face got taut and pale again. Was he afraid of the river? Lynn wondered. Or was it simply the memory that it was by going over the Falls that Alison, and their child, had died? Lynn had to admit that she might well react the same way, see the river as a living, malevolent force.

'I can't, Michael.'

'Why not?'

Ben shrugged, shook his head. 'You know – because of Alison.'

Michael slid his arm around Ben's shoulder and kneaded the knotted muscles in the shoulder. 'That's why you need to go, kiddo.'

Ben looked at him.

'It was an accident, kiddo. A terrible, terrible accident. But the river didn't do it. Alison must've gotten sick and dizzy or something and—' He left the sentence unfinished.

'You've been playing on the river since you were a little boy, Ben,' Lynn said. She knew that he would have to make his peace with the river if he was ever to get over Alison's accident. 'Maybe now would be a good time to give it another try.'

He looked at them both and then brought the three of them together in a hug. 'I know you're trying to help me, and I appreciate it. I just—. Well, I'm scared about going on the river.'

'You've got a life-jacket, kiddo,' Michael said. 'You'll be fine.'

Ben glanced at Lynn. She leaned forward and kissed him on the cheek. 'It'd be good for you, honey.'

Fifteen minutes later, Ben and Michael set off for the river.

'I loved her.'

'I know you did, kiddo.'

'And I'm never going to get over it.'

'Someday you are, kiddo. Not for a long time. But someday.'

'Maybe I don't even want to get over it.'

'She'd want you to. Alison would.'

'This fucking river. That's what did it. This fucking god damned river.'

The brothers were in a wooden rowboat they used for fishing. It was slow but reliable.

Ben appreciated how Michael just let him say whatever came to mind. They'd fish and they'd talk and then they'd fish some more. They'd been out here a little over an hour now, Michael having caught himself a carp that he'd thrown back. Some kids had come by in a fast motorboat and spoiled the fishing for a time but now downriver was quiet again – except for the distant roaring of the Falls.

'I think about the kid, too,' Ben said.

'I know you do.'

'What she would have been if she'd grown up.'

Ben hung his head, started to cry.

Michael left him alone.

So much rage, Ben thought. And I don't know what to do with it. Or direct it at.

The river, the Falls, that's what had killed her but there wasn't much you could do to a foe like that.

They drifted further downriver.

Ben could feel the hot sun start to bake his arms and face and neck. He should be using some kind of sun block but right now he didn't give a damn. He looked out at the dusty shore line, the deer and the dogs and the occasional moose you sometimes saw.

Indians. He wanted to imagine the shore line as the Indians of 5,000 years ago had known it. He'd taken such pleasure in his fantasies ... and not so long ago, either.

But that had been when he was a kid. And now he could no longer be a kid. Not ever again. He wasn't quite an adult, either – he was well aware of that – but he wasn't a kid, either.

His fiancée and his daughter were dead and you could never be a kid again after something like that.

'I know some girls.'

'God, Michael. Right now I could give shit about other girls.'

'I mean when you're ready.'

'Maybe I'll never be ready.'

Michael shrugged, turned to watch as two canoes of Cub Scouts paddled by. Michael spoke to the Den Mother who, like her charges, was dressed in a blue Cub Scout shirt and cap. She was fortyish but red-haired and still cute.

'I didn't mean to take it out on you,' Ben said after the Scouts had gone upriver.

'It's all right, kiddo. Just relax, fish.'

'I guess I'm not up to it.'

'You seem to be doing a little better with the river.'

Ben shook his head. 'It's like Mom says, how can you hate a river?'

'It was an accident, kiddo. A terrible, terrible accident.'

Ben spent the next few minutes watching the play of sunlight and shadow on the surface of the river. It was an inexplicable phenomenon but one that fascinated him – light and shadow. In Lit class he'd read a poem about it, and how the poet felt that he could never adequately describe it, or the feelings it evoked in him.

Sometimes none of it made any sense, of course. His father dying in a tractor accident. Poor little Elizabeth being born with feline leukemia. Alison and their daughter—

'They giving you a hard time about me?'

'Who's "they," kiddo?'

'You know. The town. About my drinking and the wrecks and all.'

'They're worried about you, if that's what you mean.'

'I'm not going to drink any more.'

'I'd say that's a good idea.'

'In high school—'

'I remember, kiddo. I remember.'

Ben had gone through a time when he felt like a total geek. Neither boy nor girl had wanted much to do with him, and when he passed by people, they usually greeted him with a smirk. It wasn't paranoia, either. It actually happened. The smirk. Geek Ben. Or 'Old Weird Ben' as some of the kids called him. Ben and his animals and his science-fiction books and movies. Ben and his scared hurt eyes and his overwhelming sense of isolation, as if he had been sent here from an alien planet to observe the natives ... but could never become one with them. Too different, too weird.

And somehow, he'd started to drink. Michael thought it was kind of cute at first, the little brother coming over and getting loaded. But then Ben started coming over a lot ... and then Ben started stealing booze from Michael's own stash.

Ben had ended up going to a psychologist a couple of towns away. He was too embarrassed to see a counselor here. The counselor helped. Had let Ben talk about all his fears and frustrations, and then made a few simple, practical suggestions. One of which was: give up drinking. And Ben had agreed. And his life had gone much better, then. Not a perfect life, by any means, but better than it had been.

Then, after Alison's death he'd started drinking again—

'Mom'll be glad to hear it, kiddo.'

'Yeah.'

Then, calmly, in little more than a whisper, Michael said, 'She's worried about you.'

'I know.'

'Afraid you're going to come apart.'

Ben nodded.

'I told her you were too tough for that, kiddo.'

'I hope you're right.'

'I am right, kiddo.'

Michael leaned back against his end of the rowboat. 'Someday you're going to meet somebody and you're going to fall in love, and you're going to have a baby and you're going to be happy again.'

'I can't even think about that now.'

'I know you can't. But I also know that that's going to happen to you.'

Leaning against his own end of the rowboat, Ben said, 'Nobody could have a better brother than you, Michael.'

The famous Michael grin. 'You know something, kiddo? You're probably right.'

'You asshole.'

'Hey,' Michael laughed, 'one minute ago nobody could have a better brother than me, and now I'm an asshole.'

It was nearly dusk before they came off the river. Ben hadn't felt so relaxed since the last time he'd been with Alison.

4

Over the next few days, Ben's appetite continued to get better. There was even a meal at which he accepted her offer of a piece of pumpkin pie. The last two months, he'd lost all interest in dessert.

Lynn also noticed that Ben was spending more and more time with the animals. For a few weeks, he'd even seemed beyond the solace they had to offer. But now he was putting baby bunnies in the palm of his hand, and taking some of the dogs for long walks around the farm, and setting little toys in the cages of the kittens.

She wasn't naive enough to think that any of this meant that Ben was suddenly all better again. But she did recognize the signs that things were getting at least somewhat better with him.

One late afternoon, she came home to find him at the kitchen table with a carving knife in his hands, and the guts of a pumpkin piled neatly on a newspaper. He'd carved the hollowed-out pumpkin into a fierce jack-o'-lantern. 'Alison wanted me to make one for her this year,' he said.

Lynn noted that his voice didn't quaver when he mentioned Alison, nor did his eyes glisten with tears. He'd simply mentioned her name by way of explanation.

That night, Lynn and Ben stood outside the front window admiring Ben's handiwork. With leafsmoke on the air, and the farm shadows appropriately deep, and a chill wind skittering dried scraping leaves across the lawn, the jack-o'-lantern was impressively spooky.

Her only wish now was that Ben had a friend, male or female wouldn't matter. But Alison had been his life for eight months and the few friends he'd had before her had drifted away.

But she was definitely encouraged. He was starting to get back into the rhythm of his life again. About that there could be no doubt.

Now her nightly prayers became prayers of gratitude. Please, Lord, keep him on this path.

Make him whole again, Lord.

Make him whole again.

On Tuesday of the following week, a harsh cold rain fell on Black River Falls, smashing the fallen leaves, dulling the bright autumn colors that had made the town so beautiful.

Ben and Lynn were in surgery by 7:30 that morning. There was a cat to be spayed and a dog's leg to be broken and reset. The first vet, years earlier, hadn't done a very good job.

By eleven, the workday was pretty much finished. Ben had been painting the exterior of the office but the rain canceled that for the day. Everything else was under control.

'You mind if I go into town?'

'Not at all,' Lynn said. 'Would you mind picking some things up for me at the supermarket?'

'You have a list?'

'I can make one real quick.'

As she handed him the list a few minutes later, she said, 'If you see Michael, remind him that he's supposed to come for dinner Sunday.'

'All right. I'll probably stop by the video store after I get done at the library.'

She just looked at him, amazed.

Since Alison's death, he'd avoided the library as if it held a superstitious terror for him.

She didn't blame him, of course. Walking around the place where the couple had first met, where Ben had spent so many love-sick afternoons just working up enough courage to ask Alison out.

She would still be in the library now, ghostly images of her, anyway.

This was another good sign, going to the library of his own volition.

She gave him a quick hug.

'What was that for?'

'For picking up the groceries.'

But they both knew better.

They both knew what the hug was for.

She slid into her slicker and rain hat and walked him out to the old truck. She needed to grab the mail from the box, anyway.

The rain made the engine even more high-strung than usual. It sputtered, coughed, roared, died, sputtered some more, and then finally, in a perfume of gasoline, fired properly and caught.

'You need any money?' Lynn said over the roaring engine.

'No, thanks. I've got enough.'

'Have a good time.'

'I will, Mom. Don't worry.'

When he was halfway down the drive, she walked over to the mailbox. The usual assortment of bills and advertisements.

She looked up just in time to see Ben's truck disappearing around the farthest bend.

The library.

Things were definitely getting better with Ben.

Definitely.

Denise had called twice and Michael wasn't at all happy about it. They had talked only once since the night Paul had broken into the bedroom. Michael didn't want to talk to her again. His instinct was to kill Paul Fletcherwith his bare hands ... but if Fletcher was killed, Michael would immediately be implicated. Talking with Denise just reminded him of that and made him more frustrated.

Just after lunch, the store phone rang again and Michael knew that it would be Denise.

Barb, one of his new clerks, came over to the cash register where Michael was checking out a Golden Ager (seniors for an extra discount). 'Phone.'

'Be a minute.'

Barb nodded and went to the phone in the back room.

'I hope this is sexy,' said the old coot renting the video. He grinned with clacking dentures.

Michael smiled. Good to know that even after the human body had been slowed, bent, and gnarled, the desire for sex still remained.

'I saw it,' Michael said. 'Got some nice ladies in it.'

The codger grinned again.

Michael wasn't at all pleasant to the person on the phone.

'Yeah?' he said, his voice already harsh.

'We need to talk.'

'No, we don't.'

'I haven't seen you for almost three months.'

'And you're not going to see me now, either.'

'I miss you.'

'I can't help that.'

'I didn't think it was anything except sex,' Denise said, 'between you and me, I mean.'

'We had our time, Denise. It's over.'

'You didn't let me finish.'

'Then finish and I'll hang up.'

'I think I fell in love with you.'

'Oh, God, Denise, come on. You and I are too much alike for shit like that.'

'Well, it could happen, you know.'

He sighed. 'I'll bet you've already been seeing somebody else on the side, haven't you?'

'God, Michael, I really resent that.'

'Haven't you?'

'Just once, you prick, and it really isn't any of your business, anyway.'

'Just once?'

'Well, it was a weekend when Paul was away. But I haven't seen the guy since.'

'You spent the whole weekend with this guy?'

'Well...'

Michael smiled. 'I thought you were in love with me.'

'Has it ever occurred to you that maybe I was thinking about you the whole time I was in bed with him?'

He laughed. 'Denise, please, listen. I'm too young to die. I really am. Paul's always hated me, anyway. Ever since we were little kids. Next time he catches us together, he really will kill me. And you.'

'He's such an asshole.'

Michael heard the front door open and peered out between the curtains covering the back doorway.

Ben had just come in and was looking around the store for Michael.

'I have to go,' Michael said.

'I want you inside me.'

'Aw, Denise, c'mon. Give me a break. Save that kind of talk for the new guy.'

'There isn't any new guy.'

'The weekend guy, I mean.'

'Just because we spent a weekend together doesn't mean I'm going to see him again.'

'Right.'

'Well, it doesn't.'

'I need to go, Denise. Sorry.'

He hung up and went out into the store.

'Hey, kiddo.'

Ben was over in the horror section, checking out the new Wes Craven video. Most critics said it was Craven's best picture since *The Hills Have Eyes*.

Ben looked up. 'Hi, Michael.'

'Nice to see you, kiddo.'

Ben nodded. 'Same here.'

'You in town for the afternoon?'

Ben shook his head. 'Huh-uh. I was over at the library for the last couple of hours.'

'The library?' Michael softened his voice. 'How'd it go, kiddo?'

'At first it was kind of tough. You know, thinking about all the times I'd met her in there and everything. But then—'

Tears glazed Ben's eyes. He lowered his head.

Michael offered him a clean white handkerchief.

Ben daubed his eyes, handed the handkerchief back. 'Sorry.'

'Nothing to be sorry about, kiddo.'

'Your customers and all.'

'Hey, kiddo, who's more important to me, my customers or my brother?'

Ben smiled. 'Yeah, I guess you're right.'

'So after a while, things went all right, at the library, I mean?'

'After a while, yeah. I just started thinking about how much she'd liked working there. I mean, she wasn't a real librarian or anything, and only a library this small would ever have hired her, but she loved it. She really did. She always said it was like being inside a fortress where nothing could get to you. So I just started thinking about that and—. Well, then I actually started enjoying myself. I just sat there and read some old Isaac Asimov and Robert Heinlein stories – you know, the stuff I read when I was in sixth and seventh grade – and it was sort of peaceful being there and every once in a while, I'd see her and hear her and—. And I felt closer to her than I have since—'

Tears again.

Michael's handkerchief again.

Ben using it and handing it back again.

Plump silver raindrops sliding down the gray wintry windows; the smell of the heating system being used for the first time this year; the bright faces of the videos somehow dulled even blanched by the chill, somber day . . .

'I'm sorry.'

'There you go again, kiddo.'

'Well, it can't be real good for business, having your brother in here crying.'

'I'll worry about the business, all right?' Then Michael said: 'You know what we forgot?'

'What?'

'Those damned videos at my place. The new sci-fi ones. You never did pick them up.'

'I forgot.'

'Well, hell, kiddo, you know where I keep the spare key, right?'

'In the garage, taped to the inside of your tool box?'

'Right. Why don't you let yourself into my place and get the videos? They're right on the buffet in the dining room. They should be, anyway. That's where I usually stash stuff.'

'Maybe that's what I need. Watch a sci-fi movie.'

'Exactly. And take some candy from the counter with you. Free gratis.'

Ben grinned. 'Just like going to a real movie, huh?'

'Just like, kiddo. Just like.' Michael gave him a quick, strong hug. 'Let me know how you like them.'

'I really appreciate it, Michael.'

'I'm just glad to see that you're doing better is all, kiddo. You're my only concern.' Then: 'You need any money?'

Before Ben could answer, Michael had his worn old wallet out and was thumbing through some crisp green bills.

'No money, Michael. I don't need any more.' He nodded at the wallet which had once been nice black leather but was now worn to a dull gray along the edges. The cellophane envelopes holding pictures and various forms of identification were yellowed and torn, their contents ready to spill out. 'But you sure could use a new wallet.'

'Yeah, but it's one of those things you just never remember to buy for yourself.'

Michael walked Ben over to the candy counter, filled a small paper bag with a variety of candies, and then handed it over.

'I can't eat all this,' Ben said.

'Then give some of it to the critters,' Michael laughed.

'Oh yeah, right,' Ben said. 'I can just see that hawk with the broken wing eating some Hot Tamales.'

'How much is this one?'

'Seventy-five dollars.'

'Wow.'

'It's genuine leather.'

'I know, but—'

You wanted something less expensive?

'Uh-huh.'

'How much did you have in mind?'

'Oh. Twenty-five dollars. Thirty dollars. Something like that.'

'Well, it isn't the top of the line the way this one is, but it's very nice.'

Mr Allingham, who owned Allingham's Gifts, bent down behind the counter and picked up a wallet that looked clearly inferior to the one he'd just been showing.

'Like it?'

'It's pretty nice. How much is it?'

'$27.95.'

'That I could afford.'

It felt a little coarser than the first one Mr Allingham had shown him ... but it was sure an improvement over what Michael had now.

'Could you gift-wrap it?'

'Sure, Ben. Be happy to.'

'With a ribbon and everything?'

'With a ribbon and everything.' Mr Allingham, who was short and bald and looked like a munchkin wearing a vested dark suit, tapped the wallet and said, 'That brother of yours is going to like this one. You wait and see.'

'I'll take it, then,' Ben said, checking the wallet pockets and the windows for licenses and photos. It really was very nice. And it smelled of new leather, too.

While Mr Allingham went in the back and wrapped up the wallet, Ben walked around the store. This kind of place had always intimidated him a little. His mother had never made much money so they'd always done most of their shopping at K-Mart and Target. But here in Mr Allingham's . . . Well, he'd just looked at the price tag on a piece of rather plain luggage and it had said, incredibly, $400 . . . Ben couldn't imagine spending that kind of money on a piece of luggage.

This explained why this small but very crowded shop was always used as the measure of a gift's quality. 'He bought it at Allingham's,' would say everything the listener needed to know.

The wallet made a nice little package. The bow was a deep blue, the wrapping paper a buff blue. Very nice indeed.

Ben took his own wallet out and paid Mr Allingham.

'How much for the wrap?' Ben said.

'Free.'

'Free? Don't you usually charge for it?'

'Usually,' Mr Allingham said, 'yes. But, well, you know.'

'I guess I'm not following you.'

Mr Allingham, who had rather prissy eyes and mouth, looked down inside the counter and said, 'Your young woman.'

'You mean Alison?'

'Yes, Alison.'

'What about her?'

Mr Allingham raised his eyes. 'Well, I never personally got to tell you how sorry I am, Ben. That's what I'm trying to say here, with the free wrap and all.'

'You don't need to do that, Mr Allingham.'

'I want to, Ben.'

'Well, thanks.'

'You're most welcome. You're a fine boy, Ben, and so is that brother of yours. Your mother did a fine job of raising you. She sure did.'

Ben nodded goodbye, said, 'Thanks' again, and left the shop.

* * *

Michael's was the life most high school boys dreamed of. Hot car. Hotter motorcycle. Plenty of girls. Plenty of spending money. And, thanks to a cleaning woman who came in twice a week, always neat and always orderly.

After getting the key from the tool box and letting himself into the house, Ben looked around a few minutes at the latest gadgets that Michael had acquired, the most formidable being the big-screen high-resolution TV set. Ben had never seen one as wide as this. It was called a home theater and it really was. Watch a few videos on this and you could probably never go back to a standard-sized screen.

Ben wanted to sit down and watch one of the sci-fi videos Michael had set aside for him. But he didn't consider this for long. By now, his mother could be very busy and needing him. And here he'd be sitting on his butt watching a video.

No; time to get back home.

He'd leave the gift, pick up the videos, and head to the farm.

He went into the bedroom, feeling uncomfortable as he did so. Michael was a real ass-bandit. Everybody knew that. Ben wondered how many girls Michael had seduced in this room.

As he crossed the floor to the bureau, past the king-sized water bed that was mounted on a pedestal, Ben could almost picture gorgeous naked girls in Michael's bed.

He blushed, as if he'd been caught doing something dirty.

And then he realized that this was the first sexual thought he'd had since Alison died.

Alison.

He stopped, as if paralyzed, letting the name and all its implications overwhelm him.

Alison.

And their baby girl.

And then the darkness left, and he felt able to move purposefully again.

Nothing wrong with having sexual thoughts about girls.

Perfectly natural.

Or so he told himself.

But he felt guilty having such thoughts.

Alison, and their child, dead—

And here he was imagining silky white naked girls in his brother's bed—

He gripped the gift box firmly and walked over to the bureau.

Michael had an array of colognes and after-shave sitting on top of the bureau. Obsession. Brut. English Leather. Canoe. And several others.

Michael was the ultimate ass-bandit.

No doubt about it.

Then Ben opened the top drawer of the bureau, ready to set the gift in there so Michael would get a surprise when he opened it, and then—

Then his life changed.

Completely.

For ever.

The drawer contained undershirts and underwear of such white brilliance that they had to be fairly new. Socks of various hues were rolled into the far corner.

But it was neither underwear nor socks that drew Ben's attention.

It was the red silk scarf that captivated and held Ben almost breathless.

Dana's scarf.

How had it gotten in this drawer?

And what was his brother Michael doing with it?

'Is she going to live?' asked Ida Boone, a very earnest six-year-old girl.

'Yes she is, honey,' Lynn said.

'You're not just saying that?'

'The Doctor said she's going to live, honey,' Ida's mother said. 'She wouldn't lie to you.'

'But Princess has a broken Elvis.'

'Not Elvis, Ida,' her mother said. 'Pelvis.'

'Oh,' Ida said. 'Will she have to stay here?'

'For the night,' Lynn said. 'But I suspect she'll be ready to go home tomorrow afternoon.'

They were in surgery.

Princess, a cute little mongrel with floppy spaniel ears and forlorn brown eyes, had been struck by a car about half an hour earlier.

Ida and her mother had rushed Princess out here.

Lynn had done all the basics, checked the vital signs, including heart rate, saw the pupils weren't dilated, and checked the dog's mouth to make sure the color was a healthy pink.

Then she did three X-rays and found the broken Elvis.

'Will she be on crutches?' Ida said.

'Dogs don't use crutches,' Lynn explained.

'Then will she have a bandage?'

'There isn't much we can do for a broken pelvis except let it heal,' Lynn said. 'Trying a splint or any kind of body wrap might be dangerous.'

The slight, pig-tailed girl said, 'So she can't play?'

'Not for a while,' Lynn said.

'All she can do is watch TV and stuff like that?'

Lynn smiled. 'Does she watch TV?'

'She likes professional wrestling,' Ida said.

Her mother said, 'That's true. There's something about the movement of the wrestlers that fascinates her. She sits there and watches the whole thing sometimes.'

'I'll have to remember that for the next veterinarian convention I go to,' Lynn said. 'About Princess and the professional wrestling.'

Twenty minutes later, she escorted Ida and her mother to the front door. The chill rain was still slashing down, thunder rumbling in the southern sky. Ida and her mother ran quickly to their car and piled in.

For some reason, Lynn looked east to the road that Ben would take coming home. She wondered how it had gone at the library, whether the memories had been too much for him.

She had this real need, suddenly, to see him.

She hoped he'd be home soon.

She went back inside and fixed up a nice comfortable bed for Princess the pro-wrestling mutt to sleep in.

5

Ben had to pay thirty dollars to get the guy to buy him two pints of whiskey. But he didn't mind. The sweet blind bliss of booze was well worth the price.

He sat by the railroad tracks, Ben did, and hurled rocks at the fast hurtling trains, the way he had when he was a kid and the trains were magic with the promise of such faraway lands as Mexico and California. He sat and hurled rocks until he was too drunk to do it any more.

By then, he was on his second pint, and weaving away from the rail-yards, and staggering down to the little park where, on so warm a night, a lot of high school kids hid in shadows and smoked dope and balled their girlfriends.

Ben came wobbling into all this and somebody said something that he didn't like, and so Ben took a swing at him.

And promptly fell on his butt.

And the kids crowded around for a look at him there on his back on the grass and one of them said, 'It's that friggin' dweeb Ben Tyler.'

'Geek.'

'Faggot.'

Then somebody kicked him because it seemed like the appropriate thing to do, some boy that is; some girl said, 'Leave him alone,' and then knelt down next to him to see if he was all right and Ben, all drunk and confused, put his arms out to her and said, 'Alison? Alison, is that you?'

'Friggin' geek,' one of the boys said.

And then they left him there alone in the night.

By eight o'clock that evening, Lynn was getting worried. She had called Michael three times, the library twice, the shopping center

211

twice, and two or three boys Ben had been friendly with in high school. None of them had seen Ben within the past five hours.

At eight-thirty, Michael, who was on a dinner date, called her.

'Anything new?' he said.

'Not yet.'

'You check with Chief Rhys again?'

'He hasn't seen him anywhere, either.'

'Mom, I'm sure he's all right.'

'I hope so.' Her voice trembled slightly as she spoke. 'Listen, you have a date. I know where you are. If anything happens—. Well, I'll call you.'

'Nothing's going to happen, Mom.'

'I hope you're right.'

'He went off somewhere to be alone. That's all.'

She spent half an hour with her critters, finding solace and strength in the innocent way they dealt with their pain and anxiety. She had a crush on a tiny lamb who had suffered a bad virus and was staying here a few days. She held it as she had once held Ben and Michael, in the cradle of her arm, a soft half-silent song on her lips.

When the phone rang, it startled her the way an explosion would have. She put the lamb away, and grabbed the wall phone on the third ring.

'Hello?'

'Dr Tyler?'

'Yes.'

'This is Ken Campbell.'

'Hi, Ken. Sounds like you're calling long distance.' Ken was a fuel truck driver who owned a small acreage on the north end of town. Ken and his family had a small zoo of critters and brought them to Lynn for medical attention.

'Phone in my truck.'

'Oh.'

'Dr Tyler, I've got your boy with me.'

'Ben?'

'Yes. He's pretty drunk. I found him by the roadside.'

Her hand was shaking badly. 'Is he all right?'

'Appears to be.'

'Can he talk?'

'Not much, I'm afraid. He told me he was too drunk to drive so he started walking. I think he was at the Four Corners.'

The Four Corners was a tavern where underage drinkers frequently went.

'I really appreciate this, Ken.'

'Glad to do it.' Pause. 'Poor kid. His girl dying pregnant and all—'

'Thanks again, Ken.'

'I'll be at your place in another ten minutes.'

She filled up the Mr Coffee and set him to work; she hurried and turned back Ben's bed; and she pulled her truck out of the garage and pointed it toward town in case Ben had been injured and needed to be taken to the hospital.

She saw the shape of the fuel truck silhouetted against the moon-painted night sky.

Ken pulled in, the heavy truck popping gravel as it made its way up the drive.

Ken stopped just in front of the garage.

Lynn was up and inside before the truck had quite stopped. Vital signs weren't important for just critters. She checked Ben's pulse, lifted back an eyelid, and then put her ear to his nose to hear his breathing.

His vitals all appeared to be fine.

The rest of him was not so fine, however.

He'd obviously fallen down on his walk home. His face was scuffed and cut in several places. His entire body stank of beer and whiskey. The knees of his jeans were torn out, the exposed flesh beneath bloodied, like his face.

'I'll help you get him down,' Ken Campbell said.

They took him inside and up the stairs and put him into his single bed. Lynn threw a light blanket over him and then went downstairs with Campbell.

'I really appreciate this,' she said.

'That's what neighbors are for.'

She wanted to cry and give him a hug. He seemed so simple and honest in a world that was too often complex and deceitful.

'May I give you a hug?'

He smiled. 'Pretty gal offers me a hug and I turn her down? No way.'

She gave him a hug and they both laughed.

She walked him outside.

The rain had stopped late in the afternoon and now a curious warmth filled the land – a kind of purgatory, between the seasons of autumn and winter.

'He'll be all right, Dr Tyler. I've tied a few on in my time, too, and I always survived.'

'Thanks again, Ken.'

'No problem. You take care.'

She waved goodbye and stood for a moment as his retreating headlights swept her. Then she hurried back inside.

When she got upstairs, she found the bed empty. A moment of true panic, almost disorientation, grabbed her.

Where was Ben?

Then she heard him down the hall, in the bathroom.

Throwing up.

She went in and helped him all she could. He was very sick for a very long time. He seemed to be unconscious throughout. The few times their eyes made contact, he didn't seem to recognize her.

She got his clothes off him and quickly sprayed some Bactine on his cuts and then put him to bed. The rest would have to wait until morning.

Within moments of lying down, Ben was snoring.

She went downstairs and poured herself a cup of coffee. She felt alone, and terrified, without quite knowing why.

In the morning, Ben was sick again. But he didn't let his mother into the bathroom. He was awake enough to have some pride.

Sick three times, kneeling over the john, tears stinging his eyes, images from the night before attacking him like ghosts in a deep, dark wood.

He wasn't even sure how he'd gotten home.

When he finished being sick, he took the Lysol and the toilet brush and some clean rags from the closet and cleaned up the mess.

Then he got in the shower, ran it very hot at first, then very cold, and stood there recomposing himself molecule by molecule.

He was Ben Tyler again.

Then he remembered the red silk scarf. Alison's red silk scarf. In

Michael's drawer. At least he'd been smart enough to put the wallet on the kitchen counter so Michael would never suspect that Ben had seen the red scarf in the bureau.

Michael and his mother were finishing up breakfast when Ben got downstairs.

Michael pointed to the wallet on the table. 'You really didn't need to do that, kiddo.'

Ben knew he had to act as if everything was perfectly normal. 'My pleasure.'

'Can you afford it?'

Ben forced a smile. 'All the stuff you've done for me?'

'Well, I really do appreciate it, kiddo.'

'How about some coffee?' his mother said.

'Great.'

'You think you can eat something?'

'Maybe a piece of toast.'

'A little margarine?'

'Great.'

'You know, Mrs Conroy gave us some of that strawberry jam she always puts up every fall. You want a little bit of that?'

'A little bit'd probably be all right.'

'I'll be right back,' his mother said, and started to walk into the kitchen.

Ben caught her slender wrist.

'I want to apologize to both of you,' Ben said.

'Aw, c'mon, kiddo, Michael said. 'Maybe you owe Mom an apology but not me.'

'You love me and you worry about me. I shouldn't have gone off and gotten drunk like that.'

'You had me scared,' Lynn said. 'I have to admit that.'

Ben gave her a kiss on the cheek. 'I'm sorry, Mom.'

'I'll get your coffee and toast, honey.'

Ben sat down.

How about that red silk scarf, Michael? Where did you get it?

That's what he wanted to say, of course.

But instead he said: 'I dropped off the wallet at your place but then I forgot to pick up the videos.'

215

The truth was he'd been so rattled by finding the scarf he'd forgotten all about the videos.

'No sweat. I brought them along this morning.'

'Thanks, Michael.'

'You bet.'

The chill gray of yesterday was gone. The day was sunny and in the mid-forties. The hills were bright again with the last of autumn leaves, and the horses in the hills shone sleek and chestnut as they ran.

'Had a bad spell, huh?'

'Yeah,' Ben said. 'A bad spell.'

'Anything in particular?'

Ben shrugged. 'Just started thinking about Alison and – and I couldn't handle it.'

'God, kiddo, I'm sorry. But at the risk of sounding like some old fart preacher, you're not going to find any happiness in getting drunk.'

'I know.'

'You scared the shit out of Mom last night, kiddo.'

Ben sighed. The way he'd been running his life lately, his mother was as much a victim of Alison's death as he was. She deserved better treatment.

'You ever think of seeing that counselor again?'

Ben started to shake his head but pain stopped him. A hangover like this one took at least a full day to recover from.

The smells cheered him more than anything. Coffee. Eggs. Bacon.

Lynn came back with his coffee and toast. 'I made you three pieces. Just in case.'

'Thanks, Mom.'

She set them down in front of him and said, 'I'd better get over to the office.'

'I'll join you in a few minutes.'

'Take your time. Everything'll be fine.'

She leaned down and kissed him. She got a smudge of lipstick on his cheek and then daubed it off with his napkin. 'You probably don't remember any more, Ben, but one day I gave you a kiss before you got on the school bus but I forgot to wipe the lipstick off. The kids

216

teased you until the teacher finally wiped it off. I was afraid you wouldn't ever forgive me, you were so embarrassed.'

Oddly enough, there were tears in her voice and eyes as she finished her story.

She gave them a tiny wave and then left the dining room. Ben heard the back door open and close quietly.

'She's some lady,' Michael said.

'She sure is.'

'I want you to do something for me, kiddo.'

'All right.'

'The next time you want to tie one on—'

Ben was hungrier than he'd thought. He'd already downed half a piece of toast and a third cup of coffee. 'Uh-huh?'

'Call me before you do anything.'

'Sort of like AA?'

'Yeah.'

'All right.'

'All right you will or all right you'll think about it?'

'All right, I'll do it.'

'Great, kiddo. Great. We've just got to get you through this and then you'll be fine.'

Yeah, Ben thought, someday I'll forget all about the girl and the baby you killed.

But had Michael killed them?

Ben looked at his brother for a long moment, trying to see if there was something sinister in Michael's face he'd never noticed before. But – nothing. Boy-next-door handsome. Genuinely friendly smile. Merry eyes.

Could Michael really have killed Alison?

'I still want to introduce you to some girls – you know, down the line.'

'Appreciate it.'

Michael moved back from the table, stood up.

He walked over to Ben and bent down and gave his younger brother a hug. 'I love you, kiddo, you know that, don't you?'

'I sure do.'

You love me but you hated Alison.

You always hated Alison.

She thought you killed her friend.

Maybe you killed both of them, Michael.

Maybe you killed both of them.

'I need to get to the store,' Michael said, walking to the doorway between dining room and kitchen. 'Those videos are in on the TV set.'

'Thanks again.'

'You bet, kiddo. You just remember our deal.'

'That I call you when I want to get drunk?'

'Right. And I'll be there.'

'Thanks a lot, Michael. For everything.'

'I'll talk to you later, kiddo.'

'Thanks again.'

Then Michael was gone, leaving Ben to his hangover and then his fear.

What if Michael really had killed her?

How was Ben ever going to turn Michael over without destroying his mother in the process?

Her father had been a killer.

And now her eldest son.

How could he ever turn Michael over?

6

I know what you did.
I want money. Meet
me at 9:00 tonight
at the Sheffield
Park Pavilion.

YOU KILLED THE GIRL
IN THE RIVER. I
WANT MONEY. TONIGHT.
AT THE SHEFFIELD
PARK PAVILION. 9:00.
BE THERE OR I
GO TO THE POLICE.

You didn't get away
with it. You killed
the girl. I saw
you. I want $10,000
within a month. Be
at the Sheffield
Park Pavilion at
9:00 tonight.

On the Saturday afternoon following his discovery of Dana/Alison's red scarf, Ben sat in his room writing blackmail notes to Michael.

This was the only way he'd know for sure if Michael really had anything to do with Alison's death.

If Michael showed up at the park...

Well, if he showed up, then he had something to hide. And

219

if he had something to hide ... that could mean only one thing.

Ben's word processor had several different typefaces. He experimented not only with the contents of the note but with the look of it.

A) He couldn't use his standard typeface because Michael might recognize it.

B) He wanted a typeface that would intimidate. Something bold, imposing, arrogant.

C) He wanted to position it in the exact center of the page for maximum effect – heavy black type surrounded by white space.

D) But he mustn't forget about the words themselves. They had to be like a knife in Michael's heart.

Sunday afternoon, Ben was still working on the note. He'd probably written sixty drafts of it by now, tried all eight of the type fonts available to him five times each.

Lynn came upstairs several times to inquire gently about what he was doing. As she said, she hadn't seen him this intense since he used to write those science-fiction stories of his for his creative-writing class in eleventh grade.

Then, suddenly, he simply stopped, an automaton all broken down.

He lay on his bed and thought of how crazy the notion was. No way Michael had killed Alison. For one thing, Michael wasn't a killer. For another thing, Alison had come around to seeing that Steve Conners had acted alone. There was no *reason* for Michael to kill Alison. She'd spent a few times with Michael. Maybe she dropped her red scarf and he picked it up or something.

Nothing sinister.

He was Michael.

His own brother Michael.

This was all crazy.

He got up from the bed and marched over to the computer and pulled out his chair and sat himself down.

His fingers hovered over the proper keys and then he prepared himself.

He was going to erase it all.

Then he was going to call Michael and say, A really funny thing happened, that day I picked up those sci-fi videos, you remember? I was going to put the wallet I bought you in your top bureau drawer. And guess what I found there? This red scarf that belonged to Alison. I was just kind of curious – you know, no big deal – about how you got it and all.

And Michael would say, Oh, man, I forgot to give that to you, didn't I? I gave her a ride home from downtown one day and she left it in the car. But you should have it, kiddo. I'll bring it out to the house tonight.

And it would be that simple.

And that honest.

And then the whole matter would be settled.

Alison's death had been a terrible accident.

And Michael would be—. Well, Michael would be good old Michael. As always.

Night.

The cat's-eye green letters on his screen the only illumination in his room.

He lay on his bed.

Awake.

He still hadn't erased any of the messages he'd planned to send to Michael.

He wasn't quite sure why.

There was something ridiculous about the idea that Michael had murdered Alison.

Just because Ben had found her red scarf in Michael's bureau...

Yet he couldn't quite bring himself to erase the notes, either.

He'd eaten supper, but sparingly.

He'd talked to his mom for a time, but not at any great length.

He'd gone out and checked up on all the critters, including his new kitten.

And yet none of these moments eased or balmed or gentled him as they usually did.

For now, the only reality was his bed and the darkness of his room and the green letters on the screen and the faint hum of the word processor's cooling fan. He slept.

> I SAW WHAT YOU DID.
> YOU KILLED THE GIRL
> IN THE RIVER.
> WE NEED TO TALK.
> THE PAVILION AT
> SHEFFIELD PARK. 9
> TONIGHT. OTHERWISE
> I GO TO SEE CHIEF
> RHYS.

There.

The right one.

The one he was going to send.

He was sure of it now, certain that the only way he could ever rid himself of his suspicions was to send the note and see what Michael did.

If he showed up—

But he wouldn't show up.

He hadn't done anything.

It was Wednesday before Ben actually got around to mailing it.

He used a mail box outside the pharmacy and he felt as if a dozen pairs of eyes were watching him.

And a dozen mouths were whispering about him, too.

There's the kid who thinks his brother is a murderer.

And after all his brother has done for him, too.

'You all right?'

'Sure. Why?'

'You just seem sort of – distracted or something,' Lynn said that afternoon as they were doing such romantic chores as cleaning out critter cages.

Ben forced a smile. 'You worry about me too much, Mom.'
She smiled back. 'Maybe I do.'

Michael would get the letter tomorrow morning, Thursday morning.
Then, if he decided to act on it, he'd be at the pavilion Thursday night at 9:00.
And so would Ben, watching from the woods.

'Oh, I almost forgot to tell you about Michael,' Lynn said at dinner Wednesday night.
'Michael?'
'He has to drive over to the capitol tomorrow for some kind of video exhibition.'
But tomorrow was – Thursday.
Tomorrow was the day he was supposed to get his letter and tomorrow was the day Ben would find out for sure if—
'He wonders if you could work at the store for three hours tomorrow night. His assistant will close up but Michael thinks there'll be a lot of business, so . . .'

The next day, the temperature hit sixty-plus degrees. Despite the date – it was November 6 – people were walking around in short-sleeved shirts and light jackets. A few women with nice legs to display even put on shorts. Kids in school counted the day one molasses-slow minute at a time. Think of all the neat things they could do when the sun was out and the temperature was sixty-four.
All Ben could think about was waiting till dark and getting the letter back from Michael's place.
Having been out of town all day, Michael would be confused by the letter. Did 'tonight' mean the night he'd been out of town or 'tonight' when he was back home again?
Several times during the day, Lynn asked Ben again if everything was all right.
She was obviously worried that he was having another anxiety attack about Alison, and might well start drinking again.
As he worked in the office, and helped her with the various critters, Ben tried to be as focused as possible. But it wasn't easy.

Had his brother murdered Alison?

It was difficult to focus when you had stuff like that on your mind.

Ben put four hours in at the video store.

On the way home, he pulled his old truck up in the alley behind Michael's house, then snuck up the lawn to the screened-in porch.

The mail man always left the mail inside, on the rubber WELCOME mat.

Ben had just gotten inside the porch when a car pulled up to the curb out front. Lights on. Radio playing.

Michael.

Ben dropped down so that nobody could see him from the curb or the front walk.

Shit.

What a terrible time for Michael to get home.

How would he explain his presence here?

Then he thought of a good one.

I wanted to take your mail inside, in case anybody tried to steal it. You remember what happened to old lady Painter? Somebody stole her Social Security check off her front porch.

And Michael would say, Thanks a lot, kiddo. I appreciate it.

The car pulled away.

Ben snuck a look.

Hadn't been Michael at all.

Denise's husband is who it had been.

Sleek new Buick. Forest green.

The way Denise hung around the store so much, Ben had long suspected that something was going on between her and Michael.

Her husband had apparently suspected the same thing.

He was checking up on them.

Ben grabbed the letter he'd sent Michael and got out of there.

Whew.

The impossible weather continued the next day. Sixty-seven degrees by 10:00 a.m. Light headwinds carrying warm breezes. Lots of sunshine and almost no clouds.

Ben typed out a new envelope, took it to a mail box, sent if off.

Work was erratic that day, so late in the afternoon, he went into town. The library again. He sat in the small room where he'd often sat with Alison. They'd held hands under the table and occasionally even snuck a kiss. He teared up once but for the most part it was enjoyable.

On his way back home, when he was parked at a stoplight, Michael pulled up.

'Hey, kiddo,' he said, turning the radio down.

'Hi.'

'I'm headed out to the river. Want to go along?'

'Think I'll pass today, Michael. I'm kind of tired.'

Michael grinned. 'Maybe I'll need you to save my life again.'

'I'm sure you'll be fine.'

Michael watched him a moment. 'You're not pissed at me or anything are you, kiddo?'

'No, of course not.'

'Good. Because if you are, tell me what I did and I'll change it.'

Bring Alison back from the dead, Ben thought.

The light changed.

'You sure you don't want to go? Perfect weather.'

'You go on, Michael. Have a good time.'

Michael smiled. 'I'll sure try, kiddo.'

Then he took off, his powerful car leaving a small stretch of teenage rubber.

When Ben woke up the next day, the temperature was seventy-one degrees.

The critters knew how beautiful the day was. They were going crazy in their cages. Ben soothed them as he fed them. All those who could hobble around would be taken out for a stroll today. He promised them that. This seemed to calm them down a little.

He tried not to think about Michael. Or the letter. Or whether Michael would be in the park tonight at 9:00 p.m.

Two or three days a week, Michael took a two-hour lunch break so he could go home and work out with the weight station he had in the basement. He had a good body and planned to keep it that way.

He pulled up to the curb, hopped out and walked up to the front porch where the mail was tucked under the WELCOME mat.

On his way into the house, he looked through the six envelopes but didn't see much: American Express, Sears, Wal-Mart, The American Film Society, Shell – and one plain white envelope with a Black River Falls postmark. No return address.

Michael Tyler
204 Hecate Lane
Black River Falls

No state name. No zip. Didn't need them in a burg as small as this one.

He was about to open the letter and read it when somebody began pounding on the back door.

Damn.

He wanted to get some weight-lifting in. He hoped it wasn't one of his downtown buddies just stopping by for a chat.

He looked out the window of the back door and still didn't know who it was.

Some guy in a trenchcoat and a blue Chicago Cubs baseball cap and a pair of large dark glasses.

With his head tilted down so Michael couldn't get much of a look at him.

Michael opened the door. 'Yeah?'

And from out of the right pocket, the guy produced a silver pistol and pointed it directly at Michael and said, 'This is a stick-up.'

'What?'

'Yeah. I want your body.'

Then the guy gave Michael a shove back inside, kicked the back door shut behind him, and then proceeded to strip off hat, coat, dark glasses.

It was Denise.

She still had the gun in her hand.

'You scared the hell out of me,' Michael said.

'With this little thing?' Denise said. And then pulled the trigger. It was one of those cunningly designed cap guns that at a quick glance looked like the real thing.

'God, Denise. You shouldn't be here. I thought we had an agreement after that night Paul came over—'

'You haven't been thinking of going to bed with me?'

'Aw, shit, Denise. You know it's not that. You know it's—'

But then she was all over him, right hand undoing his fly as her left hand eased him back against the wall...

The first time, they didn't even make it all the way into the bedroom.

Paul Fletcher did all his business that morning from the cellular phone in his car.

Most of his time was spent following Denise around.

The last couple of days, he'd sensed that she was about to slip back into her old ways. Their sex-life, at least for her part, was routine, and when he tried to be affectionate she seemed bored, even irritable.

No other conclusion he could draw.

She was getting itchy for a few more nights with that nobody sonofabitch Tyler.

So what else could he do?

At a discreet distance, he'd spent the morning following her around.

Beauty parlor. Shopping mall. Coffee shop. And then a brief stop at a gas station where she came out wearing this trenchcoat and Cubs baseball cap.

Why the hell would she wear something like that?

Fletcher found out soon enough.

227

Why she would wear something like that was so she could walk up to Tyler's back door and knock.

And no onlooker would know who she was.

In fact, no onlooker would even know she was a she.

They'd think she was a guy.

In some weird get-up.

So now she was inside.

He tried not to imagine what they were doing.

He tried hard.

He blamed Tyler.

Denise was a pretty face and a nice pair of tits and an even nicer pair of legs. But no brain. In fact, she was more like a child than any adult Fletcher had ever known.

But Tyler.

Despite their big scene in the bedroom that night, when Fletcher had threatened to kill Tyler if he ever came near Denise again ... despite this, Tyler had obviously been sniffing around.

And had once again lured Denise back to him.

The sonofabitch.

The dirty sonofabitch.

He thought he was something.

But he wasn't.

In Black River Falls only the Fletchers and a few of their friends were something.

And that's the way it would always be.

And if Tyler still hadn't gotten the message ...

Well, he'd get the message very soon now.

Very soon.

'You can't say you didn't enjoy it, Michael.'

'If he ever finds us together again, he'll kill us – you know that, don't you, Denise?'

'Maybe I don't care.'

'You seemed to care the night he broke in on us with a pair of guns.'

He was finishing up with his tie, putting it back on for work.

She brushed his hands away, finished knotting it for him.

228

'You're such a little boy sometimes. Can't even tie your tie right.'

She was still naked, pressing her breasts against him, as she finished her work.

'You planning to walk out of here naked?'

She reached down, touched his groin.

'You could go again, if I gave you a few minutes.'

'God, Denise, c'mon. I've got to get back to work and you've got to get out of here.'

She smiled. 'Yessir, if I just gave you a few more minutes...

She brushed his groin again.

'How's she doing?'

'Good.'

Ben had the kitten in his hand, the new one he called Romper.

'She's so cute.'

'So was Elizabeth,' he said.

They were in the barn.

The warm breeze carried the scent of hay and pine from the trees in the surrounding hills.

'You don't have to feel guilty, hon.'

'Guilty?'

'You know. About liking Romper.'

Ben sighed. 'You figured it out.'

'Most people are like that.'

'They are?'

'Sure. I was like that with your dad.'

'You were?'

'Uh-huh. After he died, people were always trying to fix me up with men but every time I'd go out with one of them, I'd feel guilty. You know, like I shouldn't be doing this – and how could I do this when my poor husband was dead?'

'I'm like that about Alison.'

'It's going to take time, hon.'

He lifted the tiny kitten and nuzzled her to his nose. 'And now I'm like that about Romper. I keep trying not to like her, find things wrong with her. That way I won't have to feel guilty about Elizabeth.'

Lynn put her arm around his shoulders and said, 'You know what?'

'What?'

'You're one darned nice young man.'

'You might be a little bit prejudiced.'

'I don't think so. I think I'm being perfectly clinical and objective.'

'Right.'

'So listen, darned nice young man,' she said, leading him out of the barn. 'Why don't we take Romper over to the house and give her a little warm milk?'

He brought the kitten up to his face and addressed her. 'You think you'd like that, Romper? Some nice warm milk?'

'I heard her,' Lynn said. 'She said yes.'

'You've got good ears, Mom.'

'I do?'

'Yeah,' Ben said. 'Most people can't hear cats when they talk.'

She laughed. 'I see what you mean.'

They took Romper over and fed her milk until her little stomach was positively bulbous.

Then the kitten lay down in an empty straw basket near the back door and went to sleep.

Michael had to get back to the store.

As he was hurrying out the door, he saw the white envelope he'd set on top of the dining-room table.

The one with no return address.

The one with the Black River Falls postmark.

He had a terrible premonition. He knew what it was.

Paul Fletcher. Harassing him about Denise.

Michael slit open the top of the envelope and took the letter out.

It didn't take him long to read. By the time he was done, both his stomach and his colon felt in danger of exploding.

His face and arms and armpits were covered with cold, sticky sweat.

I SAW WHAT YOU DID.
YOU KILLED THE GIRL
IN THE RIVER.
WE NEED TO TALK.
THE PAVILION AT
SHEFFIELD PARK. 9
TONIGHT. OTHERWISE
I GO TO SEE CHIEF
RHYS.

So somebody knew what he'd done.

He made a fist and smashed it into the wall so hard, he left a large hole in his wake.

Somebody knew what he'd done.

He was going to find out who it was. And then he was going to kill him.

231

7

The afternoon dragged.

Ben kept busy enough, doing some more painting on the office exterior when the customers slacked off, but nothing could keep him from speculating about tonight.

Please don't be at the park, Michael.

That was his primary thought: that Michael not show up.

He had suffered enough of a loss with Alison and their child. If he also lost his brother...

Just before five, he took a roan for a half-hour ride, a slow one. She hadn't healed completely yet.

He went up in the piney hills, in the fine Indian summer afternoon that smelled of autumnal smoke.

From up here, the farm and Black River Falls lay spread out below in the valley. Everything looked so peaceful, so picture-perfect, one of those little towns you saw on calendars sometimes ... towns you suspected were never visited by illness or envy or greed or bigotry ... or even death.

The church steeple, the town square, the red brick grade school, the piney hills on the far side of the valley...

Ben hoped that there was a town like that somewhere – a town so perfect that everybody kept it a secret – and that he somehow someday learned where it was...

On his way back down the hill, he saw Michael's car come up the drive of the farm.

Michael got out and walked over to the office, where his mother would just be finishing up for the day.

Ben wondered what he wanted.

He didn't just drop in all that often.

233

All this was in pantomime: the two of them walking out of the office, walking over to the car, Michael reaching into the front seat and handing her something, then giving her a kiss and getting back into the car, honking once, and then leaving.

What had Michael given her?

'Michael was here while you were out riding.'

'Oh?' Pretended ignorance. 'How was he?'

'Oh, fine.'

'Really?'

They were eating dinner. She looked up. Smiled. 'You sound surprised. That he was fine, I mean.'

'No, I just meant – well, the last couple of times I saw him he seemed a little hassled was all.'

'Well, if he was, it was his business problems.'

'What's wrong with his business?'

'Well, he didn't want me to tell you this, but one of his short-term loans is coming due and he hasn't got quite enough money to pay it off.'

'What's he going to do?'

'Well, I'm going to loan him a few thousand – as much as I can afford anyway.'

'Will that cover it?'

'Not quite. But he says business has really been picking up so maybe he'll have more cash than he thinks.'

'But he seemed all right, huh? Today, I mean.'

'He seemed fine.'

'Great.'

She took a bite of her salad. 'I just wish he'd settle down.'

'Get married?'

'Or at least get himself one steady girlfriend.'

'Maybe he likes it this way.'

'That's what scares me.'

'What?'

'Maybe he likes it this way so much he'll never change.'

They ate in silence for a time and then Lynn said, 'What's on the agenda for tonight?'

'Probably just ride around a little.'

234

'I'm glad you've been doing that lately.'

'Yeah?'

'Yes. Getting out of the house. It's good for you.'

'I don't go anywhere in particular.'

'Doesn't matter. You get out and see people. That's the thing. You need that, Ben.'

'Yeah, I suppose.'

Then: 'Have you looked on your bed?'

'My bed?'

'Uh-huh. Michael brought you a present.'

'Oh, God.'

'What?'

'He doesn't need to do that.'

'Go look on your bed.'

A few minutes later, Ben came back into the dining room holding a video tape in his hand.

'The uncut version of *Blade Runner*.'

'He said that was your favorite and that this just came out and he wanted to get you your own copy.'

Ben didn't know what to say.

All he knew was that he felt guilty for even considering the possibility that Michael had killed Alison.

How could a guy who was so kind and thoughtful all the time do anything that terrible?

He wished now he hadn't sent the note.

Standing there, holding the tape in his hand, he felt absolutely positively certain that Michael was no killer.

Lynn said, 'You sure couldn't ask for a better brother than that.'

'No,' Ben said, 'I sure couldn't.'

8

Ben wanted to be one of them, one of the lovers who were sitting in cars along the top of the hill in the park. The high school kids were going through the rites of spring, even though this was early November, windows down to let in the fresh 63-degree breezes, radios up nice and loud so that the rock and roll would make the youthful sex all the more exquisite and relentless. There were eight or nine cars, parked at discreet distances, along the top of the hill that overlooked the valley.

He realized he'd never brought Alison up here and he felt a real sadness, not just because they hadn't made love here, but because there were so many places they hadn't gone, so many things they hadn't seen, so many feelings they hadn't experienced together. He could smell her hair, feel the tender warmth of her cheek, hear the gentle reassurance of her soft voice. He ached, and felt a little insane, for the loss of her.

The night was overwhelming with the perfume of the loamy earth and the sight of the full golden moon and the melancholy sound of the lovers talking and laughing.

He felt utterly bereft, as if a part of him, an entire limb, had been amputated.

No, he could never replace Alison. Not ever.

Five minutes later, he made his way down the east side of the steep hill to where a large, open pavilion sat on a ledge of earth. Six large gas grills were set up along the northern perimeter of the pavilion. A large gravel parking lot covered the west side. You could almost hear the hubbub of family reunions here, little kids running around and screaming and giggling; the older men playing horseshoes, clank of shoe against iron post; the young

237

men boasting of their cars, revving the engines to show how hot they were. But not tonight.

Because of the month, the park service had already closed everything up for the winter. The gas grills didn't work, the water had been shut off, electricity no longer coursed through the veins of the wiring.

He was fifteen minutes early.

If Michael came, he would drive up the winding, asphalt road that led to the pavilion, cut his lights, wait for the person who'd sent him the letter.

If he didn't come up the road –

If he didn't come up the road, then everything would be fine. Ben would know that he was wrong, that he still had a brother, still had a family . . .

Fifteen minutes to go.

Ben stayed in the shadows of the forest, looking at the empty pavilion directly beneath him.

Fifteen minutes to go.

Lynn was not what you'd call a world-class housekeeper. She kept the dishes clean and put away, and she kept both upstairs and downstairs bathrooms sparkling. As for the rest of the house . . . As for the rest of the house, she sometimes let it slide. A thin skin of dust on the living-room furniture. Too many old magazines stacked on the far side of the old leather recliner. The living room sending up a faint cloud of dust whenever the kitten ran across it.

No, not a world-class housekeeper.

And sometimes she felt guilty about it, felt that she was letting down her generation of women, the last to be raised on the Donna Reed principles of homemaking.

She was thinking about all this as she walked along the upstairs hallway to the TV room.

Then she happened to glance into Ben's room.

Ben was in no danger of becoming a world-class housekeeper, either. Alison used to tease him about it, in fact. How these tornadoes used to come in his room and really throw things around.

Lynn sighed.

238

Maybe she should spend a few minutes and go in there and pick things up. If nothing else, empty the X-Men wastepaper basket, which was overflowing.

She went to the hall closet, got her dust mop, dust rag, can of wax and a plastic disposal bag and then set to work.

She'd give Ben a nice surprise.

A clean and orderly room to come home to.

She got to work.

After tidying his desk, dusting it, then spraying and polishing it with wax, she bent down and picked up his wastebasket, upending it into the plastic disposal bag.

Three pieces of balled-up paper bounced to the floor, followed by a sheet of paper that had been creased but not folded.

She picked it up and stared casually at the words centered on it:

> YOU KILLED THE GIRL
> IN THE RIVER. I
> WANT MONEY. TONIGHT.
> AT THE SHEFFIELD
> PARK PAVILION. 9:00.
> BE THERE OR I
> GO TO THE POLICE.

Who would Ben be sending such a letter to, and why?

She put down her mop and dust rag and looked inside the balled-up pieces of paper.

They were variations on the same letter.

A terrible coldness ran through her, and now she felt not only grief for the loss of Alison and the child, but fear for the sanity of her son.

Alison's death had been an accident.

Hadn't it?

Three minutes to go.

Darkness.

No sign of any car on the road leading to the pavilion.

An owl somewhere. A distant dog. The faint sound of a car radio from the hill where the high school kids were parked.

The verdant hush of the forest; the loamy heady scent of the sweet Indian summer night.

Suddenly: headlights.

Stabbing the darkness below.

Angling toward the road leading to the pavilion.

Starting to turn toward the pavilion—

Ben excited now. Was it Michael's car?

And then turning away abruptly, following the main road to the pine forest on the cliffs above.

Darkness again.

> I SAW WHAT YOU DID.
> YOU KILLED THE GIRL
> IN THE RIVER.
> WE NEED TO TALK.
> THE PAVILION AT
> SHEFFIELD PARK. 9
> TONIGHT. OTHERWISE
> I GO TO SEE CHIEF
> RHYS.

Now Lynn knew what Ben was doing: setting a trap for somebody, somebody he strongly suspected had killed Alison.

But who?

And what made Ben so sure that Alison had been murdered?

Lynn sank down on his bed, the rumpled pieces of paper in her lap. Poor Ben.

Had he snapped from all his sorrow?

And where was he now?

Was he in the park, waiting for the mystery person to appear?

Not coming.

Ben decided this when his wristwatch showed the time as 9:18.

Michael was not coming.

And Ben felt great relief.

His brother was not a killer.

Ben wanted to go home now and make some popcorn and get down the Hot Tamales and watch the video Michael had surprised him with. He wanted to be a boy again, at least for tonight. He did not want the sapping griefs of adulthood.

Good old Michael.

You couldn't ask for a better brother.

Ben came out from his hiding place in the forest, stepping down on to the grassy area in front of the gas grills.

And that's when he heard the rustling behind him.

But by then it was too late.

Because somebody possessed of astonishing strength had gotten him in a choke-hold and jammed the business end of a pistol hard against his temple.

Ben wanted to cry out for help.

But it was no use.

He was being strangled to death, rapidly losing the ability to breathe.

'Chief Rhys, this is Lynn Tyler.'

'Evening, Lynn.'

'Sorry to be calling so late.'

'No problem, Lynn. What can I do for you?'

'Well, this is a weird question.'

'That's what I'm here for. Weird questions.'

'I'll bet you get tired of them, don't you?'

'Sometimes, I suppose.'

'I'm even kind of embarrassed to say it. About Alison's death, I mean.'

'What about it?'

'Do you think it was accidental?'

'Don't you?'

'Yes, but – I was just wondering.'

'What makes you wonder?'

'Oh, just a TV show I saw.'

'Well, I have a lot of faith in Dr Mason.'

'So do I.'

'And he certainly didn't have any doubts about it being an accident, Lynn.'

'Good. Thanks for saying that. That's exactly what I needed to hear.'

'You sure you feel better?'

'I really do. And thanks.'

'My pleasure, Lynn. Any time.'

'Well, I'll let you get back to your family, Chief. Goodnight.'

'Night, Lynn. Take care of yourself.'

Ben had been thrown face-first to the ground.

His assailant was kneeling on his back.

Ben had never been treated this savagely in his life. His head hurt, his throat was on fire with pain from being choked, and his spine felt as if it would snap from the pressure his assailant was putting on it. He'd also eaten a mouthful of dirt when he was slammed to the ground.

'Why the hell did you send me that note, Ben?'

Only then did Ben realize who was on top of him: Michael.

'Oh, God,' Ben said. 'It's you.'

'This isn't funny, Ben.'

'I know it's not funny. You killed her, didn't you?'

'God damn you, Ben, you don't really believe that, do you?'

'You showed up, didn't you?'

'Only because I wanted to find out who'd written the letter.' Pause. 'I'm going to let you up, all right?'

Ben said nothing.

All he could think of was that Michael had killed Alison.

'All right, Ben?'

'All right.'

Michael jumped off Ben and stood up.

Ben was a long time getting to his feet, still feeling the physical shock of Michael throwing him to the ground so hard, and the mental shock of Michael being here at all.

Ben tasted blood in his mouth; felt blood on his knees from where a rock had slashed him.

'I'm sorry I hurt you. I didn't recognize you.'

Ben kept his head down, not knowing what to say, what to feel, what to think.

'Are you hearing me, Ben?' Michael said, pushing his face close to Ben.

Ben swung on him, connecting his right fist to the side of Michael's face.

242

Then he started punching wild, sometimes connecting, sometimes not.

Michael kept ducking and bobbing, backing up to avoid the punches. 'Ben, listen, you keep this shit up and I'm going to hurt you, all right?'

But all Ben could think of was hurting the person who had killed Alison and the child.

He caught his brother with a good left hook right in the eye.

And then Michael suddenly fought back.

Stood his ground, angled his shoulder downward, and then drove a fist deep into Ben's stomach.

Ben cried out and dropped to his knees.

Michael moved in closer, landing a very heavy punch to Ben's head.

Ben cried out again, fell face-forward, his head grazing the small sharp rock that had cut his knee.

Ben moaned, fearing he was going to vomit. He had never felt physical pain such as he had now. He was all pain – weak and dizzy and throbbing, throbbing pain.

'You hit me again, I'll hurt you even more, you understand me, Ben?'

Michael stood over his brother, his breath coming in hot ragged gasps.

He was sweaty and his hair was mussed.

Michael almost never looked disheveled this way. It was his pride.

'You killed her,' Ben said, looking up at him.

'Bullshit.'

Then Ben had to drop his head again, trying to regain poise and strength and focus.

Half a minute later, he looked up at Michael again. 'She was right. You killed her friend Dana and you were afraid Alison was going to turn you over to Rhys. That's why you had to kill her.' Tears seared his eyes and voice. 'Did you kill Conners and that private detective guy, too?'

The foot came from nowhere, a sharp toe angling up and catching Ben in the ribs.

He tumbled all the way over this time, his scream lost when his face touched his chest as he collapsed inward.

'You stupid bastard,' Michael said. 'Why the hell did you have to push this thing? Why the hell couldn't you have left it alone? Even the god damn coroner said her death was accidental.'

Ben just stared at him there in the deep shadow and moonlight, the night so sweet with aromas and animals and the ageless secrets of the night forest.

'You killed her, didn't you?'

'You want me to say it?'

'Yeah, I do, Michael. I want to hear you say it.'

Michael paced off a small circle, running his right hand through his hair. Once, he paused and looked up at the sky, as if imploring the gods for help.

'She had those letters that Dana had written her about me,' he said, turning back to Ben, who was now struggling to his feet.

'She burned them.'

Michael shook his head miserably. 'I didn't know that until it was too late.' He then raised his eyes and looked directly at Ben. 'It was an accident, Ben. I didn't mean for her to go over the Falls.'

'An accident. Right.'

'It was, kiddo. I'm telling you the truth.'

'Don't call me kiddo.'

'I've been calling you that since I was eight years old.'

'Not any more. It makes me sick to hear you say it.'

'I'm your brother, Ben. Doesn't that make any difference to you?'

'Yeah,' Ben said, the tears in his eyes and voice again. 'You're my brother and you killed my girl and my baby.'

And then he started crying. Couldn't help it. Couldn't stop himself. He put his head down and began to sob.

Michael came over and tried to comfort him but Ben pushed him away violently.

'It was an accident, Ben. It really was.'

Ben started walking then.

He had no idea where he was going.

He was just walking ... somewhere.

'Where you going?'

But Ben was not about to answer.

He just headed for the forest.

He wanted to be alone in the forest.

244

Why couldn't the real forest be like the Disney forest, all those happy fanciful little creatures there to cheer you up?

'You better think hard about it, Ben, before you go see Rhys. You better think of what this'll do to Mom. You know about Grandad – and now me.'

Ben stopped.

'She couldn't handle it all over again, Ben. The scandal and the trial. She'd never make it through and you know that.'

Ben was still frozen in place.

Michael's tone had changed now. He obviously knew that his words had had their desired effect on his brother.

Michael had played the Mother card and won the poker game.

No way Ben could put his mother through it all again.

No way at all.

Michael walked up to him, put a hand on his shoulder.

'You'll find yourself a girl, Ben. Alison wasn't right for you, anyway. She was a bitch.'

He was going to say more but Ben didn't give him time.

Ben swung his entire body around and put a fist deep into Michael's face, so hard that even Michael was stunned by the force of the blow.

He tottered backwards, arms windmilling to keep him upright.

But Ben wasn't done.

He jumped Michael and threw him to the ground and then started hitting him.

Michael cried out.

Ben felt hot blood wet on his knuckles and hands. Michael's blood. It felt great.

He kept hitting Michael and hitting Michael and so fast and so often that Michael lost his ability to defend himself.

And then somebody was there with a flashlight and a familiar female voice said, 'My God, Ben, look what you're doing to your brother!'

Ben glanced up to see his mother standing there, her flashlight in one hand, a piece of paper in the other.

'Now get up, Ben,' she said. 'Get up.'

9

After the late news, Chief Rhys took Puffy out for a walk. Puffy was a Pekinese and Rhys hated the damned thing. It was like a toy except for the fact that it all too often peed on the carpet. That was where a toy had it over a Pekinese as far as Rhys was concerned.

As usual, Puffy set the pace.

Rhys liked to walk up the hill on Highland Street and then come back along the railroad tracks. Railroad yards always reminded Rhys of when he'd been a kid and when trains had been his first love, big black fierce freight engines and sleek sylvan moon-yellow passenger trains tearing through the very fabric of the night. Flying in airplanes bored his ass off.

But then, looking down at the tiny copper-colored dust mop at the other end of the leash, he realized that Puffy bored his ass off, too.

Dogs like Puffy were strictly for women, and only certain kinds of women at that.

He'd had a great big face-licking black Lab for eighteen years. The dog had been great with the kids, but during that time he'd always had to make his wife a promise. When Genghis passed on, Irene got to pick their next dog.

Enter Puffy: mincing, crabby, self-absorbed.

But Puffy didn't hold his attention for long tonight.

He was soon enough thinking about the call he'd had earlier from Lynn Tyler.

What the hell had that been all about?

Where had she gotten the idea that maybe Alison's death hadn't been an accident?

The funny thing was, Rhys had always been troubled by the 'accident' too, but without quite knowing why.

And now Lynn called.

She was an intelligent, sensible woman, not one given to flights of fancy.

So if she had questions—

The subject of Alison was still on Rhys' mind when he topped the hill and looked down into the railroad yard below, two black engines parked silent in front of the roundhouse, several lines of boxcars parked on the tracks gleaming in the moonlight. From inside the roundhouse came the rough loud talk of the railroad men, hearty talk that for Rhys was imbued with the legends of riding the rails. As usual, he had the urge to start his life all over again, to become a railroad man instead of a small-town cop...

Puffy peed on Rhys' foot.

'Aw, dammit, Puffy,' Rhys said. 'You did it again. You're supposed to go on the grass, not my foot.'

Puffy looked up belligerently and yipped.

Not barked. Puffy wasn't big enough to bark.

She yipped.

As if to say, you should be honored that I chose your foot to piss on.

Then they walked on, back to the house, and Rhys, his left shoe a bit soggy with doggie pee, started thinking about Lynn's mysterious phone call.

Lynn grabbed Ben by the shoulder of his jacket and pulled him off his brother.

Lynn had never seen Ben this way, so angry that his fists had been smashing again and again into Michael's face.

By any standard, Michael was not only stronger but far more agile than his younger brother.

If anybody should be on top, raining blows down, it should have been Michael...

Ben finally gave in to her.

Allowed her to jerk him to his feet.

Allowed her to push him away from Michael so that she could kneel down and see what damage he'd done.

In the shadowy night, she had difficulty seeing Michael's face in any detail. But there were dark splashes of blood on his nose, mouth and chin, and the way his breath came in gasps, she could tell that he had been hurt both physically and mentally.

Michael would never have expected Ben to dominate him this way. Slender Ben, decent Ben...

She stood up to help Michael to his feet. He seemed to be recovering physically but his face was still angry, still shocked and humiliated.

'I want to know what's going on here,' she said.

Michael daubed blood from his lips. 'We had a disagreement.'

'Oh, really? I couldn't tell,' Lynn said.

'It's just between us,' Ben said. 'It's nothing for you to worry about.'

'Seeing my sons rolling around on the ground, trying to kill each other isn't something to worry about?'

She realized she wasn't helping the situation. She forced herself to take several deep breaths. Fear had settled in her stomach and was slowly working its way up into her chest.

Did Michael know something about Alison's death?

But that was impossible. Michael was no killer.

'We need to calm down,' she said. 'And get this family back together.'

Michael was putting himself back together, tucking in his shirt, running a comb through his hair.

In her calmest voice, she said, 'Now I want to know what's going on here.'

'It's over, Mom, it's nothing to worry about,' Ben said. 'We just had a little disagreement is all.'

'This was hardly a "little disagreement."'

Michael came over and put his arm around Lynn. 'After he was in my house one day, I was missing this watch and I asked him if he'd seen it. He took it the wrong way – like I was accusing him of stealing it or something – and then he just took a swing on me.'

'Why were you up here in the first place?' she said to Michael.

Michael looked stricken for a moment. 'Well, uh, I just saw him driving around and I stopped him. And that's when I asked him about the watch.'

'Then where's your car? And where's Ben's truck?'

Ben picked up now: 'We parked over there and just went for a little walk.'

'A little walk,' she said. 'And why did you send Michael this note?'

Ben and Michael stared at each other, then Michael looked away.

'We just had a misunderstanding is all,' Ben said. He sounded miserable.

'You're both lying to me and you know it.'

'There's nothing to be upset about, Mom, honest,' Michael said.

He put out his hand and walked over to Ben.

They shook, and then Michael embraced him.

They clapped each other on the back.

'I love you, kiddo,' Michael said.

'I love you, too,' Ben said.

Michael turned back to his mother. 'Now does that look like we're still mad or anything?'

She knew they were lying to her but what could she do? Because of the notes she'd found in Ben's wastebasket, she knew that he was going to meet the person he suspected of having killed Alison.

Michael.

There was no other way to explain his presence up here, no other way to explain the fight they'd been having.

But she knew there was no more to say.

They obviously weren't going to tell her the truth.

She looked again at Michael. The blood on his face, the slightly wounded aspect of his gaze – he seemed uncharacteristically vulnerable.

'So you're not going to say any more?'

'There's nothing more to say, Mom,' Ben said.

'Then I guess I'll go back home,' she said, suddenly weary.

'Everything's fine, Mom,' Ben said.

'And that's true, Mom. Everything really is fine.'

She took a last look at them there in the moonlight, her two sons, and left.

Three hours later, Chief Rhys was in his robe and pajamas eating half of a bologna sandwich with his right hand while he held a Robert B. Parker novel in his left. If only he was as good at law enforcement as Spenser. And if only he were as good a shot, as good a chef, as good a lover and as good at being an all-around great guy. Then he'd really be on to something.

After getting back from his walk earlier in the evening, he'd gone up and crawled into bed next to his wife and made a little love and read a little Parker and then gone off to sleep.

But an hour and a half later he'd been wide awake, staring at the streetlight patterns on the ceiling, needing to pee but too lazy to get up and do it, and thinking very hard about Lynn Tyler and her phone call.

Rhys had started thinking about the connection between Steve Conners and Michael Tyler.

Thick as thieves, they'd been; thick as thieves. And if one had been involved in a murder then there was a good possibility that the other was, too...

He started to bring the sandwich up to his mouth, not really taking his eyes from the book, when he heard a growl and looked over to see Puffy sitting on the table, eating the other half of the sandwich for him.

'Oh, dammit, Puffy,' Rhys said.

The dog did look kind of cute, with mustard and mayo and ketchup all over her face. She must have been eating the damned thing for the last couple of minutes.

Puffy growled again.

'She's not going to like this, you know,' Rhys said, 'me feeding you a bologna sandwich. Remember what the candy bar did to your bowels? She's gonna get us both for this.'

Rhys sighed and then started feeding the rest of his sandwich to the dog.

It sure did look cute, no doubt about it.

All the time he was feeding Puffy, his mind was drifting back to Lynn Tyler and the phone call.

Something going on there.

No doubt about it.

Something really heavy going on there and he aimed to find out what.

Puffy finished the sandwich in eight bites and then started growling for another one.

No way she could sleep.

She'd tried praying, she'd tried biofeedback, she'd tried imaging pleasant pictures ... but sleep hadn't come.

251

She was just rolling over on her side, sighing and thinking of maybe turning on the light and reading her new Dean Koontz paperback, when she heard him in the drive, gravel popping beneath the weight of his old truck.

Ben.

In moments, she was gliding out of bed and into her robe, headed downstairs.

'Oh, great.'

'A lot of people would be happy to see me.'

'Yeah, well I'm not a lot of people. I'm me. And I want you out of my house. Right now.'

'Excuse me for living.'

'I'm not up for any of your bullshit, Denise.'

'Well, I'm not up for any of yours, either. I want you to fuck me. Is that like a real chore or something?'

'It is tonight.'

She was lying on his bed in the streetlight shadows, naked except for her red bikini panties.

Her voice softened. 'Did something happen?'

'Denise, I really don't want to see you tonight.'

'Maybe I can help you.'

'I need a lot more help than getting laid, Denise. Believe me.'

'Wow. You're really down.' She patted the bed next to her. 'C'mon, lie here and talk to me.'

'Denise—'

'I won't try to take advantage of you, I promise.'

'Very funny.'

'You know how I rub your neck and your head sometimes?'

'Denise—'

'I'll do that. That always relaxes you.'

'Oh shit, what's the use?'

He lay down next to her on the bed. His entire body was plank straight, plank stiff.

He was well beyond the curative powers of sex. Well beyond.

She jumped up and then straddled him so that she could rub his temples and forehead and eyelids.

He had to admit it felt good.

As did her bottom riding his hips. She had a great butt, Denise did. A great butt.

Down the alley, Paul Fletcher thought: You bitch, you stinking bitch. You don't care what people think about me at all, do you?

A Fletcher woman running around on her husband.

As if we were just some frigging low-rent family.

You bitch; you bitch.

'You want a Pepsi or something?'

'No thanks, Mom.'

'There's cake.'

'No, thanks.'

They were in the kitchen.

'I'd be happy to make you some eggs. You know how you like scrambled eggs.'

'Mom, I'm fine. Really.'

'You want me to go upstairs?'

He glanced at her, shook his head, went over and sat down at the kitchen table. Then he stared at his fists.

The windows were open and a breeze feathered the curtains, smelling of earth and smoke from the piney hills. The kitchen was small and neat and tidy. She thought of all the times she and her husband had sat out here looking through bills that were overwhelming them. She got sad for him, dying so young, having his life abbreviated that way, and then sad for herself. It hadn't always been easy, fighting the prejudice of the town for what her father had done, and raising two boys on top of it.

'I know you want to talk, Mom.'

'I think you owe me a talk.'

He looked up. 'Are you mad?'

'A little, I guess.'

His eyes went back to his fists. 'I just had this crazy idea. I wanted to blame somebody for Alison's death – and I blamed Michael.'

'But why Michael, honey?'

He shrugged. 'Because they never got along, because he never particularly liked her.'

'And for that reason you thought he killed her?'

'I didn't say I was being rational, Mom.'

'And that's why you mailed him the note?'

'Yeah.'

'That's the only reason?'

'Yeah.'

'Are you telling me the truth, Ben?'

'Yeah.'

'I'd appreciate it if you'd look at me when you said that.'

He raised his gaze to hers. 'I'm telling you the truth, Mom.'

'You don't think Michael had anything to do with her death?'

'I don't think Michael had anything to do with her death.'

She walked over and took his head and pressed it gently to her chest. 'I'm glad you know better now, honey, about Michael. He could never do anything like that.'

'I know, Mom. And I'm sorry.'

'We have to be strong – the three of us. We're a family.'

'I know, Mom.'

She let him go and said, 'I love you, Ben.'

'I love you, too, Mom.'

'I'll still make you those scrambled eggs.'

She looked so pale and worn sometimes. 'You need some rest, Mom. Why don't you go to bed?'

'I'd be happy to—'

'I know, Mom. But I'd rather have you get some sleep.'

'I am kind of tired, I guess.'

'You go on up.'

'You sure you're all right?'

'I'm fine.'

'Michael loves you.'

'I know, Mom.'

'We're a family, Ben. After what your grandfather did – and after your father died–' Tears came then, filling her eyes and voice, weary tears. 'We have to stick together, hon.'

He went to her and held her and was struck by how fragile she felt. He'd always thought of her as forever young. But she was getting older, and more tired. And sometimes sadder.

That's why he could never go to the police about Michael. Because of what it would do to her.

'You go on up, now.'

She kissed him on the cheek. 'Thanks, hon. Thanks a lot.'

'You never had this problem before.'

'I warned you,' Michael said.

'Paul has it all the time, when he's been drinking, I mean.'

'I'm sure he'd be glad you told me that.'

'It's nothing to be ashamed of,' Denise said.

'Don't you have to be home by eleven or something?'

'He's at the Moose tonight.' She giggled. 'Isn't that a stupid name for a club – the Moose?' She paused. 'You want me to try again?'

'It's no use.'

And it wasn't.

They'd been in bed for more than an hour now. She'd used her fingers, her pelvis, her mouth. But she'd gotten no response.

He wasn't embarrassed.

He was too distracted to be embarrassed.

All he could think of was one thing: now he would have to kill Ben, and make it look as if Ben had committed suicide.

There wasn't any choice now.

'You mind if I do myself?' she said. 'And use your finger.'

'If you want to.'

'Maybe when you feel me get hot, you'll get hot.'

'Maybe.'

'It works for Paul sometimes.'

'Good.'

'Did I ever tell you that you've got a much bigger wiener than Paul has?'

'I think you mentioned that once, yes.'

She giggled again. 'He thinks he's such a big deal. He should look at himself in the mirror sometime.'

Ben stayed in the kitchen for an hour with the lights out.

He listened to the night. To the winds, which the nearby Mesquakie Indians said sang songs to those who knew how to listen. To the owls and birds and horses restless in these dark and secret hours. And to the river. Ever since Alison's death, he'd hated the river but tonight, for some reason, it comforted him, as it had comforted him all his boyhood. He needed to be one with the river again. It was time. The river had not killed Alison. The river was his friend. Michael had killed Alison. Michael was not his friend.

Sometime after midnight, there in the dark, a rain came up and made loud noises as it pelted the roof and windows, and made the critters in their cages restless and noisy.

After a long, long time of the rain, Ben put his head down and cried.

10

After Ben went into town for supplies the next morning, Lynn took advantage of the sunny day by raking up some of the rain-soaked leaves on the lawn. She'd done her chores and seen her patients. Nobody else was scheduled for the entire day.

She had worked up a healthy sweat and was enjoying herself with garden gloves and rake, and exercising the long muscles in her arms, when she saw the Chief's white Ford with the whip antenna and the official door decals pull up in her driveway.

She thought back to her girlhood.

When the police were closing in on her father, they came out twice, sometimes three times a day. They always came up to the door and knocked politely, they always asked if they could sit in the living room and talk, they always asked Lynn if she would go play outdoors.

The neighbors loved the high drama.

She always saw them behind their lace curtains, whispering and pointing, excited in the way children are excited by a gift.

This was a gift, the drama of the police closing in, closing in, and the trial to follow, and then the execution. You couldn't get much more exciting than an execution.

'Morning, Lynn.'

'Morning, Chief.'

'You got a good day for raking.'

'It's gorgeous.'

All the time they talked, he came closer, closer, crisp in his khaki uniform and campaign hat.

'This is what I do when business is slow – yard work. And I like it.'

'It's always nice to be outdoors,' Rhys said, his warm blue eyes watching her. 'I'll bet you know why I'm here.'

She nodded. 'My phone call.'

'I have to admit, you got me curious last night.'

'I was afraid of that.' She leaned on her rake and smiled. 'I saw this dumb TV show.'

'Oh?'

'Uh-huh. About this girl who drowned and everybody thought it was an accident but it wasn't.'

'What channel was it on? I must've missed it.'

She had to quickly cover her lie. 'Since we got that satellite dish with all the cable channels, I'm never sure what channel I'm watching.'

'But this show—'

'Oh, it was a silly show. I shouldn't have bothered you.'

His eyes narrowed. 'You think Alison's death wasn't an accident?'

'No. I told you, it was a silly show. And I was being silly about it.'

'Then you don't really have any suspicions?'

She graced him with her nicest, most self-effacing smile. 'I'm just getting weird in my old age is all I can figure out.' Then she composed herself and looked very serious. 'No, I don't have any suspicions at all.'

'Alison drowned?'

'Alison drowned.'

'You're sure of that?'

'I'm positive of that, Chief.'

She'd been so stupid to call him.

Now he'd be closing in, closing in – the way his years-ago predecessor had closed in on her father.

And then, thank God, the phone rang.

'I'd better get that,' she said, hurrying to the office.

She was pleased to find that Mrs Dunne's dog Henry had stepped on some broken glass last night and required a 'look-see' as Mrs Dunne always said.

'I suppose you're just terribly busy, Doctor.'

'Not at all. Bring him on out right away.'

'Are you sure? That would be great because I've got my Bridge club this afternoon and—'

'See you in five minutes, Mrs Dunne.'

The woman lived nearby.

Lynn went back out to Chief Rhys.

'Afraid I'll have to excuse myself. Mrs Dunne's Henry cut his paw on some glass.'

Chief Rhys smiled. 'Poor thing.'

'Mrs Dunne?'

'No, Henry. Because he has to put up with Mrs Dunne.' He cinched the edge of his campaign hat between thumb and forefinger, angling it just the way he liked it. 'You sure you don't have any suspicions, Lynn?'

'I'm sure.'

'It was just a TV show?'

'It was just a TV show.'

'And you were being silly?'

'And I was being silly.'

He looked directly at her. 'That's the part that surprises me, Lynn.'

'What is?'

'You being silly. You're not a silly woman, Lynn.'

'Well, I guess everybody's silly once in a while.'

His gaze was still upon her. 'Yes, I suppose so.'

'Sorry but I'd better get ready for Henry.'

A slight smile parted Rhys' lips. 'And for Mrs Dunne.' He touched the brim of his campaign hat in a kind of mock salute. 'Take care, Lynn.'

'You, too.'

Then she went in to get ready for Henry.

And for Mrs Dunne.

Until eleven o'clock that morning, Michael had no idea how he was going to kill his brother. Then he walked over to Lurleen's Coffee Shop for his morning break, and the opportunity he was looking for walked right up to him.

Ben came down the street, his arms loaded up with three bags from the hardware store.

'Hey, kiddo.'

Ben winced. 'I told you not to call me that.'

They were standing on the street, their conversation interrupted every minute or so by somebody saying good morning to them. The temperature was sixty-seven degrees again, and the sky cloudless.

'I called out to the house, and Mom said you had the afternoon off.'

'Yeah. So what?'

'I thought maybe we could do something together.'

'No way.'

'This is really bullshit, Ben. Your attitude and everything.'

'I can't believe you, Michael. You don't regret anything that happened, do you?'

'Life goes on.'

'Yeah, your life does anyway. But not Alison's – nor the little girl she was carrying.'

'You're not even sure it was a little girl.'

'Alison was sure.'

Michael smiled coldly. 'She have psychic powers, did she?'

Ben started to walk past him. Michael grabbed Ben's arm. 'Why don't you come over to my place and we'll have a talk?'

'Take your hand off me.'

'We need to talk, Ben.'

'There's nothing to say.'

'I've got some new videos you'd like.'

'I'm going on the river.'

'I thought you hated the river.'

Ben looked at him coldly. 'Now that I know you killed her and not the river – now I'm going on the river again. By myself.'

And that was when it all came clear to Michael.

How he was going to do it.

'I wish you'd change your mind.'

'I want to go now, Michael.'

Michael leaned close to him. 'Believe it or not, kiddo, I still love you. Even after all the pain you've laid on me lately.'

Ben just glared at him and walked away.

An hour and a half later, Michael came through the woods to the edge of his mother's farm.

From here he watched as Ben came out the back door of the house and got into his truck and drove away.

If this was a typical day, and he had no reason to think otherwise, his mother, having fixed lunch for herself and Ben, having done the dishes after Ben left, would be out soon.

She would go into her office and stay there for most of the afternoon.

Then Michael would sneak into the house, into Ben's room, and use his computer.

In the meanwhile, he provided a nice lunch for a dozen or so hungry mosquitos.

What the hell was keeping his mother, anyway, he wondered after he had waited an additional fifteen minutes.

Then she was there, coming down off the back porch, carrying Ben's new kitten with her to the office.

He had to move fast.

And move now.

Ben was thinking about Indians again – about what this land had been like five hundred or a thousand years ago – as he rowed his way downstream.

He could hear the drums in the deep forest; hear the war chants; see the braves in their ferocious battle paint astride their barebacked steeds.

A simpler, better time, the way Ben reckoned.

Then he tried to think of nothing at all, to simply drift on this ancient river, to note the way the weeping willows drooped along the banks at this particular spot, to note the way the deer stood atop a rock promontory and looked down on the river, a mother and her fragile offspring.

As always, he decided to put in near the Falls themselves, to stay just on the edge of the fastest current and deepest water.

Memories came to him, so many afternoons with Alison, so many words that would always remain in his mind and heart, so many visions of Alison...

Inside and upstairs in less than a minute.

And certain that he wasn't seen.

Ben's room.

The computer.

Sitting at the keyboard.

261

The screen lighting up.

Finding the proper directory, the one Ben would actually use to compose such a letter.

C:\LETTERS

There. That one.

Into the proper file.

Typing:

Dear Mom,

By the time you read this, I'll be dead. I know that my death will devastate you but I don't believe you would want me to go on suffering the way I have since Alison died.

I'm ashamed of myself for even thinking that Michael had something to do with her death. He didn't. I just needed somebody to blame. I'm just having too much greif.

I could go on and on here, Mom, but the fact is I just don't want to live any more. I'm going to go over the Falls the same way Alison did.

I love you, Mom. I hope you understand that and don't hate me too much for what I've done.

Ben

Perfect.

An envelope from the bottom right-hand drawer.

Tape the envelope to Ben's door.

And leave.

Leave quickly.

'You all right?' said the police officer Chief Rhys hated more than any other police officer in the world, his son-in-law Vic, who took advantage of being the son-in-law every chance he got.

They were in the coffee room and Vic had been sitting across from Rhys for the past ten minutes and Rhys hadn't said a word.

Vic had tried football, the dirty channel on the local cable station, the mayor's proposed cutback on the police budget and his usual hint that he'd make a great Assistant Police Chief when Verne Malley retired.

Rhys had said not a word.

Now he said, 'Huh?'

'I asked if you was all right.'

'I'm fine. Why wouldn't I be fine?'

'Because when you get real quiet like this, something's always wrong.'

'Nothing's wrong.'

'It was that phone call, wasn't it – from Lynn Tyler?'

'How'd you know about that phone call?'

'I overheard you telling Verne.'

'You know something, Vic?'

'What?'

'You're a regular spy.'

'What the hell's that supposed to mean?'

'It's supposed to mean that you're always lurking around, spying on people.'

'No call to use language like that about me. Lurking.'

'You do lurk, Vic. You lurk all the time.'

'I've never lurked a day in my life.'

'You lurk every chance you get.'

'That's a hell of a thing to say to family.'

'You're not family, Vic. You just happened to get my daughter knocked up and you knew I'd box your ears if you didn't marry her. That doesn't make you family at all.'

Vic left and Rhys went back to thinking about Lynn Tyler's strange phone call last night.

11

Michael reached the river about an hour after Ben had put into the water.

He came around a sandy bend on the shore and there Ben was, maybe an eighth of a mile away.

Fishing.

Michael took off his shoes and socks and then decided to take off his shirt, too.

He needed all his freedom for doing the job properly – fast and certain.

Fast and certain.

That's how it had to be done.

Whenever he thought about the day he gave Alison casting lessons, he smiled.

He'd made a big macho thing of doing this and doing that – using the wrist just so, angling outward this way and not that – a big macho man ... and then she'd whupped his ass.

She wasn't any expert but neither was Ben.

And she'd been at least as good as he'd been.

He'd spent half an hour sulking. A kid like Ben didn't get many chances to play the macho guy very often and then he went and screwed it all up.

But true to her fashion, Alison got him laughing about it.

'You should've seen your face,' she'd smiled gently. 'Just like Clint Eastwood.'

At first, he'd resented it, of course, the way she kidded him. But slowly he began to see that she thought it was endearing, what he'd done, and that her teasing him was just another way of expressing her love.

Alison.

Oh Alison.

I love you so much.

And I always will . . .

He was in the boat, thinking of Alison, when he saw Michael come up over the side of the boat, and turn the entire craft upside down, dumping Ben into the water.

Panic.

Getting tangled up in the fishing line.

Trying to orient himself in the dark and bubbling water.

Michael was going to kill him.

He should have known that.

He was so naive.

Fighting his way back up to the surface of the water, seeing daylight play on the top of the water like burnished gold.

Fighting for breath.

Lungs hot and heaving.

Needed air. Badly.

The surface was only moments away.

His arms and legs propelling him upward.

And then arms grabbing him, entangling him the way the fishing line had done.

Ben was able to flail with both his arms and legs but it did no good. Even when his foot made contact with Michael's shin, it seemed to make no difference.

Michael's grip was astonishing.

Moving—

At first, Ben wasn't sure where they were going, and then he realized: the Falls.

Another accident.

That's why Michael was careful not to fight back when Ben started kicking and biting.

Michael didn't want any untoward bruises or cuts on Ben.

Another accident.

Ben surfaced momentarily, taking in what seemed to be a dirigible's worth of air, fighting, crying out, trying to push away from his brother.

Then he was submerged again as Michael's sheer force over-whelmed him.

Blindness.

Lack of air.

Disorientation.

Then the water—

Faster.

Colder.

Roaring now.

The Falls were just ahead.

Knowing he was about to die gave Ben more strength.

He slammed into Michael so hard that his older brother lost his grip for a crucial second.

Ben, triumphant, tried to swim away.

He sensed freedom and began using his arms to pull himself ahead quickly.

For several feet, he seemed to be making real progress.

But then the pull of the Falls began sucking him ineluctably backwards.

And then Michael was there again, wrapping him up once again, pulling him toward the source of the deafening roar that filled them both.

Ben continued to fight, catching his brother several more times in chin and groin, but Michael was not about to lose him again.

They broke surface once more, Ben trying a last time to yank himself free of his brother's clutches.

Michael smiled. 'You're going to die, kiddo.' he shouted above the roar. 'You're going to die just the way your girlfriend did.'

And then Michael took him down beneath the water and tugged and jerked his little brother to the edge of the Falls.

'So long, kiddo,' Michael bellowed.

And then pushed him.

Ben turned around, facing Michael, but was pulled under by the force of the rushing water.

Then he vanished.

Once, twice, three times his hand came up above the foaming, frothing waters.

Then it disappeared.

After a few moments there was a scream but its sound didn't get past the wall of roaring noise.

Ben reappeared briefly, flailing wildly, just as he reached the very edge of the Falls.

Then he vanished again behind the crushing rush and tumble of the water spilling downward.

He no longer screamed.

He no longer flailed.

He no longer fought.

The last thing Michael had to do was bring Ben's rowboat down to the Falls and send it, bouncing, over.

Then he swam to shore and went back to town.

12

About three o'clock, having checked on all her animals, and not having much to do in the office, Lynn switched the phone over to the house.

She decided that today would be a good time to unclutter the TV room Ben had been using lately. Ben was one of those boys who could eat, read a paperback, scratch a cat and watch TV all at the same time. He tended to leave a mess.

She was just passing his bedroom door, just seeing the envelope taped to the door, when the phone rang.

She snatched the envelope from the door, walked into her own bedroom and picked up the phone.

'Dr Tyler.'

'It's Chief Rhys, Lynn. You need to get to the hospital as soon as possible.'

'I guess you know what I'm asking, Doctor,' Lynn said.

He nodded. 'I wish I could give you a definitive answer. Right now, I'd say his chances are fifty-fifty.'

She'd known Dr Sullivan the past twenty years. He'd treated the boys most of their lives. Right now, standing in the hallway of the ER, he looked older and grayer than ever before.

'He's a fighter,' Lynn said, obviously trying to make herself feel better.

'Yes, he is.'

'And if anybody can survive it, he can.'

'I suspect that's true, Lynn.' He nodded to the door he'd just walked out of. 'I'd better get back in there.'

She went over and sat down and read the letter again several times. Ben's letter.

The one saying that he wanted to kill himself.

Night filled the windows now. She felt a great melancholy, fear that Ben would die, and a sense of vast, almost unutterable loneliness.

Food carts clattered by, going in and out of patient rooms. Visitors started arriving. Most of them knew who Lynn was and nodded to her sympathetically. In small towns, everybody knew everything.

She read the letter one more time, and just as she was finishing, Michael came running down the hall.

'I was over in Valleyville, Mom. I just heard about Ben and I came right over. How's he doing?'

'The doctor says he has a fifty-fifty chance.'

Michael took her in his arms and hugged her. 'It's so crazy.'

'He left a letter.'

'A letter? Ben did?'

When they parted, she said, 'There's a little coffee room over there. The doctor knows where to find me. I could use some coffee.'

'Fine.'

The room was nothing more than a Mr Coffee machine and a table with four chairs. They were the only two people in it.

They got themselves black coffee and sat down.

'You said there was a letter?'

She nodded. 'He said he wanted to kill himself.'

'Oh God, Mom—'

'And he said he was sorry for thinking that you had anything to do with Alison's death.'

He reached across the table and touched her hand. 'He's going to be all right, Mom. I'm sure of it.'

She looked down at her lap, where the letter lay. 'Do you want to see it?'

'If you want me to.'

'I just didn't have any idea he was so near to – to killing himself.'

'The poor kid. I should've spent more time with him. I've been pretty darned selfish, when you come right down to it.'

'Here's the letter.'

Michael took it, shaking his head all the time. He opened it up and scanned it and said, 'I just wish he would have told me. How really bad off he was, I mean.'

'All the grief he's had,' Lynn said. Then: 'Did you notice that word?'

'Word?'

'"Grief."'

'In his letter, you mean?'

'Right. In his letter.'

Michael scanned the letter once more. 'Oh. Right. Right here.'

'It's misspelled.'

'It is?'

'Uh-huh. "I before E except after C." That old rule.'

Michael grinned. 'I thought I was the only one who made mistakes like that.'

Lynn didn't smile. 'You are. Ben didn't write that letter.'

'Ben didn't write that letter? Then who did?'

'You.'

He stared at her a long, hard moment. 'What the hell are you talking about?'

'You wrote the letter and then pushed Ben over the Falls.'

'Mom, that's crazy! I love Ben – you know that.'

'You killed Alison and he knew it and that scared you and so you tried to kill Ben, too.'

'God, Mom—'

She put her hand out. 'I want the letter back.'

'I don't think it'd be good for you to have the letter back.'

Michael folded it in half and tucked it into his shirt pocket.

'You killed Alison, didn't you, Michael?'

But before he could say anything, her hand shot out and she seized his wrist with alarming force.

'Didn't you?'

He looked at her and then away and then suddenly back at her. 'I didn't mean to.'

'The way you didn't mean to try and kill your brother?'

Suddenly he was a stranger, an angry man pushing his face into hers from across the table. 'Did you ever think that maybe I was thinking of you?'

'You tried to kill Ben for my sake?'

'Yes, believe it or not, I did. He would have gone to the police eventually, Mom and you—' He put his head down, composed

271

himself. Raised his head. Stared at her. 'Do you want to go through it all again, Mom? First your own father – and now your own son.'

'I want the truth to come out.'

'That's what you say, Mom. But do you really?'

She put her face in her hands, shook her head. 'I can't believe this. Alison and then your own brother—'

He stood up. Walked around the table. Tried to hug her. But she jerked away from his embrace.

'I'm going away, Mom. Ben'll be all right. You speak to him. You tell him not to talk to Rhys. And then you two can go on with your lives.'

'No,' she said. 'No. That wouldn't be right. You have to face up to what you've done.'

He was the stranger again. Pushing his face into hers, then squeezing her cheeks violently between his thumb and forefinger. 'Face up? Face up? Is that what you want? You really want to go through it all again, Mom? The trial and the execution? And all those people saying things about you behind your back?'

She was about to respond when somebody knocked on the door.

She assumed it would be Dr Sullivan.

'Come in,' she said.

Michael stepped back, composed himself.

The door opened and Chief Rhys came in.

'Sorry I couldn't get back here earlier, Lynn. But there was a bad accident out on the highway.'

He looked at Michael. 'Hello, Michael.'

'Hello, Chief Rhys.'

'Everything all right?'

'Everything's fine,' Michael said. 'I was just telling Mom that I need to run home and take care of a few things.'

'I'll be here with her,' Rhys said.

'I appreciate that, Chief,' Michael said. He looked at his mother. 'I'll talk to you a little later, Mom.'

She started to stand up. 'Michael—'

Rhys watched both of them.

'I'll give you a call in a little while,' she said.

Michael came over and kissed her on the cheek. 'You couldn't ask for a better Mom than this, could you, Chief?'

'She's a fine woman, Michael,' Rhys said. 'No doubt about that.'

Lynn wanted to speak up, wanted to tell the truth but somehow the proper words wouldn't form.

She let Michael give her his hypocritical kiss, let him say his hypocritical words.

And then he was back at the door again.

'I'll say some more prayers for Ben, Mom.'

He gave a sad little shrug, and was gone.

'Fine boy,' Rhys said.

'Yes,' she said. 'Fine boy.'

13

Michael wondered how far he could be by midnight. Maybe well into Nebraska. Then Colorado and the mountains. Escape. Mexico was where he had in mind. At least ultimately. He'd managed to get together more than six thousand dollars this afternoon. You could live well in Mexico on that kind of money.

He pulled into the dark house, killed the headlights but left the car running.

He planned to be out of here in less than five minutes.

He used the side door, going into the dark house that smelled of spices in the kitchen.

Through the dining room, the living room, into the hall leading to his bedroom.

She wouldn't tell, his mother wouldn't.

Not now.

Not until he was long gone.

Hurry, hurry.

He walked quickly down the hall and turned into his bedroom and that was when the man with the gun stood up and said, 'Hi, Michael. How they hanging?'

Just after Michael left, Dr Sullivan came into the coffee room and said, 'Things are going along pretty well, Lynn. His heart rate's improving and we've got him off the respirator.'

'Oh, thank God.'

'He's not home yet, but he's getting there.' Dr Sullivan nodded to Chief Rhys. 'I'll be checking back in a while, Lynn.'

'Thank you, Doctor.'

After he was gone, Rhys said, 'You want some more coffee?'

She shook her head. 'No. Coffee won't help.'

'Oh?'

'Being honest with you – that's the only thing that's going to help me.'

She told him everything and he said, 'He's at his place now?'

'Yes.'

'You want to ride along with me? Maybe he won't give us any trouble if you're there.'

'I hope not.'

Rhys put a paternal hand on her shoulder. 'I'm sorry, Lynn.'

'I know.'

'It's not going to be any fun for you. You know, the publicity and all.'

'I didn't have much choice, did I?'

'I guess not.'

'I had to tell you the truth. I had to.'

Then they left to get in his car.

'We had a deal, Michael.'

'Paul, listen, I—'

'You were going to leave her alone. That's what you promised me, anyway.'

'Paul, please, listen!'

'But oh, no. Not you two. Had to rub my face in it. Had to embarrass me in front of the whole town.'

'Paul—'

Given the stench, Paul had probably been drinking most of the day. He moved unsteadily. Even the gun in his right hand weaved from left to right.

But at this range, catching Michael with a fatal bullet wasn't going to be real hard.

'I don't love her, if that's what you're worried about,' Michael said.

'I'd like it better if you did.'

Then Michael realized that there was only one thing to say, one thing that could dissuade Paul.

'I'm going away.'

'When?'

'Now, Paul. Now – and forever.'

'Forever, hell.'

'Forever. Never coming back. Honest.' He gestured at the two suitcases in the corner. 'See? I'm all packed and everything.'

And that was when Michael noticed the shaving kit sitting on the edge of the bureau. Had a few reasonably heavy things packed into that kit.

If he could grab it—

Throw it at Paul's gun hand—

'She going with you?'

'Is Denise going with me? Of course she's not going with me! She's going to stay right here and be your wife.'

'Oh, yeah. Some wife she is.'

Closer to the bureau; closer.

'But I'll be gone, Paul. There won't be any problem.'

'She'll find you.'

Closer to the bureau; closer.

'Just let me walk out of here, Paul.'

Closer. Closer.

'You got any idea what it's like, Michael, walking in and finding the woman you love with another guy?'

'It's not gonna happen any more, Paul. Honest.'

'It's too late, Michael. You two promised me and promised me and promised me—'

And that's when Michael reached for the shaving kit. And picked it up. And flung it.

The kit landed high, catching Paul in the left biceps.

The gun roared twice in the stillness.

'No lights,' Chief Rhys said as they approached Michael's house.

And then they heard the gunfire.

'My God,' Lynn said.

They pulled up to the curb and instantly jumped from the car.

They were almost to the front porch when they saw a burly figure coming out the side door.

Paul Fletcher.

There was a gun in his hand.

'Stop right there!' Chief Rhys shouted, taking out his own gun, dropping into position to fire.

'My father thinks you're a scumbag, Rhys,' Fletcher said, 'and so do I.'

And then he fired three shots at Chief Rhys.

Lynn and the officer had to dive for the grass to escape the shots.

But as he dove, Rhys squeezed off two shots of his own, one hitting Paul Fletcher in the forehead, the other finding a home in his heart.

The shots lifted him up and slammed him into the house.

He didn't even have time to get a good scream off.

Lynn was running into the house even before Fletcher had fallen over face-first to the ground.

She stumbled and barked her shin painfully on the kitchen steps.

But she kept going.

Had to keep going.

Had to find Michael.

Had to find him.

Kitchen. Dining room. Living room.

No sign of him.

Bathroom. TV room.

No sign of him.

Bedroom—

He was sprawled on his back across the bed.

Blood that looked black in the moonlight had soaked the front of his white shirt.

He was crying.

He had fouled himself.

She reached him and knelt down next to him and took his face gently between her hands.

'I'm sorry,' she said.

He looked up at her and started crying even harder. 'I always hated guys who cried, you remember that?'

'Yes, I remember that.'

'And look at me now.'

'I love you, Michael.'

'Even after all I did?'

She nodded, starting to cry herself. 'Even after all you did.'

'But you would've put me in prison?'

'Yes, I would have.'

He grinned past his pain for a moment. 'I guess that's what makes you such a good Mom and all, huh? That you're such a straight-shooter.

'I guess.'

'Will you tell Ben that I love him?'

'Of course.'

'He probably won't believe that.'

'Maybe not now. But someday.'

'I'm scared, Mom. I'm getting real, real cold.'

'The Chief will have called an ambulance.'

'There isn't time for an ambulance, Mom.'

'I can get you a blanket.'

'There isn't time for a blanket, either.' Then: 'I don't know what was wrong with me, Mom. Why I was the way I was.'

She tried very hard not to think about her father, who had said something similar to her once.

She tried very hard not to think of her father.

And then she heard a deep sigh and looked down.

Michael was gone.

Her son Michael was gone.

14

The day of the funeral, it snowed.

Ben was still on crutches and had to be helped in and out of the hearse that carried Michael's body to the graveyard.

Sky and land were blanched of color, and the green tent of the funeral home flapped in the wind as the mourners muttered prayers for a young man who had killed at least two people that they knew of.

Lynn felt the eyes on her, and knew that all her years of trying to be a normal woman had been for naught.

She was once again a stranger to them, an oddity, a curiosity, a pariah, as she stood next to Ben and listened to the minister finish up burying Michael.

There was to be a luncheon in the basement of the Knights of Columbus following the burial.

She doubted that more than a handful would attend, and that included the eighteen mourners who'd managed to make it to the church.

In the hearse, on the way back to town, Ben said, 'I keep thinking of what you said about Elizabeth. That sometimes it's merciful for things to die.'

She nodded and patted his hand. She felt so many conflicting feelings, she was almost dizzy with her sorrow.

'I keep thinking about Michael. Thinking that's maybe why he died. Because it was merciful.'

'It probably was, honey.'

'I want to forgive him someday, Mom. You think I'll be able to?'

'Someday you probably will, honey. Someday.'

She looked away, then, because he'd started crying softly, and she knew it would embarrass him if she watched.

* * *

The hearse drove into the town where her father had walked, and took as his mistress a beautiful young town girl. And where he'd ultimately killed her.

It was this same town where her eldest son Michael had also murdered a beautiful young girl.

And it was the same town that had for years whispered about her, and disapproved of her, and disapproved of those who were seen as being too nice to her.

And now it was going to happen to her all over again – and not just to her but to Ben, too.

The hearse pulled up at the rear of the one-story Knights of Columbus hall. Protestants and Catholics alike used this place.

She helped Ben from the hearse, helped him down the stairs.

Incredible that he'd lived at all, Dr Sullivan had said, let alone with just a broken leg as the most serious damage.

Just before she opened up the door and went inside, Ben startled her by smiling.

'You've got a lot more friends than you know, Mom,' he said.

And then he reached over and grabbed the door knob and pulled the door back.

And there, seated at eight long tables, with their luncheons on plates in front of them, were at least sixty townspeople, of all ages, of all occupations, of all social positions.

And when they saw her, they stood up and began applauding.

And Chief Rhys came forward with two older women and they surrounded her and escorted her to a place of prominence at the long table up on the stage where the mayor and other dignitaries stood applauding.

'We just wanted you to know that this is your home, Lynn,' Chief Rhys said. 'This is where you belong.'

She foolishly tried not to cry.

But it was no use.

This sort of extraordinary kindness required the tears of solace and renewal; the tears of friendship and trust and joy.